I0637769

Nowhere on the Sound

Book 4 in the On the Sound Crime Series

Gemma Christina

Jpenname Publishing, LLC

Contents

Prologue

I t was a mistake to drink that thermos of coffee.

The land beyond her windshield rolled on. Mile after mile of nothing.

Chuck had warned her.

"It's a long drive And it will be forever before you are anywhere. I know how you women are with the bathroom. Don't get yourself into a pickle. That part of Nevada hasn't left the Wild West, so be careful."

She'd smiled politely while inwardly scoffing at the supervisory agent. The bladder of a racehorse — that's what her dad always said. And even though Amber couldn't say what the phrase meant in the technical sense, she knew her father meant he could take her hiking without bathroom breaks slowing them down.

"Understood, sir."

"Good." Chuck nodded satisfactorily, appraising her with his bushy brows, his eyes playing second fiddle to them. Part of her wanted to trim them, right there, in the office. She decided against it. As the newest and youngest agent in the Las Vegas field office, such a move would be a losing venture.

And while Las Vegas hadn't been her first choice of assignments, she found Chuck Leonard easy to negotiate. There was little complexity to staying on his good side. Show up. Follow the lead of your training partner without complaint, and don't screw up.

So complaining was not an option when he threw her a bone, a chance to venture out on her own for the first time since completing the bureau's required two-year probationary period. It was a task no one else wanted. That was fine with her.

But Chuck's warning about the bathroom proved true. She hadn't seen a rest area sign for the past twenty miles. The next town wouldn't appear for another twenty-five miles. Hoping it offered a restroom was a gamble.

If she pulled off, the lonely desert roadside had nothing but squatty shrubs. No trees to hide behind. Just dirt sliced open by the unending roadway, leading to the distant shale-colored mountains, unyielding and hard against the blazing blue sky.

She turned up the radio to take her mind off the pain in her bladder. If people lived nearby, they liked country music, because that was all her radio would play. Unless she counted the conspiracy talk show on 470 AM. She'd heard "aliens" and flipped back to Alan Jackson singing "Living on Love."

Country wasn't her favorite genre, but her dad loved it. Through him, she'd learned to like it well enough. At least enough to find it more enjoyable than talk of little green men.

The song eventually faded into the background as her eyes shifted to the case file on the passenger seat. It was thin, with little in the way of evidence or statements. Memorizing the details took little time when there was so little to read. Jeannette Resco disappeared almost five years ago after stopping for gas in Austin, Nevada. Recently divorced, the twenty-five-year-old former waitress at the Flamingo had packed up and headed home to Eugene, Oregon.

Austin had a single gas station available: a Texaco that still had rolling analog numbers. Belinda Peterson, the clerk working that night, was the only person who remembered seeing Jeannette. After Austin, they lost all trace of her. She never made it to Eugene or any desolate towns along the way.

Now, the same Belinda claimed she spotted the missing woman again. In Austin, as if Jeannette had never left.

Chuck would usually not send an agent fresh out of her probationary period to check out Belinda's story except that none of the Las Vegas agents believed the witness's new story. The case was cold and no longer interesting. Chuck figured it would be a long drive for a quick interview and then another long drive back.

Amber didn't care that there was likely nothing to the case. Being solo, on her own . . . It meant she could test her knowledge and investigative ability without having someone else in her ear.

The FBI assigned the two guys who handled the case originally to different offices. Amber called both, but she only got through to Special Agent Doleman in Cincinnati.

"Yeah, I remember that one. An endless drive into the desert just to come up completely empty." A long sigh hissed from the phone. "We only attempted to assist the local guys because of her ex and his ties to the mob, Bobbie Friolini in particular. But Friolini knew his days out of prison were numbered. I doubted and still don't think he'd risk taking out a hit on the girlfriend of an informant. I don't think she knew anything of value. Honestly, we were never sure she was really missing. Her ex was violent. It's possible she just disappeared so he couldn't find her." He was silent for a second before continuing. "I don't know. Maybe she stayed in Austin." Amber could hear the shrug in his voice. "I doubt her loser boyfriend or even the mob would spend time in that place looking for her."

Jeannette's parents, however, insisted their daughter would never just disappear without at least letting them know she was alive. Amber had to agree, especially when the mother became seriously ill, a heart condition aggravated by stress. No daughter who loved her parents, and from all accounts Jeannette was close to hers, would allow such suffering to continue.

Amber slammed on the brakes.

In a gravel turnout, a lone porta-potty sat just beyond an orange-and-white striped construction barrier. Pulling off the road, she let the car creep near the plastic booth of her deliverance. The area appeared to be some kind of dump site, with one dump truck off in the distance but close enough to see its empty cab. Other than the truck and a pile of displaced sand and rock, she was alone.

"Please don't be locked," she pled into the dry air as she left the car. "Or as disgusting as I'm imagining."

Both things could be true, but the alternative was peeing into an empty cup. That usually went badly for a woman.

The door swung open with ease, releasing a musty plastic odor combined with strong hints of sewage. Overall, not as bad as she'd expected.

Recently cleaned, she thought. Thank you, Lord, for small blessings.

Determined to do her business quickly, Amber hurried inside, whipped down her suit pants, careful to keep her gun and badge from falling inside or touching anything. Then she released an enormous sigh of relief.

She was just finishing up when the unmistakable sound of tires skidding on gravel made her freeze, her fingers hovering at the last step of buckling her belt.

Voices. Two, maybe three men.

Sucking in a lungful of tainted, scorching air, she finished the buckle, breathing out just as she pushed the belt end through the last loop.

This had been the perfect trap, and like a moth tempted to the flame, she'd fallen for it.

Stupid, she chided herself as the sun glared through the blue plastic walls, sweat sprouting everywhere on her skin. Using the back of her hand, she caught some of it before it leaked into her eyes.

Breathe and think. The mantra ran through her mind on repeat; the same words that had pushed her whenever she felt stuck on a test, during training at Quantico, or when other agents said stupid things to her.

No doubt the men outside planned only a car heist, but once they saw a single woman step out of the porta-potty, their animal brains would add things to the menu.

She tapped her pocket, feeling the hard outline of the car keys, glad she hadn't been completely clueless. When she had to explain this later, she'd blame the lapse in judgment on her brain's complete focus on needing to use the bathroom.

Well, girl, she thought, you got yourself into this. Now get yourself out.

Even in the heat, Amber usually wore a suit coat. Her slight frame made it difficult to conceal her gun and badge any other way. Most situations didn't require hiding her status as a federal agent. So far, she'd spent most of her new career collecting statements for crimes already investigated to some extent by local law enforcement. Today, she needed the FBI to be her little secret, at least for a minute or two. Unfortunately, her suit coat rested on the passenger seat of her car.

Standing rigid and trying to keep her movements slow, the agent unclipped her holster and gun from its current front-facing position on her belt, reattaching it below the small of her back. Then she removed her badge from the same front position and stuffed it in her pocket.

Inhaling another deep breath of the foul air, Amber pushed the plastic door open and stepped into the high-octane sunlight. Forcing her eyes to shake off the temporary blindness, she took in the scene: one cowboy-hat-wearing man in a white pickup, arm flung across the seats. Relaxed. He's done this before. One bent inside her car, driver side. Looking for keys? A third leaning against the passenger side, waiting for her with a handgun hanging on his hip. A baseball hat covers his greasy, shoulder-length hair that matches the dirt. Coincidentally, the hat reads "Raymond Dirt."

"Oh," Amber squeaked out, putting a hand to her chest. "Oh, dear. What? What are you doing?"

A smile crept across the teeth of Raymond-Dirt guy as he threw a look toward the pickup truck. Amber could almost hear his thoughts. "Look what we got here, fellas." But he said nothing, just turned back to her with dark eyes that roamed her body.

The guy rummaging for keys backed out of the car and stood, his face flushed from the search effort. He was young—no more than fourteen, Amber guessed. His eyes flitted between Raymond Dirt and her, and then over his shoulder to the pickup. The lack of keys in the car seemed to bewilder him, as if most suckers left them inside their car—maybe even left the engine running.

At least she hadn't been completely stupid.

"We thought you might be having some car trouble," Raymond Dirt drawled, his smile twisting with the lie. "And we're the helpful sort. If you, like, need a ride somewhere."

He pushed himself away from the car and started moving toward her, a hungry gleam in his eyes.

The boy by the car shuffled his feet. Both Amber and the dirt guy glanced his way.

Hands buried in his hair, he stepped back and forth. "I don't like this, Gary," he said, his words dull but full of worry.

Dirt-guy named Gary stopped in his tracks, staring at the kid as if he'd like to rip his tongue out. "What'd I tell you about saying my name?" He waited a second, eyes on fire, before adding with angry emphasis, "Robbie." Turning to the truck, he shouted, "David! Get out here and take care of your brother."

Amber bit back a smile. Now she knew all their names. And the last piece had fallen into place—David getting out of the truck. Otherwise, what came next might tempt him to take off.

David followed orders, stepping down from the gigantic pickup truck. He left the engine running as he approached the kid. "Come on now, Robbie. Just shut the door and come back to the truck."

Amber watched as he put a gentle hand on his brother's elbow. For just a second, David's eyes met hers. His look said that he didn't like what Gary had on his mind, but he wouldn't stop it either.

Robbie still held his head, shaking it back and forth, moaning but not moving from her car.

It was just as well. She needed them to stay out of the truck. Not knowing how long the kid's resistance would last, Amber knew she had to make a move.

Luckily, Gary's eyes were back on her, David and Robbie forgotten.

"Yeah," she said. "We should all get going. It's boiling out here. I appreciate your stopping. I do. But my car is working just fine. So, I'll just get back on my way."

She took a couple of steps toward the car. That's when Gary moved into her path. "I don't think so, little lady." He thrust his gun-hip forward, watching to ensure she looked at it and fully understood his meaning. "First, you and me are gonna head on back to that porta-potty, and you're going to show me the appreciation you was talking about. Then, we're gonna take your keys and all go for a ride together, until you show some appreciation to my friends, too."

"We should just get her car keys and go," David warned. "Someone might come by."

Gary scoffed. "Right. There's nothing but truckers, and they all know better than to stop."

He took another step toward Amber, close enough now for the smell of cigarettes, beer and body odor to hit her so strong that she'd rather breathe inside the porta-potty.

"I-I'm not sure what you mean," she stammered, her eyes wide with fear. Some of that fear was real. Amber knew that, but she couldn't allow herself to *actually feel* any fear yet. If she gave the fear any space, this man would become powerful and might just end up getting what he wanted. Being scared would only clutter her mind. And right now, her mind was as clear as the endless blue sky overhead.

He stepped closer, moving his hands to rest on her shoulders.

"Oh, I think you do," he said, his acrid breath hot on her face, his heavy, sweaty hands like wet fish on her shoulders. Licking his dry lips, he let his eyes wander over her face. "I think part of you is looking forward to it."

She watched the realization hit him, his eyes flying open, his right hand freezing on its way down to her breast.

"Back. Up," she sneered, pushing his own gun into his gut.

Gary jumped back, his eyes still wide with surprise, or fear, or both. The look said that Dirt-Guy Gary had not learned to practice emotional self-control like the agent had.

David cursed and shook his head. "You know how to pick 'em, Gary. She's a cop."

"Close," said Amber, her voice calm despite the thudding of her heart. "FBI. Hands up, please. All of you."

Slowly raising his hands over his head, David watched her with an emotionless stare. She motioned toward Gary with her head. "You two come over here and join your friend."

David didn't move. "I don't think Robbie here is in a state to follow your orders."

The kid still had his hands over his ears, moaning and rocking next to Amber's car.

"You can leave him there. I'm not worried about him. I'd guess he didn't ask to be here."

With a shrug, David complied. When the two men were standing next to each other, Amber ordered them down on their knees.

David sighed in boredom at the order, but Gary, as he kneeled, stared at her with vacant, wide eyes, as if a woman getting the better of him had shattered something in his brain. She would have laughed, but humor could also cloud her judgment. It was time to be focused and efficient.

Keeping the gun trained on the men, Amber opened the passenger-side door of her car, reached into the glove box, and pulled out two sets of handcuffs, the only two she had. Throwing one to David, she said, "Put this around your left hand. Then clip the other side onto his right hand."

Moving with casual indifference, David followed orders. "What's the FBI doing way out here?" he asked, his eyes focused on cuffing Gary's hand. When he turned to her, his gaze, darkened by the rim of his cowboy hat, struck her as too intense for the nonchalance of his movements.

She suppressed a shudder as a thought flashed through her mind. *This guy is the dangerous one.*

"We heard there was a car theft ring operating along this stretch of the highway," she lied.

The man snorted through a half-smile, turning to look at the road. "You should've let us steal your car then. Otherwise, you don't have any cause for arrest. Besides, the FBI doesn't care about stolen cars."

"Oh, I'm not arresting you," she said, throwing him the other set of handcuffs. "Cuff your friend's left hand to the grille guard."

The truck still rumbled, its engine running. Even at a distance, Amber could feel the heat pouring from it. David's eyes darkened even more, as if behind them he contemplated a quick move to take the gun from her.

"Top of my class marksman. And if this gun fails me, I have a backup, so just do it. Nice and easy."

Robbie's moaning had ceased. He watched David lean over and snap the cuffs on Gary and then the grill guard. His eyes narrowed, but not with suspicion. More like he wanted to touch the handcuffs himself, see how they worked, or see what they felt like.

Amber moved back enough so that she could easily cover all the men with Gary's gun.

"Robbie," she said kindly, keeping the gun pointed at the two men cuffed to the truck. "It's hot out here. What do you say we get in the truck to cool off? You can take the passenger side."

Robbie shook his head so hard, Amber thought his head might fly off. "No. No. No. Only David can drive his truck. No one else. Only David."

"That's right, Robbie," said David. "You have a good memory, brother."

"We're not going to drive it, Robbie. Just cool off and maybe talk on the CB radio. David's got one, right?" She glanced at the truck and the long antenna mounted there, hoping that meant a functioning radio.

The boy nodded, his eyes lighting up. "Ten-four, good buddy."

"Robbie," said David, drawing the name out with a parent-like warning. "You need to stay off that radio. I don't want you in my truck without me." Despite the languid way he spoke, sweat glistened on the man's face, red with heat. He had a statuesque posture, like a man bent on control, not willing to show the slightest discomfort or worry.

Gary, on the other hand, finally awakened to his situation.

"You can't do this," he said, trying to wipe his brow as David kept their cuffed wrists at his side. Gary then bent his head toward his other arm, cuffed to the truck, only getting close enough to slide his forehead back and forth across the sleeve of his t-shirt. "You have to treat us humane-like. This is too hot, man. I'm gonna die."

The whine in his voice did little to move Amber to sympathy. "You want to discuss being humane?" She turned the gun on its side, studying it as if the sins of the user were engraved there. "How many women have you threatened with this thing?"

"Just shut up, Gary," said David, stretching his legs out in front of him, crossing his dusty cowboy boots.

This casual move sent a worm of worry wriggling in Amber's stomach. Did he have something up his sleeve, or, more likely, in his pocket? A gun? A knife? She probably should have patted him down, but on her own, she liked distance as a better strategy. Besides, his jeans were tight-fitting; they hid little. But he was the type to have a knife in his boot. Yes, distance was her friend.

"That's right," said Amber. "You should probably quit talking."

As much as she'd like to take the truck keys, throw them in the porta-potty, and leave the men to the heat and whatever crawled out of the desert, doing that would tarnish her first solo outing. Besides, there was no way she'd leave the kid here to suffer with the other two wretches. He clearly had some mental deficiencies that Gary and David were exploiting.

Keeping the gun lowered but directed toward the cuffed captives, she turned her attention to Robbie. "Hey, if we get on the radio, we can contact someone to help and make sure you get home. You're not in trouble or anything." She smiled warmly. "Do your parents live around here?"

"Robbie," warned David.

"Quiet, please," said Amber, not looking at him. "This is between Robbie and me."

"Mom does," said Robbie, rubbing his hands together. "Dad's gone. Gone a long time ago. We don't know where. Just gone, gone, gone."

"I'm sorry about that," said Amber, wiping her brow with her gun-free hand. "I lost my mom when I was a kid. It was really hard."

David snickered. "She's lying, Robbie. Don't listen."

Amber kept her eyes trained on Robbie, pretending the other men did not exist. She and the kid were the only two that mattered. "I know these guys probably have you doing some stuff you don't like. Is that right, Robbie?"

Robbie shot a look at David, but his hands stilled. Then the kid nodded, his eyes darting between Amber and his feet.

"I-I think you're nice," Robbie blurted out, surprising her.

A genuine smile spread across the agent's face. "I like you too, Robbie. Do you know how to use the CB radio? I bet you do."

Another vigorous nod. "I know all the call signs. Memorized up here," he said, pointing to his head. "Channel nine, emergencies. Channel nineteen, truckers. Don't clog up channel nine. I have a friend on channel twenty-one. Desert Sandy. She's got a horse named Ms. Frizzle. Like on 'The Magic School Bus.' I like—"

Gary shouted a string of curse words before adding, "Shut up, you idiot!"

With shocking speed, David whipped out his free hand and slapped the man hard enough to hear above the rumbling hum of the pickup.

"Don't you ever call my brother an idiot," he seethed

"And watch your language," Amber said. "There are so many other words available. You sell yourself short." Giving him the once-over, she said, "Or maybe not, in your case."

The man glared at her, the searing red imprint of David's hand standing out on his cheek.

David settled back against the grille. Sweat drenched his t-shirt. The situation really was dangerous in this heat. She needed to get in that truck, contact the sheriff, or find someone who could contact the sheriff, and turn the engine off. Then she'd give the captives some water and wait it out.

Unfortunately, Gary's outburst sent Robbie into turtle mode again — head down, hands wringing, looking like he wanted to crawl under a rock and disappear. She had to get him excited again.

"Do you think we could talk to Desert Sandy? Will that work on the CB? I don't know much about how those radios work . . . how far they reach or anything like that. I could really use your help. I'd love for you to teach me."

The kid kept his head down, but he mumbled, "Range seven miles in good weather."

Seven miles. The highway stretched out bare. There hadn't been a passing car since long before she stopped and ended up in this situation. Was there even a truck seven miles behind or ahead of them? A house or business anywhere within that range?

"Just seven miles?"

Flicking a glance at her, Robbie shook his head. "You're the police. So I can't tell you."

"I'm not the police, really. And anything you tell me won't get you in trouble. I promise."

Gary muttered under his breath but said nothing loud enough to elicit another rebuke. Next to him, David seemed unconcerned with her making radio contact. Admittedly, unless the sheriff had additional information about these men, David might not face any charges. It was Gary who threatened her and Gary who had the weapon.

Though she found Robbie's brother disconcerting and dangerous, like his type of poison ran deep below the surface, his indifference worked to her advantage.

"So, what can't you tell me?"

"Seven miles," Robbie said, still staring at his feet. "Seven miles. Sometimes more. Seven miles if you don't have a booster. But boosters are illegal."

Amber smiled. "I see. Well, I don't know what boosters look like, so I'm sure you don't have one."

The kid finally met her eye, a conspiratorial grin lighting up his face.

Chapter One

The dark haunted her the most.

Was there any light? MJ Brooks couldn't tell because they'd left the blindfold over her eyes, cutting her off from the world, from seeing any oncoming threat. Every sound, no matter how small, sent a shock of fear through her.

If only she could see, then she could protect herself.

Though her hands and legs were bound, she'd wrenched onto her back and sent both feet slamming into what she learned was a metal wall.

The material made a hollow, echoing thud, and though she'd been kicking at it for at least an hour, maybe longer, no one appeared. It didn't matter. For now, it was her only way of helping herself.

Dropping her head back to breathe, MJ maneuvered onto her side to release the pressure on her hands, which were bound behind her. They were already numb from the tight plastic zip ties.

A blanket lay beneath her, but with her cheek to the floor, she breathed in the fine particles of dust that seemed to ride on every oxygen molecule. With duct tape over her mouth, breathing took serious effort. Snot already caked her nose from sneezing with no hands, much less a tissue.

Wind roiled outside. She could hear it whistle around the place they kept her, but there were no other sounds. No birds. No cars. No people talking. No chance of getting someone's attention.

A tear rolled out, trailing across the bridge of her nose and onto the opposite cheek before hitting the dirty cloth that blinded her.

She saw her mom. Blood on her face as she fell to the ground.

No! She squeezed her eyes shut to stop the mental image threatening to overtake her; crush her.

Don't think. Don't see. Keep your head.

But grief and fear gripped her heart in a way she'd never experienced.

Squeaking hinges and a rush of cold air told her someone had opened a door.

MJ scurried back, pushing with her feet until she felt the cold metal wall through the back of her thin t-shirt.

A clunk sounded as the man dropped something to the floor. MJ's heart thrummed in her ears, her breath coming in short, panicked bursts.

Heavy footsteps clomped toward her. Rough hands pushed her forward, gripping her bound fists and pulling them farther up her back. She yelped in pain. There was a snip, and then a sudden release of blood back into her hands. Then he quickly did the same at her ankles.

"Do not take off the blindfold until you hear the door close," said a man's deep voice. "Otherwise, I will shoot you."

A waft of body odor assaulted her nose, and something about the casual shuffle of the man's feet told her that no sense of cruelty burdened him. He would shoot her.

She held still, afraid to move; afraid of what he'd dropped on the ground.

"Do you understand?"

MJ gave a slow nod, holding every other part of herself still.

"There's a good girl," the man said, bending closer and using one thick finger to raise her chin. His voice held no humor. The words were dead and cold. Yes, this man would shoot her. He may even want to shoot her.

The man bent so that his face was inches from hers, his putrid breath penetrating the cloth and assaulting her cold cheeks. "And you can kick all day," he added in a low growl. "We are nowhere, and no one will hear you."

He stepped away. Then the hinges squeaked like a dying animal. He was gone.

Chapter Two

Detective Jefferson Hughes's eyes flew open at the buzzing of his phone.

Part of him hoped it would be MJ. Okay, all of him hoped it would be MJ. But she was on vacation, and she'd told him before taking off for Las Vegas that she had no intention of waking up early for the next fourteen days. And it was early, very early. Like he'd barely slept at all early. There was no time difference in Nevada, so she couldn't even have mistakenly called at this hour.

No MJ. Instead, "Larson" appeared on the screen, telling him all he needed to know. The workday would start earlier than planned. Three am early, to be exact.

He pressed the answer button. "Hughes."

"Good. You're up," came the senior detective's gruff reply.

"I wasn't."

"Well, you answered, didn't you? And you sound awake, almost like you were expecting a phone call."

Pulling back the covers, Jefferson swung his feet down to sit on the edge of the bed. "I see why you make the big bucks. What's up?"

A hard sigh drifted across the line. "Mendez is still out of town, and we got a body at Seal Point Park. So I guess you drew the short straw.

The uniforms on-scene made it sound like a messy one. Knife attack. I'm headed there now. I need you to meet me there ASAP."

Like a sane person, Mendez, Larson's partner, had taken time off to visit family in Mexico for Christmas. Jefferson had even left for a few days to see his mom and brother in his hometown of Redding, California. Larson, however, had taken no time off, choosing instead to collect the overtime pay.

"Got it. Any witnesses?"

"Two young guys called it in. I don't know yet what they saw or didn't see. Apparently, they and the victim sneaked into the park sometime last night or early this morning."

"Why would they do that? It's freezing out. Are they homeless?"

"Don't know. In fact, that's about all I know right now. I'm almost there. Get moving."

The next sound was silence as Larson hung up the call. Jefferson stared at the phone for a second, as if the device had cut him off. With a shake of his head, he dropped it on the bed.

He showered and dressed quickly. Then, reaching for his shoes, he stopped with his hand hovering over a new pair of loafers. A wry smile played on his lips as his mind conjured up a clear image of MJ, her blue eyes twinkling as she teased him about wearing expensive shoes in the sand.

This morning would offer another opportunity to ruin a beautiful pair of shoes. Seal Point Park sat on the shore of the Puget Sound. The trail to the beach would be nothing but mud this time of year. Or any time of the year, really.

He still grabbed the loafers. His trunk held the boots he'd purchased for long walks on the beach with MJ, even if they'd only had one walk so far. A perfect walk. The best walk of his life, because it ended with a kiss that left no room for doubt about his feelings for her, or hers for him.

He put the loafers on, letting his mind linger on MJ before facing the gruesome reality waiting for him at the crime scene.

***

Winter in the form of snow usually hits West Sound, Washington, once or twice a year. It could be a one-day event, melting in much less time than it took to accumulate, or it could stick around like a guest way past their welcome.

This year's early December snowstorm had the good grace to come and go with fashionable speed, just quick enough that the people who liked the white fluff were still fans, and those who hated it couldn't annoy their family and friends with more than one day of grumbling. Unless, of course, their work required venturing into the great outdoors, into the left-behind mess created by melting mountains of snow saturating an already water-logged landmass.

Jefferson fit squarely in the grumbling category as he negotiated the slimy trail down to Seal Point Beach in the still-dark morning. His flashlight revealed tiny rivulets that trickled from beneath the fern-heavy underbrush, turning the trail into a slick, muddy creek. Just the slime was bad enough, but add the steep dive of the trail as it cut through the old forest of Douglas Fir, Pacific cedar, and pine, and there was a definite danger of mucking up a knee or fanny on your way down. Even in his boots, the detective struggled to keep his footing, hitting a couple of tree roots that almost sent him sprawling. The number of police who had hiked down before him made the task even more treacherous, their feet having beaten down any potential for traction.

When he safely hit the pebbly beach, Jefferson rolled his neck to loosen the muscles kept taut by such intense focus on his steps. He immediately saw the crime scene, the yellow tape perimeter standing out like a highlighted passage in a scene otherwise awash in deep grays and blacks.

Within the tape, the white suits of the forensics team were already moving about their tasks, with a few small lights scattered around. They likely hadn't had time to get their full equipment in place. Larson looked up from a conversation with the medical examiner, Dr. Stacey Underhill, and nodded in Jefferson's direction as he approached.

The two stood in front of a bleached driftwood log, which must have been a massive tree somewhere before the ocean deposited it at Seal Point. A set of legs, attached to the unfortunate victim, rested over the dead tree. As Jefferson moved closer, the rest of the man came into view, the rocks and pebbles beneath his head covered in deep shades of red.

"Good morning, Detective Hughes," said Evie Hanson, the officer manning the crime scene sign-in. Her bright smile contrasted with the early hour.

"Morning, Officer Hanson," Jefferson said as he signed the clipboard. "You seem chipper this morning."

"Just got back from a few days off. Got to visit some family in Spokane."

"That'll do it," he said, handing the clipboard back to her.

"Were you able to get away?"

"For a few days," he said. "I saw my family and the sun."

Evie chuckled. "Not much of that around here these days." The officer let a shiver roll down her arms.

He winced in sympathy. "Do your best to stay warm."

While his home town of Redding, California wasn't particularly warm this time of year, the sun usually made a daily appearance. Right after MJ left for Vegas, he took a flight home to spend some time with his mom, his brother George, and George's wife and kids. The trip also gave him an opportunity to share the good news, or partial good news, about his brother Alex—that he'd beaten his drug habit. For now, he was alive and healthy. What he couldn't tell them was his whereabouts.

Alex became one of the DEA's key witnesses in convicting a nasty group of drug traffickers, specifically a man named Nico Lopez Guerrero. The danger this posed to Alex's life was no laughing matter, so the DEA rightly kept his location a secret, even from Jefferson.

He didn't share that part with his family, saying instead that Alex would reach out when he was ready. But even that could be a lie. His brother might end up in witness protection after the trial. The fewer people who knew the details, the more chance Alex had of surviving this risky witness role, a role to which he'd readily agreed.

Despite the heavy toll of keeping that secret from his mother and brother, Jefferson enjoyed the time away more than he usually did. Even his brother noticed a difference in his ability to relax.

"What's going on, Jefferson? Is there a lady in the picture?"

The detective answered with a smile that he knew revealed too much. His family asked a million questions, but Jefferson shared very little about MJ. Their relationship, if you could call it that yet, hadn't left ground zero point five, and while he was sure of his feelings, he also felt protective of them, and hers.

If he were being honest, a sharp sliver of fear niggled at him as well. What if MJ's parents used her visit to convince her that dating a detective was a bad idea? The fear felt irrational, except that her mother loved MJ's ex-husband, Justin, and likely harbored some dream of them getting back together.

"Good morning, Detective Hughes. I dare say you are glowing for so early in the morning," said Stacey, her face peering out from the cinched hood of her protective suit. "How is our favorite middle school teacher?"

"Sleeping somewhere in Las Vegas, I'm sure, but thanks for asking. What have we got here?" The victim, who appeared to be a youngish man, lay on his back, feet on the log. His dead eyes stared into the far branches above him as they reached for the ocean. Half of the tree's roots clung to the eroding earth; the other half hung stark and exposed against the blackness of the early morning embankment.

Then there was the gash across his throat.

"I'd say that, initially, the cause of death easily observable," Stacey said, peering down at the man. "Some sort of sharp object cut his jugular. No murder weapon that we've found so far, and tracks are tough to make out because those guys trampled all over the spot when they found him." She motioned with her head toward a group standing a few steps further down the beach, on the other side of the perimeter.

Jefferson squinted in their direction, but he could only make out a few shadows.

"It's Officer Payne," said Larson, also looking that way, his hands deep in his coat pockets. "He was first on the scene, so I've got him waiting with this guy's two buddies." He motioned with an elbow toward the body.

"So, we have an identity?"

"Yep. Name's Brayden Shuster. And this really sucks for him," Larson said with a shake of his head. "But the guy just got out of juvenile detention a week ago."

Jefferson stared down at the man again, his brow furrowed. "What for?"

"You may remember when a young mom and her daughter were T-boned by a street racer up in Everette. Hit and run. Tested positive for THC. All the worst nonsense." Larson looked sideways at him.

"Wasn't even that long ago," Stacey threw out.

"Yeah, I remember something about it. So this is him? Juvenile?"

Larson nodded, his normally bald head snug in a black beanie. "He was 17 when it happened, about three years ago. I don't know all the ins and outs of the case. Apparently, he called up his pothead buddies over there to meet him at their former secret spot for smoking. They showed up at the appointed hour, and this is what they found. At least, that's their current story."

"Do you have any working theories about how this played out? It appears the attacker sneaked up from behind? And I already know the line about 'waiting to exam him at the lab.'"

The corner of Stacey's mouth twitched up. "And you know me so well, although not as well as you used to," she winked at him. "Oops, I forgot I can't tease you anymore."

Stacey liked to remind Jefferson of their brief dating period, even though neither of them had any genuine interest in the other anymore. The woman just couldn't help herself.

"Yes," she said, pursing her lips to dampen her smile and maintain a professional demeanor. "It looks like the perp surprised the guy."

Jefferson breathed a sigh of relief when she backed off the teasing. Maybe having a new boyfriend was keeping her from turning every interaction with him into a chance for banter, always one-sided.

She stepped near the body to illustrate. "Using his left arm to grab the victim, he likely slit the throat with his right arm and then slammed the victim to the ground with his left. There's a contusion on the back of his head that supports this theory."

"Phone? Wallet? Stuff in his pockets?"

"We have his phone, car keys, wallet, and a few old gum wrappers . . . wadded tissues. Doesn't seem the killer had much interest in that stuff. They even left behind about an ounce and a half of weed," said Larson.

"Really? So not a robbery, and slamming him down suggests a level of anger. Not random then," said Jefferson as he crouched near the victim's head, examining the rocks and pebbles. He glanced up at Stacey. "Got all the pictures you need?" "Yep. Feel free to poke around. Just not too much. Forensics still needs to do the fine-tooth comb thing."

Larson sighed. "You keep checking this out. I'm going to talk with Meyers and have him take the two buddies to the station. No reason to stand out here freezing. When you've seen all you want, meet me back at the station for interviews."

"Got it," said Jefferson, still picking through the rocks. "What about this guy's car?"

"It's the old Nissan you probably saw parked on the road. Forensics will take pictures before we tow it. It's supposed to rain, of course," Larson grunted.

"And the tide will move in soon. This guy needs to get moved, too," added Stacey.

The gentle forward-and-back whooshing of the ocean pressed on despite the drama unfolding on its shore. Jefferson, still crouching over the rocks, put his elbows on his knees, his gloved hands now stained with blood. "Getting him up that trail will take some work."

"Oh, we have our ways," Stacey said, unworried by the mud and slick ascent.

Just then, Jefferson felt his phone buzz in his pocket. With his hands in their current condition, he let it go to voicemail. He'd check it as soon as he had a chance.

"You know forensics will sift through all that," Stacey said, watching him meticulously move small pebbles and rocks to the side. "Are you looking for something specific?"

He shrugged. "No. But if your theory is correct, this is likely where the killer stoo—" He stopped. Amid the dull, blood-covered stones, a small reflection of light caught his eye. "Wait a minute. Do you have tweezers?"

"Do I have tweezers? What kind of ludicrous question is that?"

Jefferson kept his eyes fixed on the tiny reflection, listening as Stacey stepped a few paces away and then returned.

"Here ya go," she said, setting them in his outstretched hand.

"And an evidence bag."

"Already have it," she said, opening the top of the clear bag. "Ready when you are."

"Thanks," he said, not daring to move his head. His knees were aching, but he had to stay still. If he jerked too much, he might lose sight of whatever this little piece of something might be. He reached toward the reflection with the tweezers, seeing now that it was something round. Grasping it between the pincers, he felt no give in the item. It was hard, and smooth, like plastic. He dropped it into the bag Stacey held open.

Turning toward the closest light, the doctor held the bag up for them both to inspect. After just a second of examination, she declared, "That's a button."

She was right. Jefferson could see it now, though dirt caked the two thread holes.

"It sure is."

"Who knows how long it's been here," she said with a shrug. "But could be significant. Good eyes, Detective." Her glowing smile was friendly, but not the flirty thing it used to be. "I'll make sure Bud gets this."

"Where is Bud?" Jefferson looked around at the hooded figures carried out various tasks. Sure enough, the tall figure of Bud Lochlann, the lead forensics officer, was nowhere to be seen.

Stacey stared at him in disbelief.

"What?"

"How do you not know?"

"Not know what?"

She shook her head. "Bud had surgery last week. Heart valve replacement."

It was Jefferson's turn to stare. Should he know something like that? Did Bud announce his surgery, and he missed it somehow? In his mind, medical procedures were best kept private. If the detective were having surgery, it would take brilliant detective work for anyone else to know about it.

"But he's okay, right?"

Stacey snorted and swiped her hand through the air. "Of course. He's a tough old bird. He's just working fewer hours right now, trying to keep his stress down." A wicked smile crept up her face. "I'm not surprised you didn't know. Does anything but MJ Brooks inhabit that brain of yours these days?"

Releasing just a hint of his crooked smile, Jefferson gazed out toward the black water of the sound. Not even a pinprick of moonlight revealed its surface.

"It's foolish to throw rocks when you live in a glass house. How is Justin these days?"

In a weird twist of fate, Stacey met and fell for Justin Brooks, MJ's ex-husband, at the same time Jefferson and MJ revealed their feelings for each other. The ex's continued presence in MJ's life had been holding Jefferson back from believing she could care about him.

"Still in the mountains. I left early to help cover for Bud. Justin stayed behind to winterize the cabin. I didn't mind the 'no cell service'," she said with air quotes, "when we were together. Now that he's there and I'm here, not so much." Stacey's lips spread into a full smile as she bit her bottom lip. "And just so you know, Justin is . . . amazing."

The breathlessness of her words convinced Jefferson to get out of the conversation before the woman could share more than he wanted to know.

Chapter Three

As Jefferson scaled the trail back to the parking lot, dawn continued her slumber. Not even a whisper of that light touched the slippery slope, the forest acting as a guardian against even a chance of moonlight.

Jefferson felt his phone buzz in his pocket as he climbed the last few feet of the muddy path. He took it out, looking over the screen as he popped the trunk of his car, where his loafers waited to replace his mud-caked boots.

A missed call and now a message from Amber Wells, the FBI supervisory agent in charge of the West Sound regional office.

Having Amber call or message him wasn't too unusual. They often worked cases with their local FBI partners. But the early hour of the phone call, followed by a text message, indicated an unusual urgency.

Jefferson's heart hammered in his chest.

Alex. It had to be something with Alex. What if the cartel had found him? The detective closed his eyes, fighting to force the worst images from his mind.

Taking a deep breath, he opened the text.

"Call me. Don't do anything before we talk."

He held the phone out in front of him, as if doing this might help him understand the message. Its cryptic nature did nothing to calm his fears. What exactly did she think he was going to do?

Only one way to find out. Call her back.

Just as he was about to hit the button, another call popped up on his screen. This call was even more strange than Amber's.

Jefferson took the call, putting the phone to his ear. "Shannon?"

"Oh, Jefferson. Thank goodness." An unusual thickness in her voice and a sniffle told him she was crying.

"Shannon." He spoke slowly, breathing between each word. The earlier hammering of his heart had become a freight train. "What's the matter?"

A sob escaped, and when she spoke, her words were a tangled mess. "MJ's dad called. Someone took her, Jefferson. They attacked her mom, and then they took MJ, right in public. MJ's gone." Her words cascaded into more crying, as if they'd been holding together just long enough to reach him.

He stilled. His car forgotten. His boots forgotten. The world forgotten. Gravity settled over him with increased force, pinning him to the spot.

The two calls. Amber, and now Shannon. They clashed in his mind, building a picture he only partially understood in the moment, shadowy shapes that fit together somehow. Even if he didn't fully know the connection, the meaning of the two calls slammed into him like a punch to the gut.

A sniff and a gulping breath. "Are you there?"

"When?" he breathed out.

"Last night, as they were leaving a restaurant. Her mom . . ." Her breaths were heavy over the line. "She might not make it, Jefferson."

The last part of the sentence, his name, came out in a whisper. "She's. . . She's in a coma."

Grabbing a fistful of hair, he paced like a madman. A flight. He had to book a flight. He had to get to Vegas today.

"What do we do?" Shannon wailed. "What if they hurt her?"

"They won't," he hissed, the words fierce even though his heart seemed to cave in on itself. "I'll be on the next flight. I will find her, and if they've touched a hair on her head . . ." He stopped before saying the brutal part. Rip their hearts out, put a bullet in their heads. It didn't matter. They would pay.

"Please find her," MJ's best friend pleaded, the raw agony like sandpaper against his own fear.

He slammed his trunk closed, slipped the phone in his pocket and jumped into his car, the muddy boots forgotten.

***

He didn't drive to the police station.

The direction was automatic. Go home, pack a couple of things, book the flight, drive to the airport. He'd square it with the chief later. He'd understand. And if he didn't, Jefferson didn't much care.

Only MJ flooded his mind as he navigated the streets of West Sound, images of her that made his blood boil. Her blue eyes, tear-filled and frightened. Her face bloodied and bruised. And worst of all, her still form lying alone and lifeless somewhere in the desert.

He blinked it away.

No, that's not the MJ he knew. She'd fight. She'd bury any fear beneath resolve and defiance. Whatever they'd done, wherever they held her, MJ would look for a way out.

And she had to know he would come for her.

The car in front of him halted, its brake lights firing red as the driver stopped at an empty roundabout.

Jefferson laid on his horn. This seemed to make the driver less inclined to move. The detective hit the horn again, wanting nothing more than to jump out and scream at the idiot in front of him. The idiot who did not know that the woman Jefferson loved was in the hands of men who kill for fun.

He knew who had her. It couldn't be anyone else.

As the car in front of him finally moved, Jefferson saw an elderly woman with a tiny, yapping dog shuffling through the crosswalk. She glared at him, having heard his incessant honking.

"Normal" Jefferson might have experienced some guilt. In fact, "normal" Jefferson would never have honked in the first place.

He might never be normal again if anything happened to MJ.

The sudden ringing of his phone over the speaker system momentarily cleared his head.

Amber.

He took the call.

"Jeff, where are you?"

"Heading home. I'm booking a flight. Don't try to stop me, Amber."

The line went quiet, and for a moment, he thought the call had dropped.

"I will pick you up. I'm already packed."

A thousand pinpricks assaulted Jefferson's eyes. "You know who it is."

"Let's not talk over this line. I'll tell you what I know on the way to the airport. Hang in there, Jeff."

***

Without knowing what he packed, Jefferson headed out to Amber's black BMW.

The trunk lifted as he approached. He slung his bag inside, slammed it shut, and jumped into the passenger seat.

Amber's foot barely touched the gas before Jefferson pounced.

"Tell me what you know."

She kept her eyes on the road, her blonde hair slicked back in her usual low ponytail. Gone, however, were the professional slacks and jacket. Instead, she had the look of a casual traveler in jeans and a plain blue sweater.

"You should have changed out of that suit," she said, glancing briefly in his direction. "We need to be under the radar."

The detective gritted his teeth. Clothes were not his top concern.

"Amber, tell me."

She glanced his way again, and the empathy in her eyes almost sent him spinning.

"I wish I knew more, but it looks bad, Jeff," she said, her attention back on the road. "I won't sugarcoat it."

The weight of these words pinned him to the seat, his breathing slow and deep. He stared at the street ahead as they moved through West Sound toward I-5 north, toward Seatac airport. A soft rain, just slightly more than mist, settled over the windshield until the wipers eventually pushed it aside. Then the cycle began all over again. He clung to this repetitive motion to keep his emotions from flying away from him.

"Have you checked your email lately?" Amber asked.

He shook his head. "No. Larson called me out early."

"Your personal email."

"No," he said, already opening his phone.

A long blink and a sigh from Amber told him something waited there. "You should check it." Her eyes shifted to him and then back to the road. "Jared is already working on tracing it, if it is the same one sent to me."

The dread made his fingers clumsy as he swiped and tapped until his inbox appeared on the screen.

"What am I looking . . ." His voice died away. It was the second email on the list. The subject line shouted at him.

SHE DOESN'T HAVE MUCH TIME.

He tapped the email, clenching his teeth as it opened.

The email contained only a black square. A video.

He closed his eyes, letting out a slow breath out, preparing for whatever showed up on his screen.

The video opened to a blank black screen and no sound. Jefferson ratcheted up the volume. Heavy breathing pulsed from the phone, but still no images appeared. Then light filtered into the scene, and he realized the camera had been following a dark figure. A woman. MJ.

A push sent her sprawling stomach first onto a dirty blanket, blindfolded and bound at the hands and feet.

The detective forced himself to watch, his teeth clamped together like an iron cage, his breath only escaping through his nose.

Without even a moan or shout of pain, MJ hinged at her hips, pulling her knees underneath her. Then she flipped over, sitting up to face her captors.

There was at least one captor, maybe more. They were careful not to reveal too much of themselves. But he would find out who they were, and they would pay.

Jefferson's empty hand clenched into a fist on his knee; the acid in his stomach churned violently, a bitter taste rising in his throat. A wave of dread washed over him; he wanted to shut the video off, close his eyes, and block out the horror of what might unfold. But to find her, he had to delve into every detail, every whisper of information. The smallest clue in the video could be the key to discovering her whereabouts.

MJ pushed herself backwards, away from the camera as the person filming moved toward her. She scrambled as well as her bound feet allowed, pushing until her back hit the wall. A metal wall.

Smart girl, MJ. Don't let anyone get behind you.

Even with her head covered, MJ's rigid posture and unwillingness to stay in a vulnerable position suggested she was as defiant as ever. Still, Jefferson's heart lurched at the sight of her. Her brown curls hanging below the hood in a tangled mass.

The man snickered at her determination, but he did not speak. Instead, a robotic voiceover came on the video to make the demand.

"Detective Hughes. If Alex testifies, she dies. You choose. You have twenty-four hours from the time we sent this video to decide."

The screen went black.

Jefferson stared at the phone. He'd known who it was from the moment Shannon told him MJ was gone. This confirmed it. They couldn't find Alex, so they'd gone after him. They'd gone after him by taking MJ.

He punched at screen, trying to get back to the email header. What time? What time did they send it?

Amber glanced over. "They sent it at midnight."

"It's not enough time," Jefferson let out an anguished groan. "Twenty-four hours! It's not enough. We've already lost almost five."

His head slumped to his chest. He should have seen this coming. Nico and his cartel connections would never go down without a fight, without inflicting pain on those responsible. Alex held the keys to destroying so much of their drug-trafficking network. They would protect that network in the most violent way possible. He knew they would not hesitate to kill her.

With the video finished, the quiet thrum of the tires on pavement made the only sound. Amber waited, giving him time to absorb the contents of the video before she spoke.

"Kota has seen the video," she said, speaking of Dakota Soucy, the DEA agent assigned as Alex's handler when he turned to an informant.

"Does Alex know?"

She shook her head. "No. It's best for him to know nothing at this point. It would only jeopardize his safety. We stand a better chance of finding MJ if we don't have to worry about Alex, too."

Jefferson nodded. He suspected his brother would refuse to testify if he found out about the video. And Jefferson was just as certain that the men holding MJ would likely kill her either way.

No, removing his brother's testimony was not an option. They had to find MJ.

"Kota and a team will meet us in Vegas," Amber continued. "They've already been analyzing the security footage of her abduction. They'll brief us when we get there."

The detective squeezed his eyes shut, running a hand over his face.

How could this be happening? How did Nico and his henchmen already know how much he cared about MJ?

Turning his head to the window, he watched the cars and buildings blow by in a blur. He would figure that part out later. First, he had to focus on finding her, his heart pounding with urgency, his mind racing with the fear of being too late.

Chapter Four

Cold's menacing fingers buffeted MJ on every side, digging into her skin until it settled deep inside her bones.

She rubbed her arms, imagining the world outside this metal box, trying to keep her mind off the numbing temperature.

Her captors had taken her far enough from Las Vegas to shift the temperature. Perhaps to the mountains. Maybe north, to Utah. Once you drove past St. George, the winter temperatures plummeted. In her younger days, MJ skied the Utah mountains in places like Brian Head, just outside of Cedar City.

But the man who'd come inside, told her that kicking made no difference, had left no wet footprints. No snow. Just the cold. Dry cold.

And there she was, back at the temperature, her teeth rattling despite her best efforts to keep them quiet.

As much as it turned her stomach, MJ pulled the dirty blanket over her legs.

After the man left, she'd removed the blindfold to find a small Coleman cooler in the middle of the room, red with a white top that twisted down to open.

Her parents had one like that. When she was a kid, MJ's mom packed it with sandwiches and fruit when the three of them went hiking at Red Rock Canyon or went swimming at Lake Mead.

Tears trickled onto her frozen cheeks. What if they'd killed her mom?

She folded her arms on top of her knees, resting her head there, letting the tears fall. She didn't know why, but this was her fault. These people wanted her, not her mother. And now her mom could be dead or seriously injured, and she'd only wanted to spend time with MJ.

Her mom had been on the phone most of the morning, handling the last few details of a home sale closing that day. When she finally ended the last call, a smile lit up her face.

"That's it! It's all done, and a big payday for me." She'd wrapped MJ in a celebratory hug. "Spa day and dinner. My treat. What do you say?"

"I say, congratulations, and I'm in; no arm twisting required."

It had been a happy day. One of the best MJ had spent with her mom in a long time. Not once had she begged MJ to move back to Vegas. She never even mentioned MJ's ex-husband, Justin. In the past, her mom's incessant need to direct MJ's life had created a firmly planted wedge between them. But something had changed, and after pleasant conversation and a hot stone massage, MJ surprised herself by revealing a personal topic—her budding relationship with Detective Jefferson Hughes.

"I knew it," her mom had said, a knowing smile accompanying a shake of her head. "I knew that day in the hospital that you'd already lost your heart."

MJ rolled her eyes. "You wish. I definitely still disliked him then." She'd never admit it, but her mom was right.

When they first met, MJ considered the detective self-absorbed and inflexible, just a rule-bound cop. But when Jefferson risked his life to save her and so many other people, putting himself in the hospital, she began to see the truth behind his character. Her feelings about him softened and grew as she got to know him, even though he still tried to keep her out of his investigations.

Her mom had raised one expertly shaped brow. "Mm-hmm," she murmured. "Whatever, dear. Moms always know."

Just as they were about to leave the restaurant, a former client approached her mother.

"Toni!" cried a silver-haired woman in a sparkly gold jacket, her heels clicking a frantic rhythm against the tile floor, as she ran toward them with tiny, teetering steps.

"Linda? How are you, dear?"

The two women embraced.

"I am fantastic and loving my wonderful home, thanks to you. Is this your daughter?"

Linda released Toni and grabbed MJ in a tight, perfume-infused hug.

"Yes, she's a teacher and has spent Christmas break with us, which unfortunately ends too soon," Toni said, grabbing and squeezing MJ's hand as Linda's spontaneous hug ended.

"A teacher? How wonderful to be in education, just like your dad. Hats off to you. That's a tough job, and we need good people teaching the youth," Linda said, her high-pitched excitement lowering to a more serious tone. "And in case you didn't know, your mother is amazing. We just love her."

Toni smiled. "You're too kind. Be sure to tell Ken hello from me."

"Oh, I will. He's off to the golf tournament today. I'm guessing that's where your husband is?"

"Of course. He wouldn't miss it."

"Well, I'll let you girls get on with your day. I just wanted to say hello and Happy New Year."

MJ and her mom returned the greeting and headed out the doors onto the awning-covered walkway.

Just as they cleared the awning and stepped onto the sidewalk, a black SUV hurtled toward them.

The two jumped back to escape the path of the crazy driver. When the vehicle screeched to a halt in front of them, MJ grabbed her mother's hand, ready to run, her internal radar screaming danger.

They never had a chance. The doors opened. One masked, burly man swung at Toni's head with the butt of a gun.

MJ screamed as her mother fell against the SUV, blood already trickling from her temple. The scream had barely left her mouth when a bag went over her head and the world went black. They shoved her headfirst into the back seat.

Hands were all over her, patting and swiping until she felt her phone being pulled from the pocket of her jacket.

She tried to yank the bag off, kicking, screaming, and punching for the first few minutes, landing at least one blow that elicited an angry howl.

"She too much for you back there," the man in front asked with a humorless drawl.

"Not at all," seethed the other as he pinned MJ face-first onto the seat. She stiffened as he pushed the unmistakable barrel of a gun into the back of her head.

"I don't mind killing you right here. No skin off my nose." The man's bulky body pushed her legs hard into the leather as he enforced his words with more pressure on the gun to her head. Like a heavy stone, his other hand jammed into the middle of her back, crushing her lungs. His voice, rough with heavy breathing, held no panic, just calm assurance that the man did not lie.

That left her with little choice but to hold still, the hood moist with her ragged breathing. He could kill her now, in five minutes, in an hour, but that didn't seem to be the plan. They wanted her alive, and the reasons for that were all too horrible to imagine. Squeezing her eyes shut, MJ pressed her lips together to stifle the sob threatening to escape.

Satisfied that he'd squelched her fight, the man shifted back, freeing her just enough that she could breathe.

"Now stay down and don't move. I've still got my gun pointed at your pretty little head."

MJ did as he said, only turning her head to the side, attempting to increase the airflow through the bag.

She allowed a few silent tears to fall, realizing the hopelessness of her situation. The initial adrenaline had receded, leaving her limbs weak and shaking. The freshly eaten pasta gurgled in her stomach, threatening to travel back up her throat.

I am going to die today.

The thought came unbidden. It dragged through her mind on repeat, surrounded by images of guns and a hooded captive. She was the hooded captive, and the death would be hers. When this car stopped, her life would be over.

MJ gritted her teeth.

Stop it. Fight. Find a way out.

Biting back the panic, she tuned out the fear and listened.

The men did not speak to each other, but she heard the heavy breathing of the gun-toting brute next to her. So eager to use his weapon, he was likely the one who'd injured her mother. MJ resisted the urge to kick, hoping to find his face.

They were moving fast. Speeding would risk getting pulled over, so she'd figured they had to be on the freeway. But the way they were pitching back and forth, eliciting honks from other drivers, maybe they were speeding on a side road.

Focusing on the sounds inside and outside of the vehicle, MJ's heart slowed and her mind became more alert.

Then the SUV slowed, turned, slowed again, and came to a stop.

Her pulse immediately shot up again. Stopping meant the end. Whatever they were going to do to her, it would happen now.

The doors opened, and before MJ could react, the meaty hands of the gunman grabbed her feet and pulled. Then, securing an arm around her neck, he dragged her for a few feet before dropping her onto a cold cement floor.

"She's yours now," he said.

"What? No zip ties?" asked a man with a high, whiny voice.

"There wasn't time." This came from the driver of the vehicle. "She's a kicker though. I'd get those on before you try leaving."

A snicker. "She kicks me, I'll cut her feet off. Hey you!" shouted the whiny man. "Get over here and help."

Slow, lumbering footsteps approached.

"Hold her down while I take off these boots."

"No!" MJ shouted, trying to wriggle away. Hands like vice grips grabbed her ankles.

Another pair of hands unzipped her boots, pulling one off and then the other. Then he looped the plastic tie, pulling it tight

"Now flip her over."

The other man grabbed MJ's feet and twisted. Reaching for the ground, MJ fought to stay on her back, but her hands only slid along the smooth concrete, and the man was far too strong.

"Which car we taking?" asked the original gunman.

"The blue truck. Keys are in it," breathed the whiny man as he fought with MJ's hands. "And drive slow," he snarled.

She heard the shutting of car doors and a vehicle pulling away.

"No. Please. Just let me go," she pleaded, as the whiny man's sticky hands wrenched hers behind her back.

A wheezing laugh exploded from him. "No chance of that, little darling. You and this ugly brute are going to be spending some quality time together."

"You should watch your mouth," came the deliberate, menacing response of the other man.

"I'll watch you do as your told if you want to get paid."

A Mexican accent? Not strong, but just a touch. It might not mean a thing, but MJ locked it away in her brain as he zipped her hands together.

The other man grunted but said nothing.

They flipped her onto her back again. Two hands grasped the bag over her head, causing a moment of elation when she thought they would remove it. Instead, one man lifted it just far enough for the other to slap a strip of duct tape onto her mouth. She glimpsed thick legs, dirty jeans and dusty boots belonging to the bigger man as he straddled her with the tape.

"Alright, the package is all tied up and ready to go," said the man who seemed to be the boss. "Here is everything you need to know about your . . . houseguest. Send the videos to the two email addresses listed. Only use the phone provided." He took a few steps away. "Throw me your keys. I'll open the trunk. You pick her up."

MJ stiffened as rough hands grabbed her, throwing her over a shoulder, her stomach hitting hard against the muscle and bone.

Despite the duct tape, she let out a muted scream, bucking her body as the man bent over, moving her from his shoulder and throwing her into the trunk. She wrenched as her head and back connected with something hard.

"I was gonna put you in all nice, but suit yourself."

The trunk slammed closed.

***

This box. This clanking metal cage—it had to be a shipping container. Though she'd never been inside one, MJ knew people bought them, used them for storage or outbuildings. She'd seen just such a thing while watching an episode of "House to Home." The crew turned a dirty shipping container into a modern backyard office for a couple in Oklahoma. Of course, the TV version included things like insulation and carpet.

She'd bet a million bucks they didn't know the boxes also made excellent places for holding prisoners.

In the center of this shipping container, MJ's captors had added only a single light bulb, which cast a grim dusky light on everything inside. Scuffs, dirt, and dents marred the walls. The double metal doors were likely also an upgrade from the original industrial roll-up. The rough wood floor seemed like slivers waiting to happen. But wood in her skin was the least of MJ's worries.

No doubt about it, her situation was dire. But she was alive. And sitting here and freezing to death while waiting for the next shoe to drop? Not an option.

She stared at the cooler.

It could be food. It could be a body part.

A shudder gripped her as the image of her mom replayed, like a scene from a horror movie she couldn't forget. A horror that was all too real.

Squeezing her eyes shut, MJ forced the scene away, knowing there was nothing she could do to help her mom. Her focus had to be on finding a way out of this place.

Flinging the dingy blanket aside, she stood and walked swiftly to where the cooler sat. Squatting beside it, she grasped the handle built into the lid. The smooth plastic felt familiar, and for a moment, this terrifying day crashed into her childhood memories.

MJ closed her eyes and sucked in a slow breath.

Whatever was in this cooler, she would not scream. They would not get that satisfaction from her.

Her eyes blinked open at the same time she turned the lid.

A bottle of water. A sandwich inside a zip-top bag.

Falling onto her bottom, MJ put a hand to her chest to calm her pounding heart.

So it was just food. Not that she could eat anything. The pasta still sat like a brick in her stomach. She counted it as a minor miracle that it hadn't come up.

With careful fingers, MJ moved the sandwich aside to reveal a bag of sour cream and onion Lays potato chips and a smaller baggie filled with apple slices.

She took out the fruit, holding the bag up and staring at the perfectly cut slices in the putrid light.

What kind of big, buff kidnapper cut his victim's apples for them?

None. There had to be someone here besides the guy who left the cooler. And MJ would bet her lunch it was a woman. And not just a woman, but a mom or other caregiver. Someone who took care in preparing food for others.

She tossed the bag into the cooler and stood. The rush of adrenaline had warmed her momentarily, but now the cold leached onto her skin with fresh energy. MJ rubbed her arms, doing her best to ignore it.

A dog barked somewhere in the distance. It could have been close or a mile away. She couldn't tell. Was it *his* dog, or were there other people close by?

She moved to the double doors at the end of the container and examined the latch. A thick metal catch held the latch in place. It looked like an enormous version of a bathroom stall lock, the kind that swings up and down. Knowing it wouldn't open from the inside, MJ still tried, holding the latch and pushing upward. It didn't budge.

Looking at the walls, she began walking along one side. With so many markings and dents, she hoped to find a loose screw or anything that could be used as a weapon or tool.

Running her feet along the bottom and her hands over the wall, she managed to find two dead cockroaches on the floor.

At least they were dead, she thought, grateful that the kidnappers had at least left her socks on when they removed her boots. Toeing cockroaches, even dead ones, with her bare foot might have elicited the scream she'd been keeping inside.

On the smaller back wall, she found nothing.

This brief investigation of her surroundings, which had filled her with energy and a fragile bit of hope, was now doing the opposite. Her mood fell further into despondency as she shuffled along the last wall.

There had to be something. There were always options, always some way to change or fix a problem if she just kept poking at it. But even she had to admit that, so far, there was nothing here. She was stuck, and her captors held all the cards.

That's when she felt it, a couple of feet from the floor—something sticky on her fingers. She recoiled in shock, unsure whether to be excited or disgusted.

Reaching down, she touched it again. Not metal, but something else. She kneeled to examine the spot. Tracing the outside with her fingers, MJ realized she'd found a small hole.

With a fresh shot of adrenaline, she pushed on the middle. Duct tape. She was certain of it.

The hole itself was about two inches wide and had smooth edges, as if someone had cut it on purpose. Maybe to hold a pole or pipe at one time. Instead of filling it in or covering it more securely, they had slapped a piece of silver duct tape over it on the outside, thinking she'd never see it along the scarred silver walls.

They were wrong. And it may not turn into anything, but right then, finding that hole felt like salvation.

Chapter Five

Detective Rory Jackson sauntered into the police station like a man well-rested after a good night's sleep—not to mention a few days of vacation. As he walked to his desk, he saw the bald head of Detective Larson hunched over, his ear to the phone. Just as Rory approached, Larson reached over and put the phone back on the receiver.

"Good morning," he said to Larson.

Larson grunted and gave him a side-eye.

"Ah," said Rory. "You're still missing your pretty partner, Detective Mendez."

"You're funny, Jackson, but good of you to finally show up for work. Some of us have already put in a few hours."

"Well," said Rory, "I came as soon as I got the call. Besides, some of us are not willing to sacrifice their looks for the job. Seems like you gave up on that a long time ago," he said, patting the detective on the shoulder.

"Ha ha ha," said Larson. "The humor continues. Anyway, we've got quite a case to be handled today, so I hope you're up to it. I hope your mind's not still foggy from too much sleep."

"Sharp as always. But where's Jeffy? He usually beats me here."

"Don't know. He was with me this morning. We were supposed to meet here at the station, but I haven't seen him yet. Maybe he stopped off at that cafe he likes so much to get a muffin."

"Yes. Callie B's. Maybe he'll bring us all muffins," Rory said with a wriggle of his brows. "That would be a great way to start the day."

He plopped down in his desk chair and twirled around a few times before pulling up to his desk. Just as he opened his mouth to ask for the details of the morning's events, Larson's phone rang.

"You are a busy, important man," said Rory.

Larson, grabbing the handset, ignored him. After a quick, "Detective Larson," the man spoke no other words. He simply hung up the phone. "Chief wants to see both of us in his office, pronto."

"Uh oh," said Rory. "Whatever it is, Jefferson did it."

When they opened the door to the chief's office, the man's eyes flicked up momentarily before going directly back to his computer.

"Sit down, you two. I have something to tell you."

Rory raised his eyebrows at Larson as he took a seat. The other detective shrugged as if to say, "I have no idea what this is about."

The chief finished typing whatever he'd been working on and then appeared to hit send. Then, he clicked a few times with his mouse before flipping the laptop around to face them.

"Nothing I can say is going to prepare you for this," he said, his tone slightly less gruff than usual. "So I'm just going to show you."

A YouTube video appeared on the screen. The chief pushed play. A fresh-faced young reporter stood holding a microphone outside a building. Crime scene tape stretched across the building's entrance, whipping in the wind behind him. When he spoke, his eyes were serious beyond their years.

"I am here in front of Mia Italia in Las Vegas. It was at this spot last evening that masked men attacked two women as they exited the restaurant. Police have identified the women as . . ." He paused and consulted his notebook. "Local real estate agent Toni Devey and her daughter MJ Brooks of West Sound, Washington."

"What the—" began Rory.

"Just listen," ordered the chief.

"Devey remains in critical condition. Her daughter's whereabouts are unknown. Witnesses reported seeing the young woman being forced into a black SUV. Police have no motive for the attack, and they are following all leads to discover Ms. Brooks's whereabouts. And time is of the essence."

The picture then switched to a Las Vegas police officer. "Given the violence of this attack, we are very concerned for the safety of Ms. Brooks. We are going through witness statements, video footage, and talking to family and friends to uncover any lead, no matter how small, to find this young woman before she comes to further harm. We will release any footage we think might help in this endeavor and call on the citizens of Las Vegas to call the number on the screen if they see or hear anything out of the ordinary. If you see something, say something. You might save a woman's life."

The reporter's voice returned as a picture of MJ, kneeling on the shore of the Sound with her dog, filled the screen. "Brooks is a middle school teacher at Mariner Middle School in Washington State. Tonight, all of Las Vegas is praying for both women and for Brooks's safe return to her family and students. I'm Seth Morris. Channel Four news."

The chief closed the lid of his laptop and folded his hands, watching the two detectives with steely eyes.

"Looks like you two are going to be partnering up for the next few days, at least until Mendez returns. And I don't know when Hughes will return."

The two men exchanged glances, the truth of what this meant dawning.

"Hughes is going to Vegas," said Rory.

The chief confirmed with a single nod. "Hughes is on his way to Vegas now. I had a quick call with Agent Wells this morning. She has a knack for knowing everything before anyone else." The thought seemed to take him off track momentarily, wondering at Amber's powers. "She predicted that once Detective Hughes heard the news, he would run to Las Vegas without a second thought. Turns out, that is exactly what he was planning to do when she finally got him on the phone."

Rory began pacing behind his chair, tugging at his ginger beard.

Larson sat back, shaking his head. "This makes no sense. Why MJ? Do they think it was random? Someone she knows—some old boyfriend, or I don't know, a family member, something weird?"

A tense silence stretched for a few long seconds when the chief didn't answer, suggesting the two detectives should answer that question for themselves.

Rory suddenly stopped pacing. "So Agent Wells knows something, which means the feds are following this case."

Without dropping eye contact, the chief spoke, each word measured. "I didn't say that, but the logic tracks."

Grasping the back of his chair, Rory bent and shook his head. "Nico. This has to be something with Nico and Jefferson's brother."

Larson grunted. "They haven't had his trial yet, right? All this dilly-dallying around. Dang. I always knew that scumbag would rear his ugly head again."

"Look," said the chief, "this whole situation requires us to deal with some sensitive information. We'll all learn a lot more in the coming hours, but we still need to keep the details to a select few. Some of the FBI team will be here today. This station is home base for the operations—technical stuff, research — anything we can do to support Hughes, Agent Wells and Las Vegas law enforcement." The lines around his eyes softened. "This is MJ we're talking about. Her life is in very serious danger, and we are going to do everything we can to bring her home. But we'll do it from here. No more of my officers will run off to Vegas." His stern eyes held theirs. "Got it?"

"My wife thanks you," said Rory.

Larson rolled his eyes. "I think you have that backwards, Jackson. She's been trying to get rid of you."

"I'm glad you can joke at a time like this." The chief's stare could've melted a glacier.

Rory swallowed. "You're right, sir. I'm sorry. It's a coping thing."

"Find another way to cope when you're in this office."

Rory stood straight. "Understood, sir."

"Right," said the chief, unconvinced. "We'll make an announcement to all the officers, since this story is now making the rounds and most of them have at least heard of MJ Brooks. But we will share no other details."

"You two can help where needed, but Agent Julia Liufau will coordinate with the team in Nevada. I know how we all feel about Jefferson and MJ, but it's important that we keep things moving with our other cases. Larson, get Jackson here up to speed on the scene from this morning. Then, interview the kids you brought in. It won't hurt to give the parents another hour of peaceful sleep before you shatter their world with the notification."

The two men stood and made to leave the chief's office. Rory stopped. He turned back to look at the man from the doorway.

"Chief," he said, "has MJ been hurt? Do we know whether they've hurt her?"

The chief sighed. "We don't know. They took her alive, but in this business . . ." He looked away, fighting the images popping into his mind. "We deal with a lot of bad people, and the longer those kinds of men have MJ, the more dangerous her situation becomes."

Rory nodded solemnly, then turned and walked away.

***

Rory leaned against his desk, his arms folded, facing Larson but staring down at his shoes. "Why didn't he at least call me before he left?"

"Think of it this way. If it were your wife, would you stop to make courtesy calls before you rushed down there?"

"I guess you're right, but still . . ." He ran a hand over his face, stopping to rub his beard. "This is bad. This is really bad."

Larson nodded his agreement. "Unfortunately, there's not a lot we can do right now, at least for MJ and Hughes. So if I'm stuck with the station joker for the foreseeable future, I need you to focus on the Seal Point case." He gestured toward Rory's laptop. "The file is already on the secure portal. There's not much in it yet, but read it over. Forensics just added some pictures from the scene. Study those too. We'll talk when I get back, before we interview the two weed jockeys in there." He stood, stretching his arms overhead. "I need some coffee."

"Your insides must be permanently covered in coffee stains," Rory said, sitting and opening his laptop.

"I can think of worse things to stain a person. Especially when they're full of —"

"Yeah, yeah. I see where you're going with that train of thought." Larson snickered as he walked away.

***

The anxious youthful face on the opposite side of the table made Rory reminiscent. It wasn't so long ago that his younger self sat in a similar position after hanging with the wrong people.

Young Rory waited anxiously in a police station just the day after he'd signed papers sending him to Marine boot camp. The trouble started when his so-called friends begged him to spend an entire night running around, seeing girls, eating fast food, hanging out in the park . . . Whatever caught their fancy. They'd used the excuse that boot camp would end his life as a normal person, and he needed to enjoy one last night of madness.

They'd pulled off at a strip mall with a Seven-Eleven. Rory bought some chili-cheese nachos, ate them in the car while his friends ate hot dogs, and then he insisted on taking a nap.

His friends shocked him awake by jumping into the car. Kent, in the front passenger seat, shook him. "Drive! That guy's gonna kill us!"

Sure enough, the owner of the liquor store next to the Seven Eleven, a short dude sporting immense muscles and the look of a big toe, marched toward Rory's car.

Seeing the whiskey bottle in Kent's hand, Rory calmly took the keys out of the ignition and put them in his pocket. "Um, no. You two get out. You are not screwing me over."

"Rory!" screamed Jack from the back seat. "Go!"

Before they could make another plea, Big Toe Guy was banging on Rory's window. Thinking he could diffuse the situation by explaining that he had no intention of being his friends' getaway driver, Rory rolled down his window.

He hadn't spoken a syllable before the man's meaty fist crunched his nose.

Everyone except Rory ended up with a record that night.

The kid sitting across from him now didn't look especially smart, but he didn't look like a killer either. Like young Rory, all those years ago, he seemed stuck in someone else's mess.

He wore a sandy Carhartt beanie, a black Nike hoodie, and baggy jeans. With a straight posture, likely unusual for him, he rested his shaking hands on the tabletop, picking at the skin around his fingernails. A whisper of sweet, skunk-like scent floated onto the air every time he moved. Rory didn't think the kid was currently high, but he certainly smoked weed more often than he washed his clothes.

"So you are Dean, right?" asked Larson, his eyes on the folder in his hands.

"Yeah. Yeah, that's right. Dean Burton." He nodded as if the words alone might not be convincing enough.

Larson's hard eyes rested on the young man. "Tell us, Dean, how did you end up at Seal Point Park this morning?"

The kid sat up straighter, taking in a deep breath as he did so, color rising to his cheeks. "Okay. So Brayden, you know, the . . . the dead guy . . . Um, he called both me and JJ, you know, the other guy that was there with me. We knew he was out of juvie, but, you know, my parents wanted me to stay away from him."

"You live with your parents?" asked Rory.

Dean's color deepened slightly. "Uh, yeah. I'm starting classes at Evergreen College soon, so . . ." He ended with a shrug.

Rory lifted a brow. "That's great, man. Okay, sorry, you can keep going."

Blowing out a quick puff of air, Dean continued. "Okay, so he called. Wanted us to meet him at Seal Point. We used to do that a lot, you know, back in high school."

"What time did he call?"

The young man pulled out his phone. "It's here if you want to see." With a few swipes and taps, he set the phone on the table, showing it to the detectives. "It was like one in the morning."

"You were awake?" Larson asked, picking up the phone and reading the texts on the screen.

He nodded. "Yeah. JJ and I were playing video games. Not together, like in the same room, but online together. Anyway, Brayden called me first. I almost didn't answer it, and I kinda wish I hadn't."

"I bet," said Rory. "Did Braydon say why he wanted to meet?"

At this question, Dean's eyes darted to the table. He stared at it, contemplating his answer.

"Remember Dean," Rory said, sitting forward. "We are here because someone murdered your friend. We are not looking to string you up for anything unrelated to that."

The young man met the detective's eye and nodded. "Okay. Braydon said he had a good stash of weed he wanted to share. He wanted to celebrate being out of jail. I didn't really want to go, but he sounded so happy, and I felt bad just dissing him. You know, he made one bad mistake. I mean, it was a really bad mistake. I know that. But we used to be good friends."

"It was drugs that got him into trouble in the first place, wasn't it?" asked Larson, his eyes boring into Deans. "Wouldn't you be better friends if you convinced him to get clean? Or maybe you like the weed so much, you didn't really care about Braydon. Did you guys get in a fight? Anything like that?"

"What?" Dean's eyes flew open. "No, man. Nothing like that. Nothing like that at all. And Brayden said he wasn't even smoking the night he hit that car. I mean, he probably did the day before or earlier in the day. He smoked it a lot." His voice trailed off as if even he didn't believe his friend's claim. "We never even talked to him last night, like, in person. We walked down the path and found him there, all the blood and his throat . . ." His eyes welled up, and he rubbed them with his palms before hanging his head. "It was the worst thing I've ever seen."

Rory and Larson shared a look, silently confirming that the young man's emotion was convincingly real.

They gave him a minute to compose himself before Rory continued. "Do you know anyone who wanted to hurt Brayden?"

The kid shook his head. "No. We don't talk to anyone else from school. And I'm pretty sure Brayden didn't. I mean, after what he did . . . No one wanted to talk to him." A light seemed to enter his eyes as he shared his next thought. "But I was wondering if it was maybe someone he met in jail, you know, like happens in the movies. Or whoever he bought the weed from." The eager interest in his eyes made him look even more boyish.

Rory smiled. "Those are some good thoughts. Where did he usually get his weed?"

Dean shrugged. "I don't know about now, but he used to buy it off the street from a guy named Toby, like years ago. People say Toby ODed on Fenty. I'm not sure if that's true, though."

"Last name," asked Larson, as Rory made a note.

"Uh, I think maybe Shop or Shope. Something like that. I never met 'em."

"Anyone else?"

Looking between the two detectives, Dean hesitated. "I don't want to get anyone into trouble."

Larson's eyes narrowed. "You should worry more about keeping yourself out of trouble at this point."

The kid sighed. "Okay. It's just that, well, Brayden's dad always had a lot of weed. He might even grow some. Or at least he used to."

Rory stared back with wide eyes. "You think he'd give it to Brayden, even after the accident? Man, that is messed up."

"I'm not saying he did," insisted Dean. "But he used to give him some. That's all."

Shaking his head, Rory made a note to look into Brayden's dad. "Did you guys see anyone else in the park that night? Did you hear anything strange or see anything that seemed unusual?"

"Nothing," said Dean.

Larson picked up the young man's phone again, turning it in his hand. "Did Brayden post on social media or any gaming group chats?"

"Not that I know of," said Dean. "He wasn't in any of our gaming groups anymore. Not yet, anyway. He'd only been out a few days." The young man's brows drew together. "I don't think he did any social media. Right after the accident, people wrote some awful sh—." He shook his head. "Sorry. I mean, people wrote hateful stuff. Like you should kill yourself. Things like that. I think he closed all his accounts."

Rory made another note to get access to Brayden's social media profiles. Some people turned their online hate into real-world violence. There were so many crazies online these days.

Larson looked through his folder again. Rory knew there wasn't much to look at, but the tactic made the question seem less formal. "Did you or JJ touch anything at the crime scene? Will we find your fingerprints or DNA anywhere?"

"No, man." His voice went up an octave as he tried to press his case. "We . . . I mean, our footprints are all over the place 'cause we checked to see if we could help . . . You know if he was still alive." His voice died out, and he stared at his hands. "But it was obvious he was dead, so we didn't touch him. We just called you guys."

"Hold on a second." Rory jumped up and left the room. When he returned, he handed Dean a pamphlet.

"What you saw this morning, it can really mess with you. If you need someone to talk to, use these community resources," he said, pointing to the phone numbers on the pamphlet. "They're free, so don't just blow it off when the images get to you."

Dean nodded. "Thanks."

When Rory and Larson interviewed JJ, they got the same story, the same answers to all their questions. In the end, the two detectives found nothing to suggest the young men had any part in Brayden Shuster's murder.

Larson sat at his desk with his fourth cup of coffee in two hours. "So what do you think? Any grand ideas in that ginger head of yours?"

Rory tapped his notepad with his pen. "Unless Brayden stole the weed, I don't see that being a reason to murder him. But we should try to find that Toby guy anyway. It's possible the overdose rumor isn't true. Also, the social media hate. We need to get on Brayden's profiles, see if anything sticks out, like the same person posting repeatedly."

Larson sipped his coffee. "I'm glad one of us is bright-eyed and bushy-tailed."

"With all that coffee, you should be doing cartwheels."

"I'll do cartwheels when you shave that beard."

"So, never."

"Never."

Chapter Six

L anding in Las Vegas took too long. The seconds ticked by as the plane taxied to the gate. More time flew as vacationing passengers laughed and chatted, taking their sweet time getting their carry-on and exiting the plane. Jefferson almost lost his mind.

"She doesn't have much time."

That's what the email had said.

As they finally left the airport, the desert perfectly mirrored Jefferson's state of mind.

The stark land, like his thoughts, had a singular color; it vacillated between shades, but never veered too far from the base color of desert sand. There were buildings and flashy casinos, but that earthy color would outlast them all.

The video of MJ colored all of Jefferson's thoughts. Sometimes with fear. Sometimes with desperation. Sometimes with hope as he remembered her strength and her determination to overcome impossible odds.

But the constant color was always revenge. Someone was going to pay.

Those thoughts scared him almost as much as losing MJ. The raw desire to punish — it felt animal, uncontrollable. He didn't know this side of himself.

"Jeff," Amber said, as if this wasn't the first time she'd said his name.

They were in the back of a black SUV. He hadn't even noticed the make or model. A man in a white shirt and tie drove. Amber had introduced him, but Jefferson only remembered the 'agent' before his name.

Since leaving the airport, he'd stared out the window at the passing buildings and cars. MJ was out there somewhere.

He turned away from the window. "Sorry. What were you saying?"

"I said we are going straight to a meeting with Kota. He's been in contact with a few local sources. So anything they know, he'll know."

The detective nodded. "Good."

Amber fixed him with a steady gaze from behind her thin-framed glasses, her expression unreadable. As usual. The woman's poker face could serve her well in the city's many casinos.

Pressing her lips together, she turned away, sitting back against the seat. "Maybe you shouldn't have come."

Jefferson watched her, unsure how to respond. Did she expect him to act normal? He ran a hand through his hair. "I'm sorry. Trust me. I'm dialed in. There's just a lot to process . . . And I . . ." He turned back to the window, the rest of the sentence too hard to say.

Silence followed.

Finally, Amber touched his arm, waiting for him to look at her.

"I know how much you care about MJ," she said when he did. "I care about her too. But I need you clearheaded if you are going to be any help here."

"I know. And I am. You can trust me."

She sat back again. "Good. Because the last thing I need is to be worrying about both of you."

***

The G Hotel in Henderson, Nevada, was not a hotel at all but a motel on a busy highway. Apparently, they would not be going to the Strip or into Las Vegas itself for this meeting.

"What does the G stand for?" Jefferson asked as they pulled into the parking lot.

"I won't even guess," said Amber. "Kota picked the place. But rest assured, we are not staying here."

"I'd sleep in a tent if it meant finding MJ. Not that I'll be able to sleep."

The car stopped. The driver turned and flopped an arm across the back of the passenger seat. "That silver Explorer," he said, motioning with his head to the car parked next to them. "That one's yours."

"Thank you, Agent Toomey. We appreciate the pickup today."

"No problem. Room two. Agent Clark should be inside with the keys."

They thanked him again, then grabbed their bags.

Door number two, like the rest of the motel, had a fresh coat of white paint. Though the building seemed like a relic of the fifties, someone had updated the place so that it wasn't the fleabag Jefferson feared on first sight. Cheap, budget-friendly, but not the worst.

A beefy man with a badge hanging from a lanyard opened the door. In jeans and a T-shirt, he looked casual enough, but his narrowed, suspicious eyes said he was all business.

"That's them, Cam. Let them in," came a voice from inside.

The big man stepped aside. Amber and Jefferson entered the room to see DEA Agent Dakota Soucy perched on the edge of a twin bed. Next to him, a woman sat near a round table covered in papers and a computer. Someone had pushed it between the two twin beds of the tiny room.

Kota pressed his lips into a grimacing half-smile. "Agent Wells. Detectives Hughes. I wish I could say I was happy to see you."

Amber set her bag down. "The feeling's mutual."

"I would imagine so." His eyes fell on Jefferson briefly before he spoke again. "Well, we're glad you're here. You may know Agent Clark here," he said, motioning to the woman. She had salt and pepper hair wrapped in a tight bun.

"Of course. Good to see you again, Dawn. It's been a few years."

Dawn stood and gave Amber a quick hug. "More like twenty-five years, lady. It's good to see you, hon. I wish we were going to be partying later like old times, but I don't think that's in the cards."

"No, I'm afraid not," said Amber, casting a quick glance at Jefferson.

The detective raised an eyebrow. "Like old times?"

"I'll explain later."

"Sorry about the meeting spot," said Kota. "Since the perps sent the video of Ms. Brooks to the two of you, they must expect you'd come. And we're mixing some sketchy jurisdictional stuff. I don't want questions from the powers that be until we have more answers. So, this will have to do for now. Do you two need water or anything before we get started?" Kota's eyes swung between the new arrivals.

Jefferson ignored the question. "Who is protecting my brother?"

"Ah," said Kota with a patient nod. "You're right to ask. This whole situation underscores the importance of your brother's testimony. They are terrified of what Alex can do to them. But," he said, putting a hand out to stop Jefferson reiterating his question, "your brother is in expert hands. He's being protected by the Marshals Service, and they are very good at what they do."

"Yes, they are," added Cam, the man who'd answered the door.

Before Jefferson could say anything more, Amber took an almost undetectable step forward, just enough to signal the end of talk about Alex. "I think we're ready to be briefed."

Clearly, she still did not trust his state of mind. He eased out a breath, willing his racing heart to slow down. If he didn't stay focused, she'd cut him out. Amber cared about MJ and him. Jefferson knew that. But she was a stickler for a well-run operation. If Agent Wells believed for a second that his emotional state would compromise their objective, she'd cut off his access to sensitive information. The detective didn't doubt it for a second. And he wanted to find MJ. And to do that, he needed these people and their networks.

Kota stood with hands on his hips. "Alright. We'll share what we know, and then we'll take it from there. Agent Clark?"

"Sure thing." She moved the mouse and typed into the computer, which brought the television to life.

Jefferson and Amber sat on the edge of the other twin bed as an image of a white building appeared stark against the night sky, lights around the building glowing eerily. The camera angle was from the side, as if the camera operated from the corner of the building. A dark awning extended from the door onto the sidewalk, and two shadowy people were frozen mid-walk toward the parking lot.

"Las Vegas Metro has made some of the restaurant's security footage public, hoping to get some tips. We have the whole video, but I'm not sure how helpful it will be." Agent Clark clicked play and then sat back in her chair as the video began.

The frozen walkers continued on their way, eventually leaving the picture. For the next few seconds, the sidewalk in front of the restaurant was empty.

Then, Jefferson felt his jaw tighten and his teeth clench as he saw the restaurant door open. Two women emerged and walked under the awning. Even with the nighttime lighting, he knew it was MJ with her long brown curls, and the dark-haired woman he knew to be Tori Devey, MJ's mom.

Before they'd even reached the end of the walkway, a black SUV sped up to the curb. MJ immediately grabbed her mother, stepping back as if she sensed danger.

Giving her no time to make a move, a masked man jumped from the back driver-side door. Within seconds, he'd swung at Toni's head, knocking her to the ground. With barely a pause, he threw a black bag over MJ's head, and then tossed her into the back of the SUV as if she were nothing more than a toy. The car sped away.

Jefferson felt his nails biting into his palms. The whole thing had taken less than ten seconds.

"I'm going to guess the license plate is a fake," said Amber.

"Your guess is correct," said Agent Clark.

"Witnesses?" Jefferson barely got the word past his constricting throat. This was a nightmare. It tore at his very center to see MJ in the hands of those violent men.

Agent Clark eyed him curiously, but if she had questions about him, she kept them to herself. "There were quite a few witnesses. These guys were not quiet in their approach. But the witnesses saw the same things we saw on the video, which you'd have to agree doesn't give us much to go on."

She closed out the video and moved to another screen. "We have some footage from other businesses."

Another video began on the screen. "These are all strung together from different angles, so it's a little choppy. Here they are on Sammy Davis Jr. Boulevard. This tells me they know the area, or at least plotted their route ahead of time. Otherwise, they'd have gone out Las Vegas Boulevard and snarled in traffic."

The SUV sped in and out of traffic; the footage came in glimpses from each side and with the low angles of business-front cameras, some better than others at capturing nighttime footage.

"They follow this route until it turns into Industrial Road, and right here . . ." Agent Clark said, narrating as the SUV shot in and out of frames. "Right here we lose it. There are fewer cameras on this stretch of road. There's no sign of the SUV after that."

"So they pulled off somewhere in this area," said Amber, watching the screen that was now a static image of the last recording of the SUV.

"Looks that way," said Agent Clark. "Since we put together this footage, Metro and other agencies have spent the early morning hours searching every warehouse, parking garage, and parking lot in the area."

"We don't think they were there for long," added Kota. "This thing was well-planned. They knew we wouldn't get much from this footage. They took no pains to hide the actual abduction. And they weren't worried about us tracking them. There have to be more people involved than the two in the SUV."

The big man at the door lifted a shoulder. "Likely just hired hands."

Kota agreed. "Less risk of the goons getting caught and then spilling their guts, especially since much of Nico's network has been arrested, is lying low or has fled the country. If the search turns up anything, I'd put money on it being a discarded SUV."

Jefferson closed his eyes. "They were watching her."

No one spoke at first, and he wondered how much these agents knew about his connection to MJ.

"They were watching her, and they took her. They took her to get to me." He stared at the screen. "What I want to know is how they knew that MJ Brooks was anything more to me than an acquaintance."

Amber turned to face him. "Jeff, many people knew, or guessed anyway. I'm sure they had eyes on you too."

"That's pretty obvious now, but nothing was ever public. We barely even . . ." The sentence died on his lips.

"Now I'm getting the connection," said Dawn, studying Jefferson with soft eyes. "Don't think about that too much, hon. These worthless pieces of trash will exploit the slightest connection because they know good people care about each other. They might not even know the extent of your relationship. They sent the video to Agent Wells, too. Right? They just know she's important to you all." She tilted her head and squinted. "Didn't she help put Nico away?"

"Yes, she did," said Amber with the hint of a smile.

Dawn folded her arms and sat back. "Ha! A crime-solving teacher. He would've thought."

Jefferson had to admit he hadn't considered that MJ's role in catching Nico played a part in her abduction. Not that he felt any less responsible for this situation.

"What else do we know?"

"Not much, I'm afraid," said Kota. "But the DEA and FBI are both tracking down assets with any connection to Nico or the cartel, or sources with a good ear to the ground."

"We need to talk to Nico," said Jefferson. "This is all him. Somehow, he orchestrated this whole thing from prison."

"We're on it," said Kota. "Marshals at the SeaTac detention facility are working the levers to question the little puss-faced gnat as we speak."

Jefferson stood, running a hand through his hair. "I want to see it. When they interview him."

Kota stiffened. "They know what they're doing, detective."

"I'm sure they do. That's why I want to see it, see how Nico reacts, hear firsthand what he says. Any little sliver of information that might hint at what they've done with MJ, even if it's meant to twist me up."

"I'm not sure we can do that, but," the other man said, "I'll check. If it was my girl, I'd be wanting to rip some heads off, man. So I get it."

Jefferson wanted to say thanks, but didn't trust himself. He gave a single nod in the man's direction. Was MJ his girl? Would she see it that way? They'd had so little time together before this.

And what would she think of him when it was over?

Dawn Clark's phone buzzed on the table next to her. She gave them a motherly look of warning as she picked it up. "Now, you all be quiet for a second."

"Agent Clark," she said, taking the call.

All eyes in the room watched her with rapt attention. Not only were they quiet, no one even seemed to breathe while she listened to the voice on the other end.

"Okay, excellent. Thanks for the call."

Squeezing the phone in her hand, she pointed it toward Kota. "As you so prophetically predicted, they found the SUV."

Jefferson suddenly went cold, afraid of what else they'd found.

"Was there anyone or anything in it?" Amber asked, not looking at the detective. He silently thanked her for asking what he couldn't.

The other woman shook her head. "Empty. And yes, that's a good thing and a bad thing."

"Means they've moved her," said Kota. "They have an interest in keeping her alive at this point. But they could be anywhere within about eight hours of here, assuming they drove the entire way."

"Mexico?" asked Jefferson. "Would they risk going south?"

The door agent jumped in. "Don't think so. The border's an iffy prospect for criminals right now between ICE, Border Patrol, and

Homeland. Metro has already sent out a BOLO with her photo. That will go to the border, prompting agents to do extra vehicle inspections. If those guys try to take her across the border, they're stupid. And so far, they don't seem that stupid."

Amber stood with one hand on her waist and the other touching her chin, a position Jefferson recognized as her thinking posture. "Tell you what I'm going to have my local tech agent pore over all the video footage, checking the roads closest to the location of the SUV. If they switched vehicles, maybe he can work some magic. I'll have Agents Benton and Liufau from my office plot out potential routes they may have taken." As she added the next part, she shared a slight smile with Jefferson. "What these guys won't count on is that MJ Brooks has a mind of her own. The girl has a lot of fight in her. I think they made a mistake with such a public abduction. All of Nevada will be on the lookout for anything strange along these highways. I guarantee you MJ will do whatever it takes to draw attention."

A weak version of the detective's crooked smile showed itself, but it was short-lived. "We should go see the SUV."

Amber nodded. "I agree. But we'll need Dawn to come with us, or the local guys might just tell us to get lost."

The woman turned back to her computer. "No problem at all. I am at your disposal until we bring this girl home. Just tell me where to send all these files."

Amber moved to the table, picking up a pen and writing Jared's details.

"Has there been any word on MJ's mom, Toni Devey?" Jefferson asked the group.

Kota pursed his lips. "News is saying she's still in a coma. We've heard nothing different."

Jefferson took a deep breath as Amber returned to his side. "I want to—"

"To go to the hospital. I figured as much. We'll go there first. When we find MJ, her mom will be her first concern."

When we find MJ. He repeated it in his mind, clinging to the word "when" with all his might.

Chapter Seven

MJ pushed the duct tape gently at first, then with slightly more force. If she rushed it, the tape could blow away, fall to the ground, or double up on itself. The last thing she wanted was for her captors to realize she'd found this tiny porthole to the outside world.

With care, she pushed one side of the tape free. Then she pinched the edge of the tape with her thumb and forefinger, now stiff with cold. Slowly, she pulled the piece of tape through the hole, one small section at a time, keeping it as flat as possible. When the end of it appeared, she stuck it on the wall to keep from losing it.

Taking no time at all to revel in her day's accomplishment, MJ squatted down and put her eye to the opening.

The tiny porthole revealed more than she expected. Her metal box sat in a yard with other random pieces of junk and equipment scattered around. With a pile of old tires beside it, a useless, rusted-out truck waited in vain to be driven again. Straight ahead of her, someone had used a few tires as garden planters, maybe for tomatoes. The land, desert as she expected, had a fresh layer of snow. She could even see up into the hills behind the property. More snow dusted them, though the sky was as blue as ever.

Beyond the hills, there was nothing. No stores. No roads. No houses. No people.

He didn't lie. This was nowhere.

Adrenaline shot through MJ as she heard a scuffing sound outside the door. She hurriedly re-covered the hole and rushed back to the blanket, hoping the man wouldn't notice the tape on the inside.

With a squeak, the door opened. Holding a blue plastic bucket, the man shuffled inside wearing a Balaklava on his head and a gun on his hip. He set the bucket in the corner.

"This is for you to do your business." His tone made it sound as if he were bringing towels for a houseguest.

MJ made a disgusted face. "You're kidding, right? That's just gross."

She sensed a slight upturn of his lips, as if he preferred an argumentative captive.

"Don't worry. There's some kitty litter in there." He kicked the bucket with his boot so she could hear the litter rustle inside. "You'll survive. For now, anyway."

Once again, his words were in no hurry to come out. Keeping a woman prisoner didn't seem to stress him in the least. He sucked his teeth and then tilted his head to stare down at her. His speech carried a casual tone, but his eyes spoke a different language. Dark and brooding, they seemed the eyes of an unsympathetic man, one who could hurt others without remorse.

She suppressed a shudder, which would signal fear. Instead, she met his gaze, deciding in that moment, even at the risk of harm, to poke him for information.

"What do you want with me? Why did you take me?"

He turned back toward the door without answering. Just as he reached for the handle, he turned back. "I didn't take you. I just get to keep you."

There was no suppressing the shudder this time. It wracked her body as she hugged her knees.

He chuckled at the effect of his words, then pulled open the squeaking door and stepped through. There was a loud clang on the other side as he locked her inside again.

***

As soon as the door closed, MJ scurried back to the hole in the wall and peeled away the duct tape.

She kneeled with one eye to the outside, watching for shadows, listening for a door opening or closing, conversations with others. There had to be a house. The junk around the yard suggested that someone lived here, and they'd been here long enough to create the rusted, forgotten mess outside. Maybe the house didn't belong to the man who kept her prisoner, but there was more to this place than her metal cell.

Maybe they weren't alone. Could she find someone to help her?

MJ pulled her eye back from the hole, the cold air having sapped it of moisture. She rubbed her eyelid, trying to produce some moisture and relieve the dryness.

She'd been living in Washington for a long time. The desert of her native Nevada felt foreign to her skin. Every time she visited, it took at least a week before her nose quit feeling like sandpaper inside.

And she was pretty sure this place was still Nevada, even though her ride in the trunk had lasted at least five, maybe six hours. Given the snow on the ground, they had to have traveled north.

Curled up in the trunk, she'd felt every bump, every change of lanes, every stop as her head and back jostled against the hard metal surfaces surrounding her.

She hadn't made it easy for the person or people driving. They stopped only once. The sound of something hitting the car, or rather being inserted, told her they were stopping for gas. MJ screamed as loud as she could through the duct tape and hood, wrenching around to throw her feet up into the top of the trunk. This must have been effective, because someone hit the trunk as a warning to her.

Knowing things couldn't get any better if they left the gas station, she kept up the kicking and screaming.

If anyone heard, they didn't do anything to help. The car started, and they were on their way again.

MJ jumped at the sharp bark of a dog. This time, she could tell it was close.

Putting her eye to the hole again, she saw a white dog with tan patches running around in circles, as if waiting for something. It had a boxy nose like a pit bull.

Not exactly the kind of help she needed. The dog would more likely attack than let her escape. But the way the pit bull danced around . . . It must be mealtime. Edgar did the same thing when he knew food was coming.

A pang of sadness hit her at the thought of her dog. Would she ever see him again? Would she ever get out of this place?

Before she could spiral into complete hopelessness, a man appeared.

It wasn't the same man who'd delivered her food and bucket. This man was shorter and stockier. He faced away from her, but his head was bare, free of a mask. He had shaggy, thinning blond hair with streaks of white. The dog danced around his legs as he held a bowl aloft.

"Just hold on, Corky. Your food's coming, you silly dog."

MJ locked on as the man bent over to set the food down. Before it touched the ground, the dog shoved its jaws into the bowl and began scarfing down its meal.

"Somebody is hungry," said the man, petting the dog's head. "You're a silly dog, Corky."

With her eye beginning to dry out again, MJ attempted to shift position and switch to her other eye. In doing so, her knee hit the wall.

MJ sucked in a breath as both the dog and the man stopped what they were doing. The dog stared straight at her, a low growl beginning in his throat. Rather than wait for the man to turn around, MJ slapped the duct tape back in place and slid onto her bottom, her back against the wall, heart thrumming.

As she breathed to calm herself, another man shouted into the yard. It was the same deep, lumbering voice as the masked man from earlier. "Get back in here and wash the dishes. Leave the dog."

No response from the man outside. In fact, no sound from the man or his dog. MJ wondered if he'd noticed the duct tape was now on the inside. She tensed, expecting someone to come bursting in the door and do who knows what to her.

"Coming," he finally called back. "Dishes time. Got to do the dishes. Bye, Corky. Corky the silly dog."

MJ breathed a sigh of relief.

Chapter Eight

"**A**re you family?"

The nurse looked at the three of them as if she'd like nothing more than to boot them from her floor.

They'd agreed before arriving that Dawn would do all the talking. Jefferson put his hands on his hips, doing his best to appear only professionally interested in the patient. He'd only met Toni Devey once. It was the same day he first met MJ, the day after the horrific explosion at city hall that killed the middle school principal and almost MJ herself.

He clenched his jaw at the memory of her close brush with death. And here she was, her life caught in the balance again. Not just MJ, but her mother, too. All because of him.

"I am sorry," the nurse continued, "but only immediate family members may visit the ICU."

Dawn flashed her badge. "We understand. I'm Agent Clark with the Las Vegas FBI field office. We just want to speak with the victim's husband, Mr. Devey. Is he here?"

The other woman pursed her lips, her expression grave as she nodded. "I'll see if he can meet you in the waiting area. It might take a few minutes. Please have a seat, and I'll see what I can do."

Dawn thanked her, and the three of them moved to the carpeted area filled with sky blue chairs and light coral couches. Framed photos of serene desert landscapes hung on the wall, meant to soothe those whose loved ones battled for their lives.

Dawn and Amber both scrolled on their phones. Jefferson sat forward, his elbows on his knees, entwining and then freeing his fingers, like an unsure prayer. What would he even say to this man? An apology felt like the only decent thing to do. "I'm sorry, sir, but your daughter wouldn't be missing and your wife wouldn't be in a coma if MJ and I had never met. If my brother weren't an important witness bringing down one of the most dangerous drug traffickers in the country. Sorry about that."

He stared at his hands until he felt Amber's gaze on him.

Looking up, he met her eye.

"Just be calm," she warned. "We ask questions. We don't give information. This is not technically our case."

Sitting up, he ran a hand over his face. "I know."

"You've been awake for a long time. Try to catch a catnap when we're in the car."

He scoffed and shook his head.

Amber's eyes went to the hall behind him. She stood, and so did Dawn. Jefferson followed suit, turning to face the hall, momentarily frozen by what he saw.

MJ's blue eyes, tired and weighed down by worry, looked at them from the face of her father as he walked toward them.

Once the man stood before them, there was no suspicion in his expression, just a weariness borne of meeting strangers. He'd probably spoken to a million different police officers, doctors, nurses, hospital administrators, orderlies, and who knew how many others. Jefferson hoped the poor man had avoided the press.

Dawn stepped forward. "Hi, Mr. Devey. We're so sorry to have to pull you away at a time like this. My name is Dawn Clark, and I'm with the—"

"The FBI," he said, not unkindly but like a man for whom sleep was a memory. "I didn't know the FBI was handling the case."

"We're just assisting at this point. Metro PD has jurisdiction."

"Are you all FBI?" He scanned Amber and Jefferson.

"I am," Amber said, reaching forward to shake his hand. "Amber Wells, West Sound FBI field office. And this," she said, motioning toward Jefferson, "is Detective Hughes with the West Sound Police Department."

The man's eyes, MJ's eyes, squinted as he stared at Jefferson without reserve. "Wait," he said, putting his hands on his hips. "You're the one? Aren't you the one she's seeing, or dating, or whatever people call it these days?"

Jefferson stiffened, bracing for an angry outburst or an accusatory, *You're the reason she's in danger.*

"Yes, sir," he answered quietly.

The man's eyes welled with tears; his hand covered his mouth, and a muffled sob escaped.

Before Jefferson could react, MJ's father reached out and embraced him in a tight bear hug as he choked out the words, "Thank you for coming."

With his arms pinned at his sides, Jefferson tried to hug back, but the man held him so tightly, he was paralyzed. At least as tall as Jefferson, MJ's dad had the build of a linebacker.

Eventually, he released the hug. "I'm sorry. It's been a terrible night. And I miss my girls. Toni's lying there, fighting for her life. And MJ . . . I can't get the moment they took her out of my mind. Who knows what those animals are doing to my little girl. At least her mother is being spared the torture of thinking about it." He used the back of his hand to wipe his cheeks. He turned to Jefferson, his eyes suddenly hard like a steady blue flame. "You're going to find her, right?" The words were more of a command than a question, wielding all the authority of a father compounded by that of a high school principal.

That look, the same expression MJ used when she wanted answers, just about broke the detective. He clenched his jaw to steady his voice.

"That's why I'm here, sir. I will do whatever it takes."

MJ's dad nodded, the momentary fire already buried beneath his worry.

Amber found a tissue box nearby and offered it to him.

He took several. "Thank you."

"How is Mrs. Devey?" Jefferson asked, praying silently for good news.

The man shook his silver-haired head. "There's pressure from the original intracranial bleed, or so they tell me. That's causing the coma." He blew his nose. "Um, a bit of good news. She's shown a few random movements in her fingers, eyes flickered a few times. The doctors say that's good."

"Mr. Devey—" started Amber.

"Please. Call me Andy."

Amber gave a slight tilt of the head. "Andy. We would like to ask you a few questions if you are up for it."

"Sure, but I don't think I can tell you much. This whole thing is a complete shock."

They were the only people in the visitor's area, so they moved to chairs in the corner for more privacy.

"These questions may seem strange to you, but we are trying to cover all the bases," Amber said. "Do you have security cameras around your home?"

Despite her warning, his brows knit together. "This didn't happen at our home."

"That's true," Amber said as she sat forward a fraction more in her seat. "We need to determine if the perpetrators were targeting MJ before they actually took her."

A twist of pain flashed across Andy's face. "You think they were watching her?"

"We don't have any evidence of their watching or following her," added Dawn, attempting to tamp down the fury developing in the father's eyes.

"It's just one possibility we are exploring," assured Amber.

Andy took a deep breath, somewhat mollified by this response. "We have a camera on our front door and one on the garage. That's it."

"Do you know whether your neighbors have security cameras?" Amber pressed.

"Most of them have the same."

Amber sat back, watching Andy, as if deciding whether to ask the next question. Jefferson knew what she was going to ask, and why she hesitated. The question would spook Andy further.

Finally, she sighed and sat forward again. "Have you had any work done in your home recently . . . Cleaners, electricians, plumbers, anything like that?"

The man tilted his head to the side, eyes narrowed. He didn't answer, but he seemed to mull over her question, the truth dawning with each second that passed.

"You think they were in the house," he said, his voice barely above a whisper. Then his eyes bounced between the three of them. "Why do you think that? What do you know that you aren't telling me?"

Jefferson bowed his head, his elbows on his knees. Could they really lie to the man? A stab of gratitude hit as he heard Dawn speak up.

"Andy, unfortunately, we know very little at this point. But if there is any footage anywhere that might shed light on who took MJ and why, we want to find it. These guys were professional in the way they took her, meticulous, leaving few clues for us to follow. But if they were watching her, that's when they might have been sloppy. And it could provide the break we need."

Andy bent forward, both hands in his hair. He had a full head of it, and by the way it attempted to curl around his forehead, Jefferson could see which parent passed down the curls to MJ.

The man sighed. "It kills me to think we were being watched." His eyes were full of anguish as he looked up at them. "And in our house?" Sitting back, he slapped his thighs. "Okay, we had some cleaners in just before Christmas. And, um, I called an electrician because some of our outside lights weren't working. The circuit seemed fried for some . . ." As his voice trailed off, his eyes widened. "That guy. I'd never seen him before. The company normally sends a guy named Chase, a former student of mine. So that's weird, right?"

"Did he go inside the house?" asked Jefferson, a surge of energy increasing his pulse.

"Yeah. He needed to get to the panel, which is in the garage, but he asked to use the restroom, too. So I showed him where it was, and then I went back outside to see if the lights came on while he flipped the breakers."

Jefferson felt like jumping from his chair and running all the way to MJ's parents' house. If there were cameras hidden inside, this guy, the electrician, could be their first genuine lead.

Amber glanced at the detective, but that was the only outward sign that she felt as excited as he did. Her voice and movements remained calm and collected, as usual.

"Would you be okay with law enforcement sweeping your house, searching for cameras and reviewing your own security footage?"

"Yes. Yes, of course. Anything to find my daughter. What do I need to do?"

"Nothing right now," Amber said. "Your local PD will probably do the sweep. Do you know the name of the lead detective on your case?"

"Um, yeah." He sat forward and reached into a back pocket, pulling free a wallet. Opening it, he pulled out a card and handed it to Amber.

For a moment, she stared at it as if she couldn't read the name. Then, Jefferson detected a slight upturn on her lips. "Detective Ryan Hatch. Interesting." She handed the card back. "Thank you."

"You can keep it if you need to," Andy offered. "I have his number saved on my phone."

"No, keep it. I'll remember," said Amber, standing.

Only someone who knew the agent well would notice a change in her demeanor. Always focused, Amber seemed a bit distracted, as though the metro detective's name had taken her thoughts elsewhere.

Andy stood too, but his gaze shifted behind them. "Oh, well. Here he comes now."

Amber kept her eyes on Andy for a long moment. Slowly, she turned to watch the man coming toward them.

Detective Hatch stopped in his tracks. His eyes narrowed before a broad smile broke across his tan face. "Well, if it isn't Agent Amber Holt."

Chapter Nine

R ory checked his phone for the tenth time since getting in the car.

Nothing from Jefferson.

"Relax, Jackson. If he's got something to tell us, we'll hear it soon enough," said Larson as he turned onto Cecil Bay Highway. "You're making me feel bad pining away for your partner like that."

"Now who's the clown?" said Rory. He shoved his phone into his coat pocket. "Anyway, I'm not pining, I'm just . . . I feel like my kid is out driving alone for the first time."

Larson burst out laughing. "Oh, never let Hughes hear you say that. Better yet, be prepared to pay me in donuts so I don't repeat what you just said."

Rory snorted. "Don't count on it. He'd never believe you over me. No one would."

Larson nodded. "True. True."

Slouching down in his seat, Rory sighed. "It's just that he's been different since admitting his feelings for MJ. I don't say falling in love, because let's be clear, he was in love with her for a long time." He let his head fall against the headrest. "He's not quite the levelheaded guy we're used to. I just hope Amber can keep him in line."

Larson cast a quick sidelong glance at him as he stopped the car. "Come on. This is Hughes we're talking about. Besides, we're here, so get your head back in the game."

Rory looked up to see a postage-stamp-size house with grass-green siding.

"That was fast," said Rory, unbuckling his seatbelt.

"Get used to riding with me, kid."

Rolling his eyes, Rory exited the car and walked up the jagged walkway. Some of the wide cement planks were flat, but others rose from the ground like crooked teeth, tree roots having jacked them up over the years. Despite the state of the walkway, the house otherwise seemed well cared-for. Ornamental cabbages with bright pink centers lined the way to a mist-colored front door. A pot of newly planted pansies sat on the porch, with flowering heather on either side.

Before knocking, Larson looked at his watch. The stated time made him grimace. "I hope they're early risers. I hate waking people up, especially for crappy news."

"Amen," said Rory.

It took only two knocks for the door to open. The woman who opened it eyed them warily through wire-rimmed glasses.

"Can I help you?" She wore a pair of leggings, sneakers, and a sweatshirt as if ready for a workout.

"Mrs. Shuster?" Larson asked.

"That's me." Her eyes narrowed further.

"I'm Detective Larson and this is Detective Jackson with West Sound PD." Both detectives offered their IDs. "May we come in?"

She folded her arms and shifted her weight to one hip. "Tell me why first."

Larson's eyes never left hers, his features soft but insistent.

This seemed to flip a switch inside. "Is it Brayden? Oh no," she covered her mouth. "Is it my son?"

"Ma'am," said Rory. "Is Mr. Shuster at home?"

She stared at them, her eyes wide with horror, before nodding slowly. As she backed away, the detectives followed her inside.

***

Notifying parents of their child's death just about made the job unbearable.

Like every other cop in the world, Rory hated this part. No two cases were the same. No two losses were the same. You could improve in your delivery of the news, but you could never get used to the sounds, the pure guttural cries of anguish.

Today was no different.

Mrs. Shuster sat on the couch, arms crossed over her midsection, rocking to comfort herself. Her husband, who'd woken at the sound of his wife's anguished cries, rubbed her back, his own face contorted with pain.

"I'm sorry," said Mrs. Shuster, getting up from the couch. "I think I'm going to be sick." Her hand flew to her mouth as she rushed from the room.

Theirs wasn't a large home, and the detectives could easily hear the poor woman's retching through the walls.

Mr. Shuster hung his head, his hands on either side. After a moment, his wife's retching stopped.

She'd likely fallen to quiet sobbing, taking the time to grieve in private.

"We know this is a difficult time," said Rory. "We want to do everything we can to find the person or persons responsible for Brayden's death. Are you able to answer a few questions for us?"

The man nodded without speaking, his head still down. Then he sat up, wiping his eyes and nose with a paper towel Rory had grabbed from the kitchen.

"I'll try." Mr. Shuster took a deep breath, which hitched in the middle as his lungs tried to recover from weeping.

Rory pressed his lips into a sympathetic smile. "Thank you. This won't take long." He readied his pen and notepad as Larson asked the first question.

"Were you aware that your son was going to Seal Point Park sometime between midnight and 3 a.m.?"

"No. As far as I knew, he was asleep. Brayden went to bed before I did, although I suspect he played video games for a while." He sniffled and wiped his nose, balling the paper towel in his rough hands. "It's usually the other way around. I work at the WS Food warehouse. My shift starts at 5 a.m. most days. Today is my day off."

"Has Brayden left home in the middle of the night before?"

The man sat back, his red eyes wide as he shrugged. "I mean, he's only been home a few days . . ."

"What about before he went into juvenile detention?" Rory asked.

Mr. Shuster closed his eyes. New tears trickled down his cheeks before he answered in a weary voice. "Yeah. He did it a few times."

Mrs. Shuster shuffled back into the room, her sneakers gone and slippers on her feet. She had a thick red and green plaid blanket around her shoulders. Sitting down, she rested her head on Mr. Shuster's shoulder. Her puffy eyes stood out like wounds on her pale face.

Larson cleared his throat. "At the time of his death, Brayden had around one and a half ounces of marijuana. Do either of you know how he got it?"

Rory noticed Mrs. Shuster stiffen as her eyes flicked toward her husband and back.

The father's eyes widened. "What? No, that's impossible. Brayden didn't have two dimes to rub together."

Mrs. Shuster sat up, her lips a thin line as she watched her husband.

He could feel her hard, battered eyes on him, but he didn't meet her gaze. "Look, I've given Brayden some weed in the past. It was stupid of me, and I would never do it . . ." He faltered before finishing, remembering there would be no more opportunities to give his son anything. The man's face twisted with pain, and he bent his head down, rubbing the back of his neck.

"Did Brayden have any visitors here at the house?"

Mrs. Shuster put a hand on her husband's shoulder. "No. No one has been by since he came home. But I dropped him at the mall yesterday on my way to a hair appointment. He wanted to get some new shoes." She glanced at her husband and let out a shaky breath. "At least that's what he told me. I gave him my debit card."

If possible, her skin lost another shade of color as she recognized her son's betrayal of trust. Her fingers went to twisting her lips before she said in a weak voice, "Do you think the drugs had something to do with his death?" More tears fell from her eyes, but she ignored them.

"Until we have more information, we can't be sure," said Larson. "The fact that the bag was still in his possession suggests it doesn't, but we would like to know who supplied it and rule them out."

Then Rory added, "We also need to search Brayden's room and collect his electronics. Computers, phones, even old ones he may not use anymore."

The parents conferred with a look, their expressions weary and lost. Mr. Shuster then nodded to the detectives.

"Take whatever you need."

"His room is still clean," said Mrs. Shuster. "He wasn't back home long enough to mess . . ." A fresh groan of despair buried the rest of her words, and she grabbed her husband around the shoulders. He held her tightly as the sobs poured out.

***

When Rory and Larson returned to the station, they had company.

"Hey boss, happy holidays," said an always exuberant Special Agent Ron Benton as Rory laid a box of Brayden Shuster's electronics on Larson's desk.

The big man had taken up an empty desk near the two detectives. He sat back, his long legs out in front and swiveled his chair side to side.

"Ron," acknowledged Rory. "It's been a while, man. Welcome to back to the hub."

"It's nice to be with such fine people again, especially since you always have amazing snacks around here, even if your coffee is awful."

"That's why we brought our own machine," smiled Special Agent Julia Liufau, her long, black mane of hair stuffed under a Seattle Seahawks baseball cap. A Nespresso machine sat on her desk. "Just chip in here and there when we run low on pods. But this stuff is the best."

"I knew I liked you," said Larson, rubbing his hands together.

Rory shook Julia's hand. "You're feeding the monster," he said with a tip of his head toward Detective Larson. "And I'm afraid the only snacks we have these days are people's left-over Christmas cookies."

"Who has left-over Christmas cookies?" asked Ron. "That's a criminal offense."

Rory walked over to the quiet young man occupying the desk next to Julia, his eyes fixed on a laptop screen. "Hey Jared. Nice to see you again."

The young agent's eyes flicked up to Rory and then back to the screen. "Thanks. You too."

"What are you working on?" the detective asked, bending to look at the screen.

"I'm searching security footage around the area Ms. Brooks went missing."

"What are you looking for?"

Special Agent Jared Hill, a tech specialist, lifted his eyes to meet Julia's. The woman nodded once, her dark eyes moving between Jared and the detective.

The young man turned back to the screen, his fingers and mouse moving with speed and precision.

"Agent Wells believes MJ was moved from the original black SUV to another vehicle and then, potentially, driven out of the city. Las Vegas Metro found the SUV. I am searching the footage available from the area for a new vehicle."

He moved between videos with lightening speed. Rory wondered how he could determine anything without taking more time to search. But he knew better than to question the young man's methods. He'd been a key part of the investigations conducted with their FBI partners.

Unfortunately, they didn't have anyone on staff with Jared's skills to check Brayden Shuster's devices. They'd need to send it out to the county technology forensics team.

Rory looked up to see Chief Carlson walking into the hub, heading straight for Julia.

"Good. You're all here," he said. "Agents. Thank you for coming. Let's brief on both cases in ten minutes. We'll do the Shuster case first, with everyone. Then just the smaller team of agents and detectives for MJ. I know the Shuster murder is not a federal case, but you all know the area. Any extra input is always appreciated."

"Of course," said Julia. "I know SSA Wells wouldn't want it any other way."

"Alright," said the chief, turning to Larson. "Decide which officers you want on the Shuster case. Make sure they're in the briefing."

"Yes, sir."

The chief turned to go, and then stopped, setting his hard eyes on each person. "Get your coffee and bathroom breaks now. Don't keep us waiting." Then he marched back toward his office.

Chapter Ten

"Detective Hatch," said Amber, a faint smile playing on her lips.

Jefferson watched as they shook hands, feeling as though a new Amber had stepped into the shoes of the agent he knew.

"And it's Wells now," Amber said as she released his hand. Her smile, however, still hovered.

"Ah, you got married," grinned Detective Hatch. "I'm not surprised that some smart fellow snatched you up." Disappointment appeared to temper the man's enthusiasm, even though he claimed to expect the news.

Amber rolled her eyes with a good-natured huff. "Always the charmer," she said.

"Well, I'm charmed," said Dawn, reaching out and shaking the detective's hand with a twinkle in her eye. "I don't think we've met. I'm Agent Dawn Clark, Las Vegas field office."

"Nice to meet you," said Hatch, taking her hand in both of his. "I know a few of your colleagues. It's amazing we've never crossed paths."

Dawn chuckled. "I spend a lot of time in the outer reaches, so to speak. Nevada's a big state."

"Yes, it is." As his eyes moved to Jefferson, a flash of confusion wrinkled his brow. "Another FBI agent? I'm curious what brings you all here."

Jefferson reached out a hand. "Detective Jefferson Hughes, West Sound PD."

"And," broke in Andy. "He's been dating my daughter."

Detective Hatch's attention fell on him with fresh interest. "Is that so?"

Jefferson knew what the detective was thinking. If the roles were reversed, Detective Hughes's mind would have gone to the same place. The family, romantic partners, friends — all could be complicit in this crime. Start there and move the circle outward.

Before Hatch could ask another question, Amber took over. "Look, Detective Hatch—"

"For heaven's sake, Amber, call me Ryan."

"Fine, Ryan." That smile played on her lips again.

Detective Hatch was a good-looking man. His dark hair had spots of gray in all the right places, like a well-groomed professor. Las Vegas had provided him with glowing skin that stretched across his features without an ounce of fluff, suggesting a lean figure. Jefferson couldn't help but wonder about the past between these two.

Amber continued. "I'm sure you came here to share an update with Andy. If you prefer, we can step away and let you two talk."

A good-natured scowl crossed his face. "I'll sit on a cactus if you don't already know what I came to say."

"Ooh, I've done that by accident, friend. That's no picnic. You should take that back," warned Dawn.

Amber just smiled. Jefferson could swear the turn of her lips had an added bit of sass that the agent didn't normally display.

"Well, you might as well stick around," shrugged Hatch. "As long as Andy doesn't mind."

"I'd prefer it that way," MJ's father said.

With his hands on his hips, Hatch turned to Amber. "Why don't you tell him?"

Amber shook her head. "This is your jurisdiction."

"As long as we're all clear about that," Ryan said, looking between them. When no one disagreed or commented, he turned to Andy.

"We found the SUV."

Instead of feeling elated, the man paled. "Was she . . ."

"No. I'm sorry to say, and I'm not sorry to say, that it was empty. I wish we had found her unharmed in the SUV, but I'm also thrilled that they didn't hurt MJ, or worse, and then leave her there. Using a different vehicle to move her to another location, perhaps out of the city, confuses the trail. But, the forensics team is going over the SUV and the scene right now."

"But it's a lead, right?" asked Andy, with a glimmer of hope lighting his expression.

"Yes, it's a lead. I will let you know if anything comes of it, or if we find something else."

"Here," said Andy, reaching into his pocket. "Take my keys. These people here seem to think you need to get my security footage. Take whatever you need."

Detective Hatch turned narrowed eyes on Amber, but he took the keys. He clearly wanted an explanation. "Thanks, Andy."

***

Andy Devey returned to his wife's bedside, leaving the detectives and FBI agents to their own devices.

Detective Hatch spoke first. "Spill it, Amber. What aren't you telling me."

"We should sit down," Amber suggested.

"Not me," said Dawn. "You have a better chance checking out that vehicle with this guy than me," she flung her head sideways at Ryan Hatch, "I'm going to go on back to the office to check in with my boss. If you need something, just give me a holler."

"Thanks, Dawn," Amber said as she gave the other woman a brief hug.

"Of course, Darlin'. Detectives, it's been a pleasure. I'm sure I'll see the two of you again before this thing is all wrapped up."

When it was down to just the three of them, Amber's demeanor seemed more her usual careful self.

"I need to tell you first that I cannot tell you everything," she began.

"That's not a very promising start," frowned Hatch. "Does Detective Hughes know everything. I don't see him tagging along simply as a worried boyfriend."

Jefferson felt his hackles rise, his expression turning stone-like. They could be wasting time with this guy. "I know what I need to know."

With her characteristic, unquestionable authority, Amber said, "Detective Hughes knows more than I'm going to tell you."

The man's teeth glared against his tan skin as a grin split his lips. He watched Amber with a mix of admiration and ambivalence. "Still savage, I see."

Amber stared back, not disagreeing. Jefferson wondered again at the history between these two.

"Okay, fine," the other detective sighed. "Continue."

She told Hatch about MJ, how she'd helped put away a dangerous drug trafficker connected to a powerful cartel. That MJ's role may have made her a target. Jefferson chimed in where needed, but he mostly listened, regretting again that MJ ever became entangled with the case against Nico.

Amber never mentioned Alex. She said nothing about the DEA's involvment, the trial or the US Marshals who hid Jefferson's brother from the world.

"That's why we don't think this was random. There had to be more planning involved. They knew where MJ would be that night."

Hatched mulled this over. "That's why you want the security footage."

Amber nodded, watching as Jefferson stood and walked to the window. The hospital had a sweeping view of the city. Even in the daylight, the strip stood out like a colorful butterfly stuck to the desert sand. There would be thousands of people there now. New Year's Eve was just three days away. MJ didn't have that long to live if he failed to find her. He pushed his sleeve back and checked his watch.

Less than fifteen hours left.

Chapter Eleven

D espite her best efforts to stay awake, MJ drifted off to sleep.
Her mother came to her in a dream, reaching out for an
embrace awash in floral perfume. When she pulled away, MJ noticed
the bleeding gash in her head. Blood pooled at her mother's feet, but
Toni continued to smile as if unaware of the injury.

"Mom!" MJ tried to scream, but her voice failed. Her body seemed
under pressure, underwater, underground.

"Mom!"

She sat up, her heart racing to the rhythm of a dog barking. Sweaty
curls clung to her face.

It wasn't real.

Then she felt the frozen floor through the blanket, saw the four
walls of her prison. The reality hit with a force that turned her stomach.

Pulling her knees up, MJ rested her head there, willing the tears to
pass. She wouldn't give in to despondency. If she were going to make
it out of this alive, she had to be strong. People would look for her. She
knew it.

Jefferson would find her.

An image of the detective filled her mind. Those soft but determined sea-blue eyes of his. From the day they first met, he'd tried so

hard to be strident with her, but his eyes always gave him away. He could never hide the gentleness, and even sadness, there. In her mental picture, his face broke into that crooked smile, and she felt her heart glow as she smiled in return.

She loved him. Or at least she thought she did. There hadn't been time yet to explore their feelings for each other. And after her failed marriage to Justin, MJ distrusted her heart's ability to know what actual love felt like.

But she suspected that her feelings for Jefferson were genuine. With him, she could be herself. And that didn't scare him. It frustrated him. The thought made her grin mischievously. Oh, how he'd scowled the first time she'd stepped on his investigative toes. Back then, she was just the bossy teacher lady getting in his way. That changed over time, and he accepted her insight as valuable. He opened up to her, and MJ saw parts of Jefferson that were hidden from the rest of the world. That's when she knew Jefferson, the man, had crept into her heart.

The "Detective Hughes" part of him still hated when she took chances and put herself in harm's way. And that was fair. He carried a heavy sense of responsibility, and his desire to do the right thing made her love him even more.

This abduction would torture him.

MJ wiped her eyes. Self-preservation wasn't the only reason she needed to free herself. Jefferson, her father, and her students, who likely saw everything on the news; none of them needed more grief or chaos in their lives. The Christmas break would end soon. MJ had every intention of being in her classroom when students returned.

The cooler still sat on the floor. Turning the top, she opened it to find all the food still there. She ate the chips first, her stomach grumbling in thanks for the calories. Then she downed the water.

Opening the sandwich, she sniffed it. It was probably fine, but she wasn't desperate enough to trust it or the apple slices.

Instead, MJ took the sandwich and moved to the duct-taped hole. With the tape removed, she peered at the scene outside.

The dog, Corky, quiet now, lay in the dirt beside the rusted-out truck. No one else seemed to be outside.

MJ licked her lips, not sure if her next move was a good one.

"Corky," she called in a whisper. "Corky, buddy."

The dog's head shot up, and he stared directly at her. His curiosity outweighed his territorial instincts, and his head tilted side-to-side without a growl or bark.

MJ held a piece of the sandwich through the hole with the tips of her fingers. "Here, Corky."

A dog knows food when it's offered. Corky jumped up, tail wagging in a slow downward movement that signaled his uncertainty. He approached carefully at first, but in the last foot, he lunged and grabbed the sandwich between his powerful jaws.

MJ snatched her fingers back as the sandwich disappeared. Then she grabbed another piece, the dog watching the hole expectantly.

Before offering it to Corky, MJ rubbed it between her palms, ensuring her scent was all over the food.

"There you go. Good boy," she said as he snatched the second piece.

With the third piece, MJ opened the bread and smeared some peanut butter on her fingers. With a silent prayer that the dog wouldn't rip her fingers off, she offered the smeared peanut butter to Corky.

After a moment of sniffing, MJ felt the warm, wet tongue as the dog licked away the food. She was making friends.

"Oh, good boy," she praised while giving him another piece of sandwich. As he stepped back and chewed, MJ swept her eye over the yard again. Nothing had changed since the last time she spied through the small hole.

When Corky came close again, MJ sat back, narrowly missing an eyeful of wet dog nose. As she stuck the last sandwich piece through to the dog, he again backed away, and MJ returned her eye to the portal, hunting for any clue to where she was being held. That's when she realized what was on the truck.

A license plate.

A door slammed from somewhere on her left. MJ snatched her head back and slapped the tape back over the hole, praying that Corky wouldn't stand there staring at it.

But the next sound was a rattle of the shipping container doors.

MJ scurried back to the blanket and then used her feet to push until her back hit the wall.

When the doors opened, the same masked man appeared, carrying a phone in his hand. He nudged the cooler with the toe of his boot. "I see the food is to your liking."

His deep voice came out in a monotone that somehow still communicated mockery. "That's good," he said, dragging out the last word. "You're going to need energy for this next performance." His teeth filled the mouth hole of his mask like a faceless devil.

MJ's stomach lurched, but anger roiled in her gut. No matter what, he would not get out of this room alive if he tried to touch her.

He snorted at the look on her face. "Don't worry, honey. You ain't my type." Then he pulled a piece of folded paper from his pocket and threw it at her. "Your lines."

She stared at it, but didn't move.

"Pick it up," he said calmly.

Still, MJ stayed with her back to the wall.

The man heaved a sigh and reached behind his back, pulling a gun from his waistband and pointing it at her.

"Pick. It. Up." Though he punctuated each word, his voice remained unhurried. "I don't much care if you live or die, so if you're going to be too much trouble, I'll just shoot you and bury you out back."

"What will your boss say?"

Another flash of teeth. "Lady. I don't got any bosses. I work for me."

MJ glared. "What did I ever do to you? I don't even know you."

He chuckled. "We are not discussing my business arrangements, so pick up the paper in the next two seconds or I will pull this trigger and spill your pretty little brains all over that wall." His statement showed the first sign of impatience.

With her glare still zeroed on the masked man, MJ reached for the paper.

When she read it, her heart froze.

In sloppy, thick penmanship were the words, "Please, Jefferson, do what they say."

Chapter Twelve

"Well, you got your way," said Hatch as they walked through the rolled up warehouse door. "We've got a team headed to the Devey residence. They'll grab any security footage and search for signs of surveillance inside the home."

"Excellent," said Amber approvingly.

Other than the SUV, the place was completely empty with only lingering odors of fuel and dust. The unpleasant smell of sewer gas also permeated the buildings in the area.

After Hatch introduced Jefferson and Amber to the crime scene investigators, they got the early report. And the findings offered few new leads.

"Strands of long dark hair were readily available from the back seat, but there is little else that is easily identifiable. We've scoured the immediate area for similar hair samples, but so far have come up empty," said the CSI supervisor, a short man named Harsha with thick tortoise-shell glasses. The cinched hood of his protective suit amplified the roundness of his face, on which drops of sweat ran together down his nose. "We will keep looking, but if I were to hazard a guess . . " He gave one sweeping look around the room. "I'd say this is not where they swapped cars."

"So they just parked the SUV here knowing we'd find it eventually," said Hatch.

"I'd say so," answered the man. "We'll run some tests on debris found in the carpet, and other such micro-analysis, but there must be another location. If they were carrying the young woman, if she squirmed at all, I'd expect to find something. I don't even see obvious signs of a clean-up."

"I can guarantee you she squirmed," offered Amber. "MJ is a fighter."

"Well, then, you make my point," said the supervisor.

Jefferson looked away, not wanting to contemplate the image of MJ fighting her attackers. "Who owns the warehouse? How did the officers get in?" he asked, stepping to the open doors of the SUV. She'd been here. In this back seat, bound with her head covered. He squeezed his eyes shut against the image before turning around for a response.

"Sammy!" called Hatch.

"Here," said a young female officer standing near the rolling warehouse door.

"We have some questions for you. Do you mind stepping over?"

"Sure thing," she said, making her way to them.

With a tilt of his head toward Jefferson, Detective Hatch said, "Our visiting detective would like to know how you got into this place and what you know about the owners."

Her eyes narrowed slightly in confusion as she faced Jefferson. "Um, okay. . . Well, we tried to contact the owners for permission, but the company on the list didn't have a phone number, just an email. So Bonnie and I walked around the building and found a window. That's when we saw the vehicle. The license plate, even though it's fake, is the same as reported from the video footage. So . . ." She took a deep breath. "Sarge sent some back up, and told us to break the lock to get in since we had exigent circumstances . . . You know, that the victim could have been harmed and still in the vehicle."

"We're not questioning that decision at all," assured Hatch. "You did the right thing."

Jefferson pulled out his phone. "What's the company name?"

"Uh," said the officer as she retrieved a piece of paper from her vest and opened it. She ran her finger down the list. Then she stopped, folded the paper at the correct spot and handed it to him. "Here you go. It's Sunshine Partners, LLC."

"Sounds like the name of a shell company if I've ever heard one," said Amber, her phone already in her hand. "I'm going to send this to Ron and get him digging."

"We're already on it," said Hatch. "No worries."

Amber nodded. "I'm sure you are," she said. "But my guy, Ron. He has special powers and contacts in the shell company world."

Hatch met her eye, a ghost of a smile playing on his lips. "Your guy? Special powers?" He smirked. "Game on."

Amber rolled her eyes. "It's an investigation, Ryan. Not pickleball. But if it were . . ." She left the sentence hanging.

Before Ryan could respond, Amber's phone buzzed. She looked up at Jefferson. "It's Julia." Taking the call, she turned and walked a little distance off.

Jefferson followed, hanging on each word from Amber's side of the conversation.

"What did you find?" Amber looked sideways at Jefferson as she listened.

The conversation took less than a minute, and Amber said no other words except to tell Agent Liufau to send the information to her email.

"What is it," Jefferson asked, pouncing as soon as she ended the call.

Amber glanced toward Hatch and the others. "The CSI guy was right. This isn't where they brought MJ. Jared thinks he's a found a second vehicle that came from a different area, a sedan they may have used to drive MJ out of the city."

Jefferson took a step back. "Then let's go. We have to get that information out. Maybe we can still find it."

She put a hand up. "Wait. I'm not done. He said the license plate is also a fake, so this will not be as easy as finding the vehicle's owner."

"Fine," he said. "But it's a lead, and the more eyes we have on it, the better."

"Agreed. I just want you to understand that this is still going to take time."

Jefferson stepped back toward her, lowering his voice. "That's exactly what we don't have, Amber. MJ doesn't have time. It's running out."

She looked down, away from the naked fear in his eyes. "I know."

Jefferson hated the desperation in his voice, that he seemed to be aiming his fear and anger at someone who wanted to find MJ almost as badly as he did.

"I'm sorry," he breathed, running a hand through his hair.

A face full of patience, Amber waved him off. "Don't be. I know this is tough. But . . ." she glanced toward the group again. "I want to give Kota a heads up before we share this with anyone else. He has assets all over the state," she said, already tapping a number into her phone. "Like you said, the more eyes, the better."

Chapter Thirteen

Larson was the last into the briefing room, a steaming cup of coffee in his hands.

"That machine is incredible," he said taking a sip. "We need to get one."

"Have you really been so good-coffee deprived?" asked Ron, his dark brows steepled on his forehead.

"You know how bad our stuff is," Larson said with disgust.

Chief Carlson grunted. "Feel free to add that machine in your budget request."

"What budget request?" asked Rory, staring at Larson next to him.

"Exactly," the detective replied dryly.

"Everyone here?" asked the chief, looking around the table.

The FBI agents sat across from Rory and Larson. Officers Liam Fogarty, Evie Hanson, and Jacob Meyers took up three more chairs.

"Yes, sir," said Larson.

The chief took his seat. "Good. We'll get started with the Shuster case. Larson, fill us in."

After taking another gulp of coffee, the detective set his mug down. "The victim, Brayden Shuster, was twenty years old. After serving three years in juvenile corrections for vehicular manslaughter, he was released just a week ago to the residence of his parents. Two buddies who were supposed to meet him at Seal Point Park, found him with a gash in his throat. On his person we found 1.5 ounces of weed, a wallet containing ten bucks, and car keys. That pretty much rules out robbery as the motive."

Larson stopped, raised a finger in the air, and took another drink of coffee. "So good," he said, smacking his lips. "Detective Hughes found a plastic button near the victim. We are not sure if it has any relevance as this is a public and well-used beach, but there you have it. We also have an initial report from Stacey Underhill, which my excellent colleague Detective Jackson will share."

Rory looked at him askance. "Chief, we need to keep feeding him this coffee. That's the nicest thing the man has ever said to me."

Chief Carlson stared at him with hard gray eyes. "Get on with it, Jackson." Before Rory could continue, the big man turned to look at Meyers.

The young officer played with his watch, pushing buttons and then scrolling on the screen. Evie Hanson gave him a soft elbow to the side.

"Son, you should be taking notes for the crime board."

Meyers flinched. "Oh . . . right. Sorry, sir."

The young officer hoped to become a detective one day. He'd proved efficient at keeping the details of their cases straight by maintaining an accurate crime board. Taking on that responsibility gave him opportunities to learn from the chief and the detectives.

"No worries. Carry on, Jackson."

"The doctor's first conclusion, not any real surprise, is that the cause of death is exsanguination, loss of blood because of damage to the jugular vein, followed by asphyxiation caused by the inhalation of blood." Rory cleared his throat and tugged at his collar. "Weapon used is likely a sharp kitchen or hunting knife with a medium-sized blade. She also found fabric fibers under the victim's fingernails, which suggests that Brayden may have grabbed some part of the killer's clothing in the struggle. Those are undergoing further testing."

Rory looked up to see Officer Hanson whispering something to Meyers, whose skin had taken on a distinct mossy color. Soon, they had the entire group's attention.

"Everything okay there, Officer Hanson?" asked the chief, looking on with a wrinkle in his bushy brows.

"Yes, sir," she said, taking Meyers's pen from his hand and pulling his notebook toward her. "I'm just going to take notes for Meyers while he gets a drink."

The other officer shook his head. "No. I'm fine."

"I think it's best, son. Take all the time you need." The chief left no room for argument

With an annoyed sidelong glance at Evie Hanson, the officer reluctantly stood and left the room.

When Meyers was gone, the chief let out a sigh. "This is a nasty one and hard for the young guys. Everyone else doing all right?"

Fogarty sniffled as if he wanted to say something, but didn't dare.

"Officer Fogarty?" The chief narrowed his gaze in the officer's direction.

The natural pink hue of the young man's skin increased slightly at the chief's directness, but not as much as it would have a year ago. He was getting used to answering superiors.

"Well, sir. I'm not going to be sick or anything. Shuster's death was gruesome, for sure, and what happened to him isn't right. It's just that I remember when he crashed into that lady and her kid. That was pretty awful, too."

"It was," agreed the chief with a quick dip of his chin. "But nothing justifies murder, especially for a young man who served his time as required by the law. We will not tolerate such things in this city."

"No, sir. Of course. I wasn't saying that. Sorry." Fogarty retreated to his notebook.

The boss's hard eyes lingered on the officer for a few seconds longer before turning his focus to Larson and Rory again. "So what are your next steps?"

Larson had polished off his coffee and now sat back from the table, his foot resting on the opposite knee. "We've spoken to his parents and are fairly confident that they knew nothing of Brayden's plans last night. We are looking into a guy he used to buy his weed from, a fellow by the name of . . ." He sat up to consult his notes.

"Toby, last name unknown," Rory filled in. "But Brayden's pals said it was something like Shop or Shope. We'll have Fogarty and Hanson hit the street today to see what they can dig up. We will head to the juvenile detention center to see what they can tell us about Brayden and anyone he may have met there."

"Got it," said Fogarty, writing the name, his cheeks back to their normal pink.

"Phone? Computers?" asked the chief.

"Waiting on the county and a warrant for the phone," said Larson. "We'd love to use Jared, but he's a little busy."

The young tech agent looked up briefly from his laptop, his eyes meeting Larson's before darting back to his screen.

"Yes, he is," said Julia, her dark eyes shadowed below the bill of her hat. "We'd love for our work to be finished and MJ found safe and sound, obviously."

A couple of people quietly agreed, but otherwise the room fell silent as they all reflected on the reality of MJ's abduction.

Just then, the door opened and Meyers returned, having regained his normal complexion.

The chief raised his palm, stopping Meyers from returning to his seat. "I think that's it for Shuster. Hanson, share your notes with Meyers. Let's get that board going. You three officers are free to go."

The officers stood, but before they filed out, Fogarty cleared his throat, preparing to ask another question.

The chief put his palm up. "This better be good, son."

"Yes, sorry, Chief. I'm just wondering if there's been any update on MJ." He turned to look at Julia. "I know she's not safe yet, but do they know where she is or have there been any demands or anything, for like money or something?"

The older man shook his head solemnly. "Not that we know of, son."

"Okay. She's just always been so nice to me. I wish I could do something."

"We all do, man," said Rory. "Just pray for her, you know?"

"Yeah," said the officer. "I can do that. I think."

Confusion flickered in his eyes, as if the young man was unfamiliar with the practice of prayer.

Without another word, the three left the room.

***

When the officers were gone, Rory couldn't hold back.

"Tell us what's going on. I haven't heard from Jefferson, and there has been nothing new reported by the media."

"Whoa there," said Ron. "Take a breath."

Julia hit Ron with an elbow. "Hey. I hope you're that worried when I disappear."

Ron shrugged. "I'd probably stop eating."

"That's a lie," she said, shaking her head as she opened a folder on the table. "We have a few updates," she said, looking at each person. "They found the SUV used in the abduction." Pulling a picture from the folder, she passed it to Larson, who studied it before passing it to Rory.

"The Las Vegas CSI team found hair samples that likely belong to MJ. They are testing those now. So far, they have identified no other relevant evidence, but the more complex tests take more time."

The chief looked up from the photo. "Where is this?"

"A warehouse owned by a shell company," answered Julia. "Ron has the name and is researching links to find the people connected to the company."

Ron flashed a confident smile. "Trust me. We'll find the miscreants. These guys think they're so clever. It insults the intelligence."

"I have all the faith in you, Ronnie," said Julia, pulling another paper from her file. "We think the abductors switched cars. Jared studied hundreds of videos and images of the area. I'll let him explain what he did."

Jared's mop of brown curls suddenly jerked up, a scowl flashing across his face. The young man hated speaking in front of people, but Amber wasn't there to intercede on his behalf. "I can if necessary."

"Please do," said Julia. "I don't really understand it, so I think it would be helpful. You've done a lot of great work."

He pressed his lips together, keeping his eyes on the laptop screen. "Well, I selected a radius directed outward from the last camera sighting of the SUV. Then I used a program to analyze which vehicles entered the radius from within the radius itself, so not coming from anywhere outside." He wiggled forward to sit higher in his seat, still tapping keys on his screen. "That narrowed the field significantly. I checked license plates, and when I found one that did not match the vehicle description, I flagged it up. There were two during the hour directly following MJ's abduction. One was a compact pickup truck. The other is a sedan."

Rory let out a whistle. "My head is spinning. That's a lot of footage surfing."

Jared shrugged one shoulder. "It wasn't too hard."

Julia grinned like a proud mother. "Thank you, Jared." She passed around another picture. "This is the vehicle in question. We've checked the pickup, and it seems the least likely option for hiding a victim. Amber will forward the description and plate number of the pickup to Las Vegas law enforcement for follow-up. We think the sedan holds greater interest."

Larson took the photo while Rory leaned in, attempting to get an advanced look. "A bit of a rust bucket," said Larson, passing the picture into the eager detective's hands.

Rory sat back, studying the photo intensely. Though the image was supposed to be color, the nighttime recording washed it out, making the car at first glance appear white; the color could just as easily be silver or beige. The angle did not offer a clear view of the driver. "That's an old Toyota Corolla. Probably eighty-something. Is this the best image you've found?"

Tilting her head with a lifted brow, Julia said, "Someone knows his cars. You're right about the make and model. It's a 1989, to be exact. And, unfortunately, yes. That's our best image."

"Were you able to track it?" asked Larson.

Surprising everyone, Jared piped up. "That part of Las Vegas turns industrial and less dense quickly. Fewer cameras are available past a certain point. If the driver took the freeway or a highway, we don't know yet which way they went. I am working on obtaining more footage, if it's available."

Though he usually spoke with a matter-of-fact tone, a hint of disappointment colored the young agent's words. Everyone in this meeting knew MJ Brooks. Her abduction weighed on them all. Jared's words seemed to remind them, and a quiet settled over the group.

Julia broke the silence. "I don't think it will be long before we have something on the sedan. Amber sent a text update just before the briefing that Las Vegas Metro is putting out an all-points bulletin for the Corolla."

"I know this isn't exactly on topic, but do we know how MJ's mom is doing?" Rory asked. He still remembered meeting Toni Devey after MJ's close call with the city hall explosion. An all-around classy lady, sleek and styled to perfection, Mrs. Devey always had a pleasant word for the detectives. He prayed she would make it.

With a solemn expression, Julia let out a sigh. "I'm afraid she's still in a coma. There have been some positive signs. Her husband said doctors were optimistic, but it's definitely touch and go."

The agent rolled her shoulders back. "Okay, but we have some other news."

"Bring it on," said Larson. "We need a pick-me-up after being reminded what that animal did to MJ's mother."

"I'm not sure if this will do the trick, but Amber and Detective Hughes believe MJ was watched and followed previous to the attack. They have a lead on an electrician who had access to the home. They suspect he may have placed cameras inside the house."

"Have they found cameras?" asked the chief, sitting back with a dark look in his flinty eyes.

"Las Vegas officers are sweeping the property now. I expect to hear any minute. I also expect they will find cameras."

Rory blew out a breath. "This has organized hit written all over it."

"Yep," agreed Julia.

"So, Nico?" asked Rory, his eyes moving between Julia and the chief.

The agent met the chief's eyes and gave a subtle nod.

Taking a deep breath, the chief spoke in a hushed tone, unlike his usual booming voice. "What you hear now cannot leave this room. You are to share this information with no one who is not already in this room. Is that clear?"

The detectives nodded. Rory sat forward, his arms crossed on the table.

The chief's face became still. His voice was tight and controlled, as if anything less would unleash the anger behind his words. "A few hours after MJ's abduction, both Detective Hughes and Agent Wels received a video. It showed MJ, her face hooded; her hands and feet bound. She was in what appears to be a shipping container. A voice on the video warned that if Jefferson's brother testifies against Nico and his network members, they will kill MJ. They are giving him twenty-four hours to make a choice. MJ's life or Alex's testimony."

Rory sat back heavily, pulling his hands down his face. "This is so much worse."

With a glance at Rory, Larson said, "No wonder he shot out-of-town like a bat out of hell."

"And unfortunately," added Julia. "We are already about ten hours in."

"Then he can't testify," said Rory, throwing his hands up in a shrug, as if it was the most obvious answer of all.

Everyone looked at him, but no one spoke. Their eyes eventually drifted away, because no one wanted to state the truth. Even Rory knew his statement was ridiculous.

Ron spoke first. "I worked on a kidnapping case early in my career in South Texas. Brownsville area." For once, the big man had no humor in his expression. His eyes were on the table, but he seemed a million miles away.

"A young Mexican girl came across the border with some friends for her birthday." He looked up with a sad smile. "Her name was Camila. It was her thirteenth birthday." He sighed. "Her 'friends' were not the good people she thought they were, and for few bucks they sold her upriver to a pair of men from a rival cartel who'd followed them into the U.S. Of course, they promised no harm would come to the girl if her father ceded the territory to them."

He turned hard eyes on Rory. "The father did all they asked. But you can guess what happened. We found her in a dumpster, and I'll just leave it at that."

"Sorry, man," said the detective.

"Not as sorry as I am." Ron stood up. Dropping a pen on the table, he said, "I need some water." Then he walked out.

"He's right," Julia said, her dark, intense eyes shaded with sadness. "Remember, Nico tried to get Detective Hughes's own brother to kill him. And not just kill him, but torture him in front of Nico, all for some kind of sick entertainment." Breathing in through her nose, she pressed her lips together, her eyes now bright with intensity. "MJ's best hope is her own intelligence and strength combined with us—law enforcement teams working together to find her. And that is what we are going to do."

Chapter Fourteen

When Detective Hatch asked if they'd eaten, just the thought of food made Jefferson's stomach turn. Eating struck him as vile as long as MJ was in danger. How could he do anything normal while some animal put his hands on her?

But as much as he resisted, Amber would hear none of it.

"You won't be any good to me at all if you can't function, Jefferson. At least drink something and have a small bite to eat."

Hatch took them to a diner in downtown Las Vegas called Ameri-Brunch Cafe. When Jefferson saw the line outside the door, he stopped.

"Nope," he said, shaking his head. "A McDonald's drive-thru makes more sense if you really must get food."

"I have to agree, Ryan," said Amber. "Even if we just get takeout, waiting in this line is a waste of time."

Hatch grinned. "Trust me, guys. I know people." He turned and took a few steps backwards. "Breakfast bagels all around?" He said, pointing at the two of them.

When Jefferson said nothing and Amber gave him a half-hearted "sure," Hatch turned and strolled confidently past the waiting patrons, heading straight for the cafe entrance.

"How do you know this guy?" Jefferson asked, watching the spot where Hatch disappeared inside the cafe. Several people in line were casting annoyed glances their way.

"We worked a few cases together back in the day," she said, her eyes on her phone.

Before he could ask a follow-up question, Hatch was back, a white paper bag in one hand and a drink carrier in the other, a grin plastered on his face. "Shall we head back to the car?"

"Okay, that was fast," said Amber.

"I might have texted ahead," said Hatch with a wink. "There's a coffee for you, Amber, a Coke for me and one for Detective Hughes. Sorry if that's not your thing. I guessed."

Though he didn't want the drink, Jefferson took it, offering a muted thanks. Amber took her coffee, and Hatch discarded the carrier tray in a nearby trashcan.

The three of them returned to the borrowed FBI SUV to discuss their next steps over breakfast. Hatch took up the backseat while Amber and Jefferson were in front. Hatch passed the bag around and then dove headlong into his food.

After he'd demolished half his bagel, Hatch took a sip of his Coke as he studied Amber. "So has she ever told you about the time she wrangled an entire herd of bad dudes all by herself?"

"Ryan," Amber warned.

The Las Vegas detective chuckled. "I'll never forget rolling up on you that day. It was hot as blazes, and you had them two dudes shackled to their own pickup truck." A smile played on his lips as he shook his head slowly back and forth at the memory. "Savage." His white teeth gleamed with an appreciative grin.

"Let's not bring that up," she said, glancing at Detective Hughes with obvious discomfort.

"Yep, that's when we first met. I was a deputy for the Nye County Sheriff's Office when I got the call for help. The call came after some lady relayed a message from her CB radio. FBI agent in distress." His eyes met Amber's. "I'd say them fellas were the ones in distress."

Hatch took a huge bite of his bagel and egg breakfast. On a normal day, Detective Hughes would be right there with him, digging into his own bagel. Instead, his food still sat in the bag, untouched. Today was not a normal day, and the sight of the food only fueled his impatience.

As the other detective dug into his food, Jefferson watched as Amber studiously avoided looking at either of them. Despite himself, he couldn't help the curiosity bubbling up.

"So what did the guys do, the ones you 'wrangled?'"

Amber chewed her bagel, glaring at Ryan Hatch like she might murder him right there and then. "We are done talking about that." She said bluntly, going back to her food. "Now eat."

Jefferson took a drink of Coke, not tempted by the food. The knot in his stomach wouldn't allow him to digest anything.

Sitting back and wiping his mouth with a napkin, Hatch looked more serious. "Just one more point on the matter. Did you know that Gary Ottis died in prison?"

Amber stopped mid-bite. Lowering the bagel to the wrapper in her lap. Then she wiped her hands in slow motion. "No. I did not know that."

"Yeah," said Hatch. "He mouthed off to the wrong guy. Some people never learn." He looked down as his phone buzzed in his jacket pocket.

"Hatch here," he said, answering the call, holding the last nub of his bagel in the other hand as he listened. His eyes flicked to Amber and then Jefferson. "Uh-huh. I see. Good work, Sammy." After a few seconds, he said, "No. No. We'll follow up with them. Text me the info. Thanks."

When he hung up, his eyes gleamed like a man ready for the hunt. "I think we've got ourselves a proper lead."

***

Despite his initial excitement about a new lead in the case, Detective Hatch seemed content to finish his breakfast in their car. Watching the man chew, Jefferson felt his muscles tighten like a cat ready to pounce. Not being in his own jurisdiction meant he had to rely on others, work on their timeline. But the need to do, to get moving, was eating him alive. Finally, he could stand it no longer.

"Are you going to share this new lead?" he asked, his voice laced with impatience.

Hatch sat back and swigged his Coke. "See. The way I figure it, the second I tell you about the lead, you are going to jump your good-looking self up outta here to chase it."

"You're pretty smart," Jefferson said, his expression as cold as his breakfast.

Hatch's lips spread in a toothy grin, but the rest of his face didn't follow. "If I've learned one thing, it's that running all over like a chicken with its head cut off, not taking care of yourself, mind and body, only wastes time and gets people hurt." He winked at Jefferson and shrugged, taking another drink. "I was hoping to see you eat something before we take off."

Not amused, Jefferson said, "I've learned that you waste time by wasting time, and this," he motioned to the bag of food, "is wasting time."

With another shrug, Hatch looked at Amber. "Does your boy here ever eat?"

Amber had wrapped up her half-eaten bagel. Holding her coffee in both hands, she watched the two of them like a bored babysitter.

"You're both right," she said. "We could have gone straight to the station to sort out our next steps, get updated information, etc. Then again," she added, glancing up at Jefferson, "you are not doing yourself or MJ any favors by refusing even a morsel of food."

He put his hands up in surrender. "Fine." Unwrapping his bagel, he took a huge bite before dropping back in the paper bag. "Now, tell us the new lead," he said to Hatch through a mouthful of food.

With a tilt of her head, Amber raised her eyebrows expectantly at the Las Vegas detective.

Hatch balled up his empty wrapper. "I'm done anyhow."

Wiping his mouth with a napkin, he sat forward, lowering his voice. "A woman called the tip line. She'd been pumping gas at an Arco out in Beatty, on Highway 95. According to her, there were strange sounds coming from the trunk of a car, and her description matches our sedan."

Eyes wide, Jefferson stared at the man. "And you were just content to wait on that? Sitting on the most actionable lead we've had? You are putting MJ at risk with your negligence."

Without warning, Hatch dropped the good-natured expression, his voice taking an angry turn. "I know my job, detective. We're not just sitting on anything. A Ney County deputy is on his way to take a statement from the witness as we speak. Another is headed to the Arco for the security footage. Like I said, a chicken with its head cut off just wastes time. We have partnerships for a reason."

Amber appeared to ignore the two detectives' sharp words, focusing instead on her phone as she typed information. "What is the witness's name?"

With his eyes pinned on Detective Hughes, Hatch said, "I'd rather not say just yet."

With her fingers still moving, Amber kept her eyes on her task. "Ryan, don't make this a thing. Just tell me."

Despite his tough talk, the Las Vegas detective had no armor against Amber's demands. He released Jefferson from his gaze and picked up his phone.

"Gina Sweeney of Austin, Nevada."

"Thank you," said Amber, still not looking up from her phone.

Jefferson didn't care that Hatch was right. Withholding the lead was just arrogance. "I appreciate the teamwork, but I prefer to check out this lead myself. If that's the direction they went, then heading that way is our best hope of finding MJ, and that's all I care about right now."

Hatch turned to Amber. "Do you want to tell him?"

Amber put her phone down and pushed her glasses on top of her head, rubbing her eyes with her fingertips. "Jeff, the town of Beatty is almost two hours away, at normal speed. With blue lights, maybe we'd make it in an hour and a half. But once you get past that tiny speck of civilization, there is nothing out there. That part of Nevada is not the place you run to without a plan."

Just then, Jefferson's phone vibrated in his hand. At the same time, Amber's buzzed on her lap. Their eyes met, each fearing what was waiting in their in-boxes.

Jefferson swiped his screen, unable to disguise the slight tremor in his hand. Before he could go any further, he felt a slight hand squeeze his wrist.

"Don't open it yet," Amber said, her steady eyes full of compassion but also demanding.

Though it killed him to wait, he knew the agent was right.

"Ryan," she said to Hatch, "can you give us a minute?"

The other detective still looked rankled from his exchange with Jefferson. "Now who's hiding leads."

Amber closed her eyes and took a breath. "Please."

Once again, Hatch's resolve melted away. "Fine, but only because *you* asked," he said, opening the door.

"I need to make a phone call, anyway." Then he stepped out of the car and left them alone.

***

"I don't think he should see this video," Jefferson said in a low voice, looking straight ahead. "It could be sensitive."

While they'd shared a lot of information with Hatch, no one in Las Vegas law enforcement, besides Agent Dawn Clark, knew the real motive behind MJ's kidnapping. Jefferson wanted it to stay that way. His brother being safely hidden away with armed and capable U.S. marshals allowed the detective to focus on finding MJ. Having both in immediate danger might be more than he could handle.

"I would normally agree, but if we want Ryan Hatch to increase his urgency to the same degree as ours, then I think it's time we let him in."

Jefferson gritted his teeth, not liking the agent's answer. "I just don't know why you trust this guy. He seems . . ." He stared out the windshield at Hatch talking on his phone.

"Arrogant," she supplied.

He shook his head. "Nah. I work with Detective Larson. I can deal with arrogant. It's more like lackadaisical, like he's got it all figured out when he doesn't."

Her face became serious as her eyes locked on his. "Do you trust me, Jeff?"

"You know I do."

"Then believe me when I tell you we can trust Hatch."

His eyes narrowed as he considered this. Then he looked upward with a resigned sigh.

"I know it's hard to trust when people you love are in danger."

The detective shied away from meeting her eyes. She'd said the word, and he knew it was true. He loved MJ. He wouldn't deny it. The feeling lived so deep in his bones that letting it show had felt like revealing dangerously vulnerable parts of himself. But when he'd finally relented, there was freedom and happiness like he'd never known. And now, he might lose the very woman who meant the world to him.

Instead of looking at her, he watched as Hatch made his way back to the car. "Well, someday, you are going to tell me the complete story of you and Detective Hatch. If I agree to trust this guy, I deserve that much."

She chuckled lightly. "I might tell you more, but certainly not everything."

The detective turned to her with no small amount of shock in his raised brows. She ignored him as Hatch opened the door and jumped into the back seat.

***

Jefferson could hardly keep his eyes on the screen as the video played the first time through. Without the head covering, he could see every mark, every speck of dirt, every waver of MJ's lips as she made the forced plea.

"Jefferson, please do as they say."

Hatch rubbed his chin, looking between the driver and passenger seats in front of him. "All right, Agent Wells. What aren't you telling me?"

With her eyes on Jefferson, Amber gave him a subtle nod, her way of saying that she would do the explaining.

Hatch listened without interruption, his eyes narrowed and his lips pursed as if he were working to keep his own mouth shut. He clearly did not like being left in the dark this long.

When Amber finished, the man stared at Jefferson. "This explains so much. Until now, I had a hard time understanding why Amber let you tag along."

Jefferson offered a deadly, crooked smile that held no humor. "Tag along?"

Hatch put both his palms up. "Sorry. Bad choice of words."

"Look. I agreed to tell you only because, for some unknown reason, Agent Wells trusts you. I don't. And if you do anything to jeopardize the safety of MJ or my brother, you'll have me to answer to." Jefferson didn't raise his voice, but the seething calm behind it left no room for questioning his sincerity. He held up his phone with the frozen image of MJ. "This," he said, thrusting the phone into the detective's face. "This is all I care about right now, not your hurt feelings at being left out of the inner circle."

"Oh, so you're the one deciding who gets to know what?" He chuckled. "I don't think so."

"Gentlemen," said Amber, waving a hand in the air between them. "Enough of this . . . this man thing. Just stop it. We have work to do."

She was right. Jefferson stared at his screen again, deciding to ignore Hatch.

The other detective slid down in his seat, his hands on his knees. "Well, do you think MJ knows what they want Jefferson to do?"

Amber shook her head. "I doubt it. Listen to her voice. It's a little shaky at the end, but MJ's every bit as defiant as ever. These were not her words," she said without looking up from her phone. "I'm sending a copy to Jared right now."

Jefferson started the video again. MJ still sat against the wall, keeping the captor or captors in front of her. Amber was right. Her voice was firm, and her beautiful blue eyes flared as she spoke into the camera.

They'd threatened her with something. Just the idea of it lit a flame of hatred inside him. Whoever had MJ would pay.

He watched it again. And again. And again.

A light touch on his shoulder made him look up. "Jeff," Amber said with concern.

When he turned, her eyes widened in alarm. "Jefferson, you've lost at least three shades of color. You need to stop." She put a hand over his phone. "Please."

"No, wait," he said, yanking his phone out from under her hand. "Look. She's doing something with her hands."

"What?"

He played the video again as Amber looked on. Sure enough, MJ's fingers were moving so subtly that the agent hadn't noticed at first.

"What is that?"

Jefferson stared at the phone. "I'm not sure."

"Can I get another look?" asked Hatch.

Glancing back at the man, Jefferson felt the earlier irritation directing his features.

"Show it to him," said Amber. "I'm going to call Jared."

Relenting, the detective handed Hatch his phone. Within seconds, Jefferson could hear MJ's plea again as the Las Vegas detective played the video.

"That's sign language," said Hatch.

"What do you mean?" asked Jefferson.

"I mean, it's sign language. Well, some of it is. At least one of her signals is a letter. The rest are probably numbers. I have a nephew who's hard of hearing. I don't know many words or anything, but I know the ASL alphabet."

"Hey, Jared," said Amber. "I'm putting you on speaker. Have you watched the video?"

"Yes," came the clipped response. "MJ is signaling a partial license plate number with sign language and numbers."

Jefferson shot a glance at Hatch, who shrugged with an "I told you so" smile.

"How do you know it's a license plate?" asked Jefferson.

Silence on the other end, as if the question had stumped Jared.

After a few seconds, the young man spoke. "It's the only logical conclusion. Otherwise, the numbers and letter are meaningless."

In reality, the question only stumped the tech agent because he'd thought the answer obvious.

"Can you track the video's source?" asked Amber.

"I'm working on that now. Agent Liufau is searching license plates using a filter. It will pull all catalogued plates containing the figure and numbers shown by MJ, which are A434."

"How long will that take?" asked Jefferson, pulling out his notepad and writing the plate numbers.

"Could be minutes. Could be days. The make and model would help, if the plate is even in the system. This depends on the age of the vehicle, the date of last paid registration, whether used in the commission of a crime, and other factors."

Amber pressed her lips together, not liking their odds. "Thanks, Jared. We'll pass the plate information to Las Vegas Metro so they can search on their end as well."

"They shouldn't bother. Our system is faster," came the deadpan reply.

"Okay," muttered Hatch. "Doesn't pull any punches, does he?"

With a suppressed smile, Amber thanked Jared again and ended the call.

Hatch opened the car door and put one foot on the ground. "Follow me to the station. We can check in with Nye County and the team at the Devey house. There is no time to waste." He said the last part with a wink at Jefferson, and then he was gone.

Chapter Fifteen

The spider dangled in open space, testing its surroundings. MJ wondered what the tiny creature saw when it gazed with all of its eyes. If she remembered right, spiders had eight eyes or something.

This inability to remember such facts is the reason I teach English, she thought. Not that she had a terrible memory; it was more that she just didn't care how many eyes spiders had. Things she cared about stuck in her mind like lifelong glue. She never forgot the difference between affect and effect, or the Greek and Latin suffixes that turned verbs into nouns. How locate became location.

The spider dangled for a few seconds before deciding the descent wasn't worth the risk and retreated to the ceiling.

"I wouldn't come down here either," she told it. "But if you can figure out how to unlock that door, I'd be forever grateful. Or maybe make a big web outside that says 'help?'"

Her spider was likely too little to do anything as spectacular as Charlotte.

Letting her head rest against the wall, MJ laughed at herself. She hadn't even been here long enough to go insane. Maybe that was her natural state of mind.

She ran fingers through her tangled mass of hair, wishing she could wrangle it with a hair tie. Maybe she'd ask for one when Mr. "I don't mind killing you" comes back. If there were a woman cutting her apples, perhaps she could spare an elastic band.

So killing her wasn't the end game. At least not yet. What did they want Jefferson to do? How had they even known to kidnap her in order to get to him? It wasn't like they'd had a long relationship or something. One date. A lunch date at that.

One kiss. One magnificent kiss. She ran a finger over her lips, remembering the warmth of Jefferson's mouth on that snowy day. The gentle uncertainty at first, and then the force of it as they both yielded to their pent-up feelings.

Covering her face with her hands, MJ rubbed her eyes, dispelling the images and bringing herself back to reality. Such memories only stirred up the fear that she would never get out of this place.

Corky barked outside. She had no new food to give him, but she went to have a look anyway.

After removing the tape, she put her right eye to the hole. It was snowing. The flakes, however, were so tiny and weightless that they floated on the air, almost melting before they hit the barren ground.

MJ shifted slightly and tried to cast her gaze as far to the left as possible. All sounds of doors opening and closing came from that direction. There had to be a house there, but no matter how far she stretched her vision, it never came into view, not even a corner.

The cold air once again sucked the moisture from her eye. She sat back and rubbed it, making tears form to give it some relief.

Something in her movement must have reached the dog's ears, because when she put her left eye to the hole, she saw Corky trotting toward her. His tail waved behind him, which gave her some hope that he'd already formed a positive connection to her.

"Hey, boy," she whispered as he approached. "Sorry, no food, buddy." Gingerly, she stuck her fingers partially through the hole. That way, if he decided to bite, she could pull her hand out quickly.

But Corky was a smart boy. MJ smiled as she felt his warm tongue on her fingers. Maybe he smelled a remnant of the peanut butter.

"That's a good boy," she said, reaching her fingers as far as possible to scratch his nose. After a few seconds, she felt only air and realized he must have pulled back or left when he realized there was no treat forthcoming.

She bent down to look. To her shock, MJ came eye to eye with a human.

Jumping back, she stared wildly at the hole, her breath coming in spurts.

"What's your name?" said the person. It sounded like the man from earlier, the one who had fed Corky.

MJ could feel herself trembling, sudden nausea gripping her. The potato chips threatened to return. Swallowing, she forced herself to respond.

"My name is MJ," she said, the fear still obvious in the waver of her voice. "What's yours?" She bent so that her face was in line with the man's eye.

"I'm Robbie. Why are you in there? I don't think you should be in there."

MJ covered her mouth as a sob escaped. "No," she said, trying to control her emotions. "I don't think I should be. Can you help me get out?"

The man's enormous eye stared at her, and then it narrowed slightly. "I'll have to ask."

"No!" MJ said in a loud whisper. Then she calmed herself, not wanting to scare the man away. He was not a young man, but his manner of speech suggested he might be autistic or have another mental disability that made him childlike. Such persons were often bound by rules and routine. If she had any hope of eliciting his help, she had to appeal to his sense of fairness. "I mean, please don't say anything. You wouldn't want to get me into trouble, right? I mean, I just want to go home, Robbie. Then I'll go away and not bother anyone."

He seemed to think about this for a minute. Then he said, "I think Corky likes you. Are you friends with Corky, the silly dog?"

MJ felt herself relaxing. Robbie, if she could keep him quiet about this conversation, could be her saving grace.

"Yes. I like Corky a lot. He is silly, but he's a good friend."

"He sure is," said Robbie. "I would be really sad without Corky. He's my only friend. Everyone else is mean. Except the other lady. She's nice, but she's scared all the time, too."

So, there was a lady. She knew it!

"I can be your friend, Robbie. But you can't tell the mean person that we talked, or he might not let us be friends. What is the lady's name?"

Before he could answer, a man's voice bellowed into the yard. "Get in here and eat."

With that, MJ could hear Robbie running away. She could only hope that he needed a friend badly enough to risk keeping her a secret.

Chapter Sixteen

The Rainier County Juvenile Detention Center sprawled across almost twenty acres. The age of the place meant that some buildings were not functional or suitable for housing youth. As a result, the center housed less than fifty percent of its 100-person original capacity, an acute shortage for all the surrounding communities that relied upon it.

The front entrance always reminded Rory of a church with its steep overhanging roof and narrow elongated windows. Not any church he would want to attend, not without offering to paint it and do a little upkeep. The place emanated depression rather than God's light and hope.

Once inside, they checked in with the officer at the registration window. She called the center administrator, who was expecting them.

Within seconds, a tall Black man strolled down the hall toward them.

"Detectives." The man gave a hurried smile as he approached them. Then he pointed one arm in the direction from which he'd just arrived. "I'm Cliff Jones. We can head on down to my office this way."

The hall to Jones's office was navy blue to the middle, topped with a thin line of lime green, similar to the Seattle Seahawks color scheme. The top half of the wall was white and remarkably clean. It had been a long time since either detective had been inside the facility, but Rory seemed to remember the walls being a putrid moss color. The paint job must be relatively new.

The Seahawks theme extended to the man's office with posters and even a throw blanket over his chair. He was clearly a fan.

"Gentlemen, please take a seat," Jones said, motioning to the two chairs in front of his desk.

"Thank you for taking the time to see us," said Rory. "I'm sure you're busy." He looked at the wall next to him. "I like the new paint job."

The man picked up a file from his desk and handed it to Larson. "Well, it's about a year old now, but the kids like it. Most of them." He grinned. "We have a few rando fans of other teams, so they like to hold their noses at it." He sat back, turning a paper clip between his fingers. "That file there is all we have on Brayden Shuster. In summary, he was a model inmate. Never got in any trouble. Kept his head down, did his schoolwork to finish up high school. I'd say that's why he got an early release."

Larson looked up from the file. "What about drugs?"

Cliff Jones nodded his head slowly. "Yes, he was definitely addicted when he came to us. Mostly a weed and alcohol guy. I don't think he routinely did any hard drugs, though I'd hesitate to say he never did, but that's not the type of treatment program he was in."

"So he got clean in here?" asked Rory.

"Sure did," said Jones, with a quick dip of his head. "Didn't take him very long either." He lifted his shoulders in an enormous sigh. "Man, I really thought that kid was going to make it."

"He might have," said Larson, "but someone else didn't give him the chance. Can you think of anyone that Brayden had a friendship with while here, or any enemies?"

"No enemies, really," said Jones. "I mean every kid gets in a scrap here and there over dumb stuff, but there were no consistent issues with anyone. As far as friends . . . He ate his meals occasionally with a kid named Oscar. Oscar Carmelo. He's still here if you want to talk to him. Oscar got here about a year after Brayden."

Larson closed the folder. "Yes, that would be helpful."

Jones stood. "All right. Just give me a minute."

***

Shuffling into the office wearing a baggy blue jumpsuit and orange croc-like slippers, Oscar Carmelo looked like a scared rabbit caught in a trap. His wide brown eyes scanned the room, landing on the two unfamiliar men.

"It's alright, Oscar," assured Jones. "These detectives just want to ask you some questions about Brayden Shuster. It has nothing to do with you." The man carried a chair, which he set down to the side of Rory and Larson. "Take a seat. I promise everything is fine."

The boy sat, but he kept shooting furtive glances toward Cliff Jones.

"Hi Oscar," said Rory. "I'm Detective Jackson, and this is Detective Larson. We are from the West Sound Police Department. Do you know where West Sound is?"

Oscar nodded numbly. "That's . . ." The word came out with a squeak. The boy cleared his throat. "That's where Brayden was from."

Rory smiled. "That's right. You two were friends?"

This time Oscar seemed less willing to commit, giving a half-hearted shrug.

"The boss here tells us you guys ate meals together," Larson said. "And you're not in any trouble, so don't feel you have to hide anything."

Oscar rubbed the back of his neck, his eyes on the floor. "Yeah, sometimes we ate together. Neither of us really had any other buddies or anything."

Rory glanced at Cliff Jones to see if he wanted to be the bearer of bad news. The man gave a quick nod.

Jones returned to chair, folding his hands together on the desktop. "Oscar, how are you doing?"

The boy shrugged again, but he met Jones's eyes briefly.

With his eyes locked on Oscar, the man said, "I'm afraid there has been some disturbing news about Brayden. Are you okay with my telling you about that now?"

Concern or curiosity, it was hard to tell which, seemed to bolster the young man's confidence. He sat up and gave the administrator his full attention. "Yeah."

Cliff Jones took a breath before continuing. "I'm sorry to say that Brayden died. Someone took his life last night."

At first, Oscar just stared, his expression unreadable. As emotion softened it, the boy dropped his head again. A sniffle and a wipe of his nose were the only outward signs that the news had affected him.

Jones handed him a tissue, which Oscar balled in his hand but didn't use.

"We're sorry to bring bad news," said Rory.

Refusing to look at any of the adults, Oscar said, "I didn't really know the guy that well."

The young man was already getting defensive, putting his guard up against his somehow being involved with Brayden's death. This kid had obviously been in trouble enough to strategize a meeting like this.

"Look," said Larson. "We're not here to accuse you of anything. And maybe you and Brayden weren't lifelong buddies, but during his time here, something might have happened that could help us find the person who did this." He sat back, clapping his hands on his thighs. "Or maybe not. Who knows?"

Oscar finally glanced up at the two detectives. Even though he claimed he barely knew Brayden, his eyes were red-rimmed as he fought the urge to cry.

"So, can you answer a few questions for us?" Larson asked.

Licking his lips, Oscar gave two slow nods.

"Thank you," said Rory. "Did Brayden have any fights, altercations with anyone or groups of people?"

Oscar answered with a slow back and forth of his head. "He kept quiet, and nobody bothered him. At least since I been here."

Rory continued. "Did Brayden ever talk about anyone that he was afraid of, whether here or outside?"

The young man seemed about to shake his head again, but stopped. His eyes flicked to the ceiling as he seemed to recall a memory.

"He never said any names, but he got a letter once. I never saw it cause he threw it away. It freaked him out, though."

"What was in the letter?" asked Larson.

Oscar's eyes narrowed. "It was something like, 'Do the world a favor and die in there.' Something like that."

When the detectives turned to Jones, the man's lips were a tight line. "The mail scanner should have caught that. Did Brayden report this letter?"

With a shrug, Oscar said, "I don't think so."

"Does all mail go through the scanner?" asked Larson.

"Absolutely," Jones said. "I'm not sure how this letter got to Brayden. The scanner looks for words depicting violence, letters that violate no-contact orders, drugs, weapons, etc."

"And he threw it away," muttered Rory. "How long ago was this?"

Finally accepting that the detectives were not here to bust him for something, Oscar grew more animated, answering with confidence. "It was right before he got released, like maybe a week?"

Larson turned to Jones. "Someone may have bypassed the scanner. Can we get the security footage you've collected from the pertinent areas around the facility? I'd like to know who has been in and out, and get a copy of your visitor logs. Maybe someone gave him the letter during a visit."

"I doubt that, but we will get you everything you need," promised the administrator.

Reaching out a hand to Oscar, Rory said, "You've been a great help, man. We appreciate it."

Relaxed with relief, the young man's face took on a boyish innocence. "I hope you catch the guy."

"Oh, we will," said Larson with a nod of certainty.

Chapter Seventeen

J efferson stared at Hatch's taillights. "Do we really need to go to the station? I thought we wanted to stay incognito."

With only a brief sideways glance at the detective, Amber focused on the road ahead. "I think that idea failed," she said almost too quietly for him to hear. "Besides, it's more important that our other partners stay off the radar. We don't want to answer questions about the DEA or anything that could lead to your brother."

She negotiated a left-hand turn before flicking a glare in his direction. "That's why it's important that you do nothing rash that gets us pushed out of the loop." The agent shook her head as they slowed for an upcoming red light. "I can't believe this is the level-headed Jefferson I'm talking to "

The detective looked away, turning his attention to the world outside the passenger-side window. This part of Las Vegas had no dazzling lights or themed casinos. Monotone buildings lined the streets like any other city in America.

My head is anything but level, he thought. But there was no way he was going to say that to Amber. His gut continued to tighten around a constant acidic ball of stress that refused to leave. Every minute that ticked away felt like a minute subtracted from MJ's life.

To keep his voice calm, he clenched his jaw. "The loop is just going to tie itself into knots that will slow us down. We know which way the guy took her. Let's go in the same direction and see what we find."

They followed Hatch into the station parking lot. Amber put the car in park and turned to face him.

"You know as well as I do, Jefferson, that running off without more specific information is a less than brilliant plan. We'd just be chasing our tails out there. Trust me. You do not want to drive Highway 95 with no destination in mind."

He felt the studying gaze of her hazel eyes, but Jefferson couldn't look at her. Instead, he watched Hatch exit his vehicle and stand by his car door, waiting for the two of them.

With a quiet sigh that Jefferson could only describe as disappointed, Amber said, "And if you know me at all, then trust that I will not leave MJ's life in the hands of people who do not know and love her like we do."

Those words. "Love her." It was a gut punch. MJ's curious blue eyes jumped into the detective's mind, making his head swim. His hand shot out to the car door, and he closed his eyes to find his equilibrium.

"Jeff? Are you okay?"

With a deep breath of dry desert air, he grabbed the door handle and pulled. "Let's go."

***

Detective Hatch directed them to a side entrance of the massive four-story building, which dwarfed the West Sound Station, and not by a little. That was not unexpected. The Las Vegas Metropolitan Police Department was a combined county and municipal force that covered 400 times the area and forty-two times the population compared to West Sound PD.

Pulling a card from his jacket pocket, Hatch swiped it across the receptor next to the door.

"I'm probably going to catch my share of trouble for this, but here we go," he said, grinning mischievously at Amber.

"Have you ever not been in trouble?" asked Amber as he held the door for her. She walked in without waiting for a response.

The man gave Jefferson an innocent shrug as he followed Amber inside.

After a quick elevator ride, they entered a room that, to Jefferson, felt very much like home.

Uniformed officers moved with purpose while others worked at desks, either on the phone or at a computer. The mingled scents of microwave meals and coffee completed the similarity.

The constant motion and buzz of voices said every officer was busy. And Jefferson could only hope they were all looking for MJ.

"Hey, Hatch," said a man leaning back in his desk chair, hand over a phone receiver. "We got some info about the security and in-home cameras. Kingston wants a briefing, but he wants you in his office first." The guy winked at him. "I won't ask what you did this time."

With a quick glance at the closed office door on the other side of the room, Hatch deadpanned, "Just my job, Bobbie. Just my job as usual."

The female officer from the garage approached. "Hey Lieutenant, we got —"

"Info on the security footage and cameras?" Hatch said.

Her face fell at his already having received the news.

"I appreciate the effort, Sammy," Hatch said, flashing a smile. Then he drew the woman's attention to Amber and Jefferson. "Could you show Detective Hughes and Agent Wells where to find coffee and restrooms while I go check in with Captain Kingston?"

"Sure thing." Her face brightened again, and Jefferson had the distinct feeling that nothing much could keep Sammy down. "Come with me," she said with an amiable smile.

Jefferson desperately wanted to follow Hatch instead, but he put on a friendly face as he and Amber followed the officer.

"So it's Sammy?" he asked as they turned into a long corridor.

"Yeah, that's what everybody calls me around the station. It's Officer Salas in public." She grinned with her wide Osmond-like smile. "Here we are. Restrooms there. Our small lounge is just across the hall. There is tea and coffee, and today, we have some cookies that Angel's wife made. They're really awesome. And that's it," she said cheerfully. "I'm sure Hatch will be out soon. If you wait in the lounge, I can let him know where you are."

"Thank you, Sammy. We'll do that," Amber said, heading toward the women's restroom.

When she was gone, the officer watched Jefferson, who hadn't moved yet.

"Can I help you with anything else, Detective?"

"I'm sure we'll find out shortly," he said with a forced crooked smile. "But I was wondering if they found cameras in the Devey home? Since you mentioned it earlier, you must know." He didn't mean to stand over her, but the woman was tiny, barely reaching his shoulder.

Her smile faded as her eyes darted behind Jefferson, perhaps hoping Amber might reappear.

Sensing her discomfort, Jefferson stepped back and waved off his question. "Sorry. I shouldn't have asked. I'm just worried, you know. The longer these things go . . ."

The sentence trailed off, letting her fill in the blank, in part because he didn't want to say it.

"I know," she said, biting her bottom lip. "It must be terrible for her family." Her dark eyes bounced from Jefferson to the wall, to the floor, and back again.

"Okay," she said, lowering her voice. "I mean, you'll find out anyway, right?" With a quick look behind her, she continued in a whisper. "They found three cameras in the house. One in the kitchen. One in the family room. And one in a bedroom — I don't know whose bedroom, though."

It took superhuman effort, but Jefferson willed his features to remain calm. Her answer had triggered a rush of adrenaline that flooded his bloodstream, and he feared his own reaction.

Her bedroom? Some scumbag had spied on MJ in her bedroom.

The thought made him want to tear out of this place and find someone to pummel until the feeling subsided.

Not trusting himself with drawn-out sentences, he offered a clipped thank you to Sammy before escaping to the men's restroom.

Once inside, he flipped on the water and stood with his hands on either side of the sink, gripping it with all his strength. The roar that escaped him came from the deepest part of him, a primitive sound that was foreign to his own ears.

His head hung low, and his body shook, but there were no tears. Pure rage flowed through him now. Rage that needed an outlet.

The water flowing into the sink felt like ice. Gathering some in his hands, Jefferson splashed his face, trying to douse some of the anger there. He did it again. And again. Until finally, he realized he'd drenched his jacket, shirt front and tie.

He didn't care. He'd waited long enough.

***

When Jefferson left the restroom, Amber was nowhere to be found.

He traced their steps back to the main room, where he found her huddled in conversation with Hatch.

"The captain has agreed to let you attend the briefing," Hatch was saying, "but we have to give a copy of your credentials to the desk clerk for some paper trail mumbo jumbo. So give them to me. I'll have Sammy make copies and take them down."

When he had both of their identification cards, Hatch stepped away, found Sammy, and returned.

"All right. You two ready?"

"More than," answered Jefferson.

Hatch eyed the West Sound detective, his lips twisting as if working out a puzzle. "You all right, man? You're looking a little . . . Uh . . . Peakish. I've got some pork rinds in my desk if you want them."

Jefferson threw his hands up. "Would everyone stop trying to feed me. I'm fine. I couldn't be finer. Really. I mean, who wouldn't want to eat pork rinds when someone they care about is being held by maniacal killers?"

Hatch backed up. "Just asking, buddy. No need to bite my head off."

Amber stood between them. "Ryan, you can head to the briefing. We're right behind you. I need to have a word with Detective Hughes."

"Whatever you say, dear." Hatch grinned as he backed away. "Right through that door over there," he said, pointing toward the open door of the briefing room. "Don't be too long."

When they were alone, Amber turned on Jefferson. "He's right, you know. You look awful, and I don't mean that your hair is out of place or your suit is . . ." She took in his jacket and shirt. "Soaking wet.

What I mean is that you have no color in your cheeks. Your eyes are as bloodshot as someone on a week-long bender, and your attitude, frankly, is unhelpful and downright caustic."

Somewhere beneath the fear, Jefferson felt the weak pulse of shame. He wasn't being himself. It was true. Amber deserved better from him, but he struggled to find his way back to normal. He knew the right things to do, the correct way to handle an investigation; he wanted to clear his mind and see the facts objectively. But how could he?

He rubbed his eyes. "I'm sorry. This is . . . I don't even know."

"But you *do* know. You are an experienced, excellent detective."

"This isn't some random case, Amber." He took a step back, looking skyward. "It's my fault." When his eyes met hers, Jefferson knew he looked like a crazy man, but he was past caring. "It's my fault she's even in this mess. And we now have less that eleven hours." He said, pointing to his watch. "I have to fix it. I have to find her."

The agent watched him quietly, her expression serene except for the tiny lines of worry around her eyes. Her next words were gentle but firm. "You did not do this, and taking on the evil of others is not heroic, Jefferson. Doing all you can to defeat it—that's the Detective Hughes I know."

She turned to see Hatch standing at the briefing door, waving them on.

"Look, Jeff. We both know that part of the job is regulating your emotions, even when the stakes are high. If you can't do that, I will have to remove you from the case. I don't want to. Trust me, I do not want to do that. But we can't risk making mistakes. MJ can't afford mistakes."

With that threat, reluctantly given, Amber headed to the briefing room.

Chapter Eighteen

The Las Vegas Metro briefing room took up almost as much floor space as the entire West Sound hub. Lines of tables, end-to-end, extended almost to each wall. Many chairs had people in them, but not all. A wiry, mustachioed man sat near the front, looking every bit like someone in charge. Jefferson guessed this to be Captain Morrow. Hatch introduced Amber and him to the group, and in that way, confirmed his assumption.

"Welcome," said the captain. "I trust everyone here has treated you well?"

"Yes, Captain. Thank you," said Amber with a tip of her head.

"Well, that's a surprise," he joked.

"Hey, now," shouted someone from the group.

The captain waved him off, but his demeanor said he enjoyed razzing the group. "I guess we also have your colleague, Agent Clark, on speakerphone?" The man spoke as if he weren't sure the tech had played out.

"I'm here," came the bright voice of Dawn Clark from a nearby phone. "Howdy, everyone."

After sweeping the room with his eyes, the captain seemed satisfied they were ready. "I know we have several teams working on different leads, so who wants to start us off?"

For a few beats, no one spoke. Then, a uniformed officer near the front raised a hand. "I can start, Cap."

"Thank you, Anderson. Your crew is working on the security or other footage at the Devey residence?"

"Yes, sir." The man walked to the front and faced the group. "We still have officers walking the neighborhood asking for door cam footage and whether neighbors noticed the suspect SUV in the neighborhood. That's ongoing, but I have a few important things to report from our work so far."

The captain, part sitting and part leaning against a table, folded his arms and crossed his ankles. "Go ahead."

"The Deveys live in a gated neighborhood, so we got footage from the camera at the main gate. From the video, we saw our suspect vehicle, with the same fake license plate, access the community with a key card."

"Any idea where they got the card?" asked Hatch.

"Yes. We followed up on that right away," said Anderson. "The card is registered to a Ron Tyler. We found Mr. Tyler at his home in the neighborhood. He told us that someone had stolen his wallet about a week ago. It was in his car while he and his wife were hiking in Red Rock Canyon."

With a glance at Amber, Hatch said, "I guess the planned attack theory is on target."

"It would seem so," agreed the captain. "What else, Anderson?"

"The security footage from the Deveys and two neighbors supports that theory. It showed the same SUV parked outside the Devey residence on the night Ms. Brooks and her mother were attacked. As soon as the two women left the house, the SUV followed. We saw the SUV continue to follow them out of the community, through the main gate."

The officer shuffled through his notes. "That's about it for outside footage. Inside the home, we found three video and audio capable mini-cams in the home. We found one in a light fixture in the kitchen. There was another one hidden among some books in the living room. The third was inside a tissue box in the bedroom occupied by Ms. Brooks."

Jefferson could feel Amber stiffen next to him. Then, without a word, she grasped his forearm, keeping her eyes on the speaker.

She was right to fear his reaction. Hearing about the camera in MJ's bedroom a second time was no less jarring to him than the first. But the tip-off from Sammy helped him control the impulse to pound on something or someone.

"What?" asked the captain, incredulous. "Why? We must be missing something about this teacher. Why would anyone go through so much trouble?" Without even a blink, the man's attention pin-balled to Amber. "Special Agent Wells, is there anything you can add to this discussion?"

Amber released Jefferson's arm and clasped her hands in front. "Not at this time." She smiled cordially.

That look of hers. Jefferson knew it well. In keeping sensitive information under wraps, no one could question the secure lips of Supervisory Special Agent Wells. She would tell them nothing that she did not want them to know.

The West Sound detective appreciated her secrecy for his brother's sake, but Jefferson knew that in the shoes of the Las Vegas captain, he would find it maddening.

Not liking her response, the captain pushed harder. "Just so we're clear, we can't adequately do our jobs if you withhold pertinent information."

The strange thing about Amber, Jefferson realized, is that the more you question her, the steadier she becomes, seeming more unflappable the ever. She showed this unique gift when she responded with a deadly calm, "I understand, Captain."

The man's jaw muscle pulsed as he kept his eyes locked on Amber. He knew there was more to MJ's abduction, and he knew the special agent in front of him would reveal nothing.

Officer Anderson cleared his throat. "Sir, we don't know where the video was streaming, but we have another promising lead that I'd like to share."

Reluctantly, the captain dragged his gaze back to his officer. "Go ahead."

"Thank you. This is regarding the man sent to fix Mr. Devey's outdoor lights. We sent Officers Ford and Diaz to Silver Hills Electric Company to get information about the employee. The owner . . ." Anderson checked his notes. "Uh, Ray Avila . . . He said the guy never showed up again after working that job. Just disappeared."

"Did you get a name?"

Everyone turned to face Jefferson, who had asked without thinking. He could have kicked himself. Of course they got a name.

"Sorry," he said, putting a hand up. "I'm sure you did. That was a stupid question."

Anderson grinned, a sparkle in his eye. "You're right. We got a name. But, as we suspected it would be, it was fake."

"Then why do you look so pleased with yourself?" asked the captain, willing to bite on whatever the officer was holding back.

"First, we already had an image of the man from the Devey's home security footage. But the guy wore a hat and did a good job of keeping his head down and face away from the camera."

The captain rolled his hand at him, telling him to speed up his story. "I'm still not getting the good news."

"What this guy didn't know — there is some dubiousness here by the company owner . . . But that's another issue. Anyway, uh, Mr. Ray Avila, though reluctantly, did eventually tell us he had installed a camera inside the company offices. According to him, some of his employees were stealing supplies, you know, wires and cables and such. So that footage has a beautiful full-face photo of our fake electrician."

This news sent a jolt of excitement sweeping through Jefferson's body. He knew instinctively that this was the first genuine lead; the first time he sensed that the bad guys had messed up.

The energy spread around the room, and Anderson soaked it in with a wide grin of satisfaction. "So," he continued. "We sent the image to the tech lab, and they're running it through facial recognition as we speak. If this guy was arrested anywhere in Nevada or the United States, which I'll wager he has, we will find him."

Chapter Nineteen

The yard beyond MJ's prison remained quiet. No Corky. No Robbie. Only the lonely wind wailed and rushed against the metal walls around her. The temperature continued to drop, and the captive shivered as the one disgusting blanket provided little warmth.

She was cold. She'd had to do her "business" in a bucket full of cat litter, but so far, MJ knew her situation could be much worse. It could still get much worse.

The worst thing right now was that she had nothing to engage her mind. Without Robbie or the dog to focus on, her thoughts wandered to dark places, like the possibility that her mom was dead.

The teacher wiped away a tear. This would crush her father. While a mountain of a man as principal, someone everyone looked up to, he had a nurturing heart. The man had never said a cross word to MJ in her entire life. And he loved her mother with complete devotion.

Why couldn't the men have kidnapped her without hurting her mother?

And Jefferson. What if they hurt him too? What if he refused to or couldn't do what they wanted?

She already knew the answer. The man holding her hostage would kill her.

Strangely though, he didn't seem to be the one making demands. The masked man acted more like a middleman, detached from her and the reason for her abduction. Did he have a price at which she could buy her freedom?

Throwing the blanket aside, MJ went again to her tape-covered peephole. Looking out, she saw gigantic snowflakes swirling in the wind. A good two-inches already blanketed the ground.

No wonder Corky and Robbie were still inside. She imagined the man and his dog curled up together watching TV. While that might not be what they were doing, the thought of it made her shiver again, missing her home, missing her own dog, Edgar.

She replaced the tape and returned to the blanket just as noises at the door told her someone was there.

A blast of icy wind hit her before she saw the masked man stepping inside the container. He carried the cooler, which he'd taken with him earlier, and a sleeping bag.

He threw the rolled-up sleeping bag at her before setting the cooler down. "Can't have you freezing to death before our next video."

"You're so kind," MJ said sarcastically. She held the sleeping bag in her lap but didn't move.

"No kindness. Just business." He kicked the cooler with the toe of his boot. "Make it last. There won't be much else coming, especially if this ends the easy way."

"And what's the easy way?"

The man grinned and made a smacking noise with his lips. "I'm sure you can guess." Then he made a gun shape with his fingers, pointed it at her, and imitated the sound of a gun firing.

MJ ignored the gesture as best she could, given the shiver of fear that rolled down her spine. "How much are they paying you?"

An amazed chuckle rumbled out of the man. "You think you can negotiate? That's humorous."

"I don't have much, but my parents have money. If you let me call, I know they will pay whatever you want." The desperation in her own voice made her wince. She'd tried so hard to keep her fear under control.

He took a step closer. "It's sweet of you to offer, darling, but, uh, money isn't that important in this case. It seems you picked the wrong boyfriend."

As he stared down at her, his intense brown eyes filled her with a sense of patient evil. No matter how long he contemplated killing her, no sense of justice, fairness, or humanity would change the outcome.

"See, you're wrong," seethed MJ. "I picked exactly the right man; the sort of man an evil person like you could only dream of being. He will find me, and when he does, you'll see how wrong you are."

As she suspected, her words had little effect on the man. The crinkling at his eyes told her he found her outburst amusing.

"The detective has no hope of finding you, even if he drags along his trusty sidekick, Agent Amber Wells."

MJ drew her eyebrows together. "Amber? What does Amber have to do with this?"

He was already shuffling back toward the door. "Time's ticking. Enjoy your last meal."

And then he was gone.

Chapter Twenty

E ach with a paper bag in hand, Rory and Larson walked into the hub and made for their desks.

"I smell Agua Azule," said Ron, his nose wiggling and sniffing like an enormous rabbit. "Did you guys go without taking orders?"

"Come on, Agent Benton. Do you think we'd do you like that?" asked Larson, setting the bag down and removing his coat.

Rory held up his bag. "Sorry, we guessed at what you might want. There's a burrito for each of our federal friends."

"I never doubted you," said Ron, already up and following the smell like a hound.

Once they dispersed the food, the group ate in silent work mode. In a ridiculous short amount of time, Rory had half of his burrito devoured. He walked to Ron's desk while eating the other half.

"Found anything interesting?"

The big man looked up at him. "Are you going to finish that burrito?"

Rory scowled. "Of course I am."

"I had to try," said Ron, turning back to his computer. "I'm still trying to nail down anything solid. The first company, the owner of the building where metro police found the SUV, is itself owned by another company based in Mexico. Yeah, so that's muddied the waters of the investigation."

Swallowing a hunk of burrito, Rory read the information on Ron's screen. Las Palmas Shipping LLC, address listed as being in Nuevo Laredo, Mexico.

"Mexico. Sounds like Nico's got some big Mexican fish helping him out."

Ron clicked a new tab on his computer. "I'd say so. It takes some money and a wide enough network to bury the company deep enough that we can't touch it." He glanced back at Rory. "But never fear, my ginger-bearded friend, I will find them. See this here," he pointed to the screen. "I've gone three layers down, and I have one name. Javi Tenedor, a Mexican accountant. He's just a nominee, a person who stands in for the owner. I'm not sure he's a real, breathing human. But if he is, and if he is in the U.S., that's a lead, baby!"

"How will you find him?"

"Very carefully," Ron said, wiggling his bushy black eyebrows.

"Could you be more specific?" Rory asked before eating the last bit of his burrito."

"Well, how about a little tutorial." With that, Ron opened another screen. "For today's lesson, I am going to cross-reference the accountant's name with travel data, specifically visas and passports belonging to Mexican citizens with the same name, or variations of it. Javi may also be Javier. He may also use another surname with Tenedor. The cartels and other illegal entities like their nominees to keep their noses clean. It makes the whole operation look more legitimate, and it allows people like Javi to cross the border without trouble."

Rory watched as the agent hit return after entering the accountant's name and a few other details. Within seconds, a list came back that appeared to be several pages long.

With a groan, Rory said, "Man, have fun with that."

Ron glanced back at him with mock hurt on his face. "Are you failing out already? We haven't even started lesson two."

The detective tilted his head toward Larson, who was hailing him over. "I think my temporary partner needs me."

"Suit yourself," said Ron. "You are going to miss out on a serious data mining tutorial."

***

"What's up?" asked Rory as he sat across from Larson.

"I just got off the phone with the Everett detective who handled the Shuster case. She is sending the file to me right now." He sat back in his chair as an enormous yawn took over. "Man, I need a nap. Anyway, the threatening letter Brayden got in Juvy could definitely be connected to his murder. Maybe even hired hit."

"I had the same thought. And, it could be the family or someone connected to the hit and run," said Rory.

"Bingo," said Larson.

Rory sighed. "Man, I do not treasure the idea of digging in that garden."

Larson screwed up his face. "Digging in that garden?"

"Yeah, you know. It's a metaphor. See, we are going to be disturbing what little growth the family has made in finding peace. Get it?"

"Oh, I get it. I just don't know why you had to get all poetic on me."

Rory grinned. "I don't know either, but you should write it down. I could be famous someday."

"Well, get your gardening gloves on, because we have some calls to make."

"Whoa," said Rory, his eyes round with surprise, "that was good."

***

Cassie Dyer and her three-year-old daughter Lily didn't have a chance. When Brayden Shuster slammed into the driver's side of their Ford Escape at ninety miles per hour, they both died at the scene.

The family had no time to say goodbye, no desperate hope in a hospital waiting room. One minute the mother and daughter were alive and the next, they were in the morgue.

After speaking on the phone with Cassie's sister, Taylor Stevenson, Rory could tell that the passing of two years had barely put a dent in the family's suffering.

"I wish I felt sorry for him," Taylor said after the detective shared the news of Brayden's death. "It might make me a horrible person, but I'm glad he's dead. He didn't deserve to live after what he did to my sister and her baby."

Despite her feelings toward Brayden, the woman had a solid alibi on the night of his murder. She was in Yakima visiting her husband's family.

He would check it out, of course, but the detective had little reason to doubt her.

Larson had taken on calling Cassie's husband, Daxton Dyer. While Rory was interested in hearing how that conversation went, he was even more interested in the person Officers Fogarty and Hanson were now escorting into the station. He glanced at Larson, who had just hung up his phone. "Isn't that Franco?"

"Yep. Let's go see what they've got to say."

As the detectives approached, Evie escorted the dealer to the processing desk. Fogarty broke off and met Rory and Larson halfway.

"So what's the story with Franco?" asked Larson.

Fogarty's blue eyes were wide with excitement. "The story about Toby dying of an overdose turned out to be true. So we asked around, and everyone said — well, everyone who would talk to us — that Franco there," he glanced to where Evie filled out a form as the dealer stood by in handcuffs, "took over all of Toby's regulars."

Larson and Rory glanced at each other, disappointment written on their faces.

"What?" asked Fogarty.

With a doubtful squint, Rory asked, "Did you get anyone on record or bring anyone willing to make a statement as such?"

The officer's face colored. "Well, no, but . . ."

"It will be really hard for us to hold him then," said Larson.

"I know," said Fogarty, getting frustrated, "but there's something else."

"Go on," said Larson.

"You should see it," he said, walking back toward Evie and the arrestee.

Rory shrugged. "I'm game."

They followed the officer, neither man feeling confident the arrest would hold up.

"Turn him around," Fogarty was saying as they approached.

Evie did as requested, though Franco jerked his arm free and turned around on his own.

"Hey, Franco," said Larson. "What'd you do this time?"

"Nothing" was the only reply.

"Of course."

Rory and Larson looked him over, wondering what they were supposed to be seeing.

"Ain't you never seen a man before," sneered Franco. "I guess not with all the —"

"Shut up," demanded Larson. The detective turned, grabbing Rory's arm, and walked a few paces away.

"Did you see it?" Larson whispered.

"Yep."

Larson nodded with a thoughtful look. "Go grab your laptop. I want to see that close-up photo of the button again."

"Sure thing, boss."

Larson rolled his eyes at the use of "boss" as Rory hurried back to his desk, returning within seconds, his laptop already open.

"Here it is."

Larson stood next to the other detective, studying the image before him. The black plastic button held few distinct features. Wide and flat, it had four holes, and a raised edge for an outside border. On the top half lay the only thing to set it apart from every other button in the average household's junk drawer: tiny, raised letters that spelled "Dry Guy."

"What are you all looking at? I have a right to know why I'm here," insisted Franco.

Without a word to the man, Detective Larson walked up to him and bent down, inspecting the man's coat.

"Hey, that's just weird, man," said Franco.

The detective stood up, his lips twisting into a satisfied grin. "Well, well, Fogarty and Hanson, that's good work."

"Thank you, sir," said Fogarty.

Franco's mounting frustration at being left out of the loop showed on his face, gradually reddening in anger. "You don't have no right to keep me here."

Stepping back, Larson put his hands on his hips. "We most certainly do, Franco. And we'll tell you all about it in a few minutes." To Fogarty and Hanson, the detective said, "Read this man his rights and place him under arrest. Be sure to offer him one of our fancy jumpsuits and bag his clothes."

"Got it." Fogarty was all smiles.

Chapter
Twenty-One

Within minutes of the briefing's end, the Las Vegas tech department had names.

"Names?" asked Jefferson.

"Yeah," shrugged Hatch. "The guy uses a few aliases or variations of his actual name. But only one has a Las Vegas address." He held out the paper for the detective and Amber to read. "Geno Cook. He's got a few priors here in the area — DUI, driving with a suspended license, shoplifting. Same sort of stuff in Utah and New Mexico."

"Do you think the address is credible?" asked Amber.

Hatch nodded. "I know exactly where this is." He flicked his eyes up to Jefferson before zeroing in on Amber again. "You remember Naked City?"

With a huff of irritation, Amber closed her eyes. "So they're still calling it that. I'm pretty sure there have been no naked showgirls lounging by pools in that area for decades."

"Now days they'd just be lounging next to cement. No pools left."

"That's it then. Let's go," said Jefferson, stepping away and looking for the exit.

"Hold your horses, Hughes," said Hatch, not moving. "I think it's best if Agent Wells and I handle this. You're too close. I don't want to risk your mucking it up."

Even while his inner-self knew the detective was right, that he, Jefferson, would say the same if the roles were reversed, there was no holding back the anger that shot to the surface. "All we have been doing is following your lead," he said between clenched teeth, "following you to breakfast where you dilly-dallied over your bagel, letting time just tick away as if MJ's life means nothing. If you want to stop me from coming along, you'll have to try putting your cuffs on me, but trust me, it won't be easy."

"You might be wrong about that," said Hatch with a reckless gleam in his eye.

Jefferson, the taller of the two detectives, took a step closer. "Try it."

Amber let her head fall back with a sigh. "Would you two just stop? Jeff, you're coming. Ryan, don't say another word."

With that, she walked away, leaving the two detectives to stare after her.

***

They arrived at an off-white two-story apartment complex in the shape of a giant U. Desert peach played accent color on the doors, railings and select bricks of the facade. The building had the look of a converted motel from the sixties. In front of the complex, a strip of asphalt allowed a few cars to pull-in for prime front parking. Only two cars took up spots; the rest were empty.

Hatch pulled in next to one car. The old sedan had a shattered back window held in place by vast amounts of duct tape. According to the Las Vegas detective, this neighborhood had one of the worst crime rates in the city. It seemed quiet to Jefferson, but he knew from experience that criminals didn't have to be loud to be dangerous.

As a precaution, Hatch planned for a patrol car to be in the area for backup, keeping the officers at a distance to avoid spooking Gene Cook, if he was even in the apartment given as his address.

"All right. Here is the plan," Hatch said, turning off the car. "I will go to the door. Hughes, go to the back in case our man tries to jump out a window. He's in number three, so on the bottom floor, which makes the window a likely possibility. Amber, you drive. Cut him off if he runs, and radio the guys in." He studied the two of them. "Got it? Are we on the same page?"

They both agreed. Jefferson could feel the adrenaline already beginning to pump through him. A part of him . . . No, all of him. All of him hoped the guy tried to take the window.

Hatch opened his car door. "Let's go."

At a natural, unhurried pace, Jefferson strolled to the alley between their target apartment complex and the one next to it. Hatch was right. Unlike the building next door, the back windows of Cook's apartment did not have metal bars. It also lacked a screen, making for a perfect getaway exit.

The alley held two dumpsters, one of which was turned on its side, empty but for a few pieces of paper stuck to the inside wall and flapping in the gentle breeze. A couple of bikes were secured to metal poles next to the building.

The distinct sound of knocking came from the other side of the building. Hatch gave it only seconds before Jefferson heard knocking again. On the third time of no answer, the other detective was pounding on the door.

"Metro police! We just have a few questions. Open the door, please."

Even though Hatch raised his voice, he sounded a hundred times more patient than Jefferson was feeling. Every nerve in his body tingled, ready to spring into action at a moment's notice. As yet, all he heard was Hatch.

Another round of pounding on the door. A man in a baggy hoodie strolled slowly across alley entrance pushing a bike. He stared into the shadows at Jefferson.

With a wild flagging of his hand, the detective warned the man to back up and leave the area. The onlooker gave one dip of his head before retreating.

The slow slide of metal on metal caught the detective's attention. He backed into a shadow to watch the window of apartment number three as it slowly opened. Within seconds, a man sat crouched on the windowsill, surveying the alley in each direction. His attempt at disguise included a baseball hat covered by the hood of his sweatshirt. It wasn't enough. The man in the window was clearly Geno, the man who installed a camera in MJ's bedroom.

Not seeing Jefferson, and believing himself to be in the clear, the guy sprang from the window, sticking the landing effortlessly, as if he'd practiced this move a hundred times.

The detective pulled his firearm. Though anger roiled through him at what this man had done . . . What he might have seen . . . there was no way Jefferson would shoot him. They needed him alive; they needed him not to run. He hoped the weapon would keep Geno from doing anything stupid.

It did not.

As soon as Jefferson stepped out of the shadows with his gun raised, and shouted for him to stop, the man took off in the opposite direction, running out of the alley and toward the front of the building where Amber waited in the car.

Bolting after Geno, Jefferson saw him turn right at the end of the alley. The West Sound detective raced after him, and squealing tires said that Amber had joined the pursuit. He didn't know where Hatch had gone. He hoped the other detective knew of a cutoff point.

Having never changed his shoes from the morning, Jefferson pounded after the sprinting figure in his boots, which had more traction and grip than his loafers would have had on the fine layer of sand covering the sidewalk, as it did everything in this place.

Geno turned sharply down another alley, pulling a gate closed behind him. Even though it wasn't locked, the barrier earned him a few feet of separation. Jefferson stepped through and quickly made up ground. He gained on the man with every step despite the scrappy fugitive's impressive speed. Having inched closer, Jefferson could tell Geno would be easy to take down, if he could catch him.

They zigzagged through alleys between run-down apartments, all marred in labyrinths of chain-link fencing and gates. Geno seemed to know every opening in every fence, which gates were locked and which were not.

Jefferson knew he should have caught the man by now. The acidic burning in his legs chastised him for his lack of food fuel. If he lost this guy, he'd have no one to blame but himself, and Amber would be justified in force-feeding him a loaf of avocado toast. With a grunt, he pushed himself harder, kicking his body into a higher gear.

After rounding the corner at the end of the latest alley, Geno also added a fresh burst of speed, sprinting like a madman across a four-lane highway. Jefferson had no choice but to dart across the road with only the briefest check for traffic. In that swift glance, he thought he saw Amber driving toward him, but he didn't dare take the time to confirm. Geno was already scaling a fence into a construction area, where heavy construction equipment sat motionless in the khaki-colored dirt.

Once again, with practiced precision, Geno scrambled to the top of the fence and dropped onto the other side. He took one glance back to see Jefferson hot on his heels. The detective might not be as agile as Geno, but his long legs lifted him over the fence with ease, and soon the two were spraying loose dirt from their shoes as they raced across the building site.

Another fence waited up ahead while the sky-scraping Stratosphere Tower loomed over them like a desert Space Needle.

They were both quickly over the fence again, and Geno took a right turn, hurtling down the asphalt path. After another minute of full-on sprinting, Jefferson felt himself flagging, his breath coming in hard spurts as the higher elevation seared his lungs. No doubt this was Geno's plan — run him around until he collapsed.

But the detective followed on, suddenly buoyed by what he saw ahead. The asphalt path ran into a side street, and there waiting was a car he recognized as the FBI loaner driven by Amber.

I've got you now, he thought.

Geno also saw the car blocking his exit, and he attempted to cut through the parking lot of an economy hotel on the corner. What he couldn't see, until it was too late, was the patrol car hidden beside the building. Hatch also suddenly appeared, running up behind Jefferson.

The fugitive stopped, his eyes flicking between Amber, standing with the driver-side door open, the detectives, and the two officers, who were now shouting commands and moving toward him with weapons drawn.

That's when Jefferson saw the knife gripped in Geno's right hand.

"Stop!" he shouted to the officers. "He's got a knife."

Hatch also had his gun pointed at Geno, but at Jefferson's warning, he raised his hand to the officers, signaling for them to stand by.

"Geno!" Jefferson shouted. "There's no way out. Just drop your weapon."

The man stood still, his head moving on a swivel as he searched for a way out. His wild eyes landed on the West Sound detective, and Jefferson could see the calculation brewing there. He was the only person with no weapon raised, and behind him, another chain-link fence offered a means of escape.

"Don't do it, Geno," said Jefferson, with as much calm as he could manage. "I could pull my gun, and these other officers already have guns pointed at you. But none of us wants to see you get shot. You understand? We just need to talk to you."

"No way," said Geno, his voice high and squeaking as he shook his head. "If I get caught, even if I don't tell you anything, I'm a dead man."

"We can protect you, Geno," Jefferson said. "You are not the person we're after, but we can't let you run away. Your choice is to trust us, put down that weapon and hope for the best, or run at me with that knife, and get a bullet right now. You decide."

The man's dark eyes moved around the perimeter again as he held the knife pointing down next to his leg, the blade catching flashes of the winter sun as he turned it nervously in his hand.

"Do as he says," added Hatch. "No one wants to hurt you here. Just drop the knife and kick it to me."

Indecision mixed with despair played on Geno's face. Jefferson could feel the fear radiating from him. *Would he really risk being shot by the police just to avoid being caught?* There had to be more.

"Have they threatened someone else, Geno? Someone you care about?" Jefferson asked.

Despite a violent shake of his head, the truth escaped as tears rolled down the man's cheeks.

"Just tell us who it is. We can pick them up too. We'll keep you both safe." Glancing at Hatch, Jefferson knew full-well that he might be promising too much. "Come on, Geno. Give yourself a chance."

The man stared at Jefferson, sizing him up. Despite the doubt still shrouding his face in shadows, Geno dropped the knife.

Chapter Twenty-Two

With Geno set up in an interview room, the detectives and Agent Wells gathered the pertinent files and discussed strategy before questioning the man.

"The officers said Geno cried about his mama all the way to the station," said Hatch with a disgruntled look at his West Sound counterpart. "I've sent them to pick her up, although heaven knows what we're going to do with her."

Jefferson lifted his shoulder in a half shrug. "It was the right move. If we hadn't agreed to pick her up, he'd be a closed book. I think he'll talk if he thinks he can trust us."

Amber nodded her agreement. "He's scared. We'll have to go heavy on building that relationship, or we still might get nothing out of him."

"Oh, we'll get something," said Hatch. "I'm just not sure we'll like it very much."

"Let's find out," said Jefferson.

When they entered the interview room, Geno set down a bottle of water, swallowing hard.

His dark eyes were red-rimmed and swollen. While not a kid, he still seemed young. Jefferson would put his age somewhere in his mid to late twenties. The baseball cap and hood were gone, revealing a headful of black, chin-length braids capped at the ends with white beads.

"Did you get her?" he asked, almost jumping from his seat.

Hatch put both his hands up, stopping him in his tracks. "Just have a seat, Geno. Our officers are on the way to your mom's house right now. As soon as they have her, they're going to call me." He held up his cell phone and set it on the table between them as he pulled out a chair and sat down.

Amber and Jefferson sat on either side of the Las Vegas detective.

Geno leaned back with his arms folded. "I'm not saying anything until I know she's safe."

With a casual shrug, Hatch also sat back from the table. "Okay. Well, how about we get to know each other while we wait? Can we do that?"

The other man turned his face to the wall without responding.

"Looks like it's up to us," he said, looking between Amber and Jefferson. "I'll go first. I am Detective Ryan Hatch with the Las Vegas Metropolitan Police." He turned to Amber, who picked up the baton.

"And I am Supervisory Special Agent Amber Wells of the FBI."

That got Geno's attention. His eyes narrowed as he turned to face her, seeming to notice the agent for the first time.

"I am Detective Jefferson Hughes of the West Sound Police Department in Washington State."

If the FBI being in the room confused or concerned Geno, it was nothing compared to the confusion now scrunching up his features. He still said nothing, but his face told a story. This man did not yet know the depth of the hole he had dug for himself.

"So, Geno," said Hatch, sitting up and resting his elbows on the table. "How did you learn to do electrical work?"

Geno snorted and shook his head but said nothing.

"No, I'm serious as a heart attack here. You did some good work over at the Devey's house. I mean, you actually fixed the broken outdoor lights. Of course you knew what was wrong with them, didn't you, Geno?"

Facing the wall again, Geno stayed silent.

"You were the one who cut the wires in the first place," said Hatch. "Worked like a charm. The Deveys never suspected a thing."

The silence from the interviewee continued, and for a few seconds, no one spoke.

Geno almost jumped out of his skin when Hatch's phone buzzed in the middle of the table.

"That should be our guys." The detective answered the call and went quiet as he listened, his eyes falling on Geno. "Sure. He's right here. Put her on."

Hatch put the call on speaker and set the phone down. "Seems your mama doesn't want to come with the officers."

"Geno? Geno, honey," said a woman's voice. "What's going on? Are you there, Geno?"

Suddenly sitting straighter, relief flooding his features, Geno responded. "I'm here, Mom."

"Oh, Geno. What have you gotten into, son?"

"Listen, Mom. You have to go with the police. I can—" He stopped and glanced at Hatch before continuing. "Someone will explain soon, but you need to just go, okay?"

They all stared at the phone, waiting for Geno's mom to say something. A few sounds came across the line that sounded like sighing and tut-tutting.

"Fine," she said. "But I'll have to call Auntie Bea to take care of my cats."

"Good, Mom. Just do it from the car. You need to go."

"Why do you sound so scared, Geno? What is going on?"

Hatch jumped in. "Mrs. Cook?"

"Mizzz Cook," she corrected. "I'm not a Mrs. unless that good-for-nothing man shows up and starts paying some bills."

Hatch had to work at holding back a smile. "Okay, Ms. Cook, it is. We've got to continue our interview with your son here, but he was very concerned about your safety. Now that we know you are on your way to the station, we'll make sure the two of you get a few minutes together when you arrive. Sound good?"

"Okay, but—"

"See you then." Hatch quickly ended the call, and in that moment, Jefferson decided he might like the detective slightly more than before.

Hatch spun his phone on the tabletop. "That there is our side of the bargain complete."

Geno ran his hands down his face, clearly less anxious but now facing the very real trouble in front of him.

The Las Vegas detective continued. "So we've already booked you on evading an officer and felonious assault with a deadly weapon against a police officer. More charges are on the way, but how serious those will be depends on your help today."

"You also said you'd keep me safe," Geno said, his eyes shifting to Jefferson. "*You* said I would be safe. Was that just a lie to get me here?"

Detective Hughes's steady gaze met the other man's accusing glare. "Not at all, but we can't know what 'keeping you safe' looks like until we know who we are keeping you safe from."

Geno turned his attention back to Hatch. "Why am I even talking to this guy? Washington? This isn't Washington with all its rain and Bigfoot crap. Why is he even here?"

And just like that, a wave of irritation washed over Jefferson. The thought of babying this guy, this criminal, for another hour trying to get information would drive him insane.

"Hi, Geno," said Amber before Jefferson could respond. The detective rubbed his eyes in disbelief. It was like she had some kind of patience meter on him, and she knew exactly when he was about to lose it.

"I'm also from Washington," she said. "Have you been watching the news?"

"Nah. What would I do that for?"

A patient smile floated on her lips. "Well," she said with a tilt of her head. "If you had, you would know that a young woman was abducted last night. Here, in Las Vegas. That young woman is from Washington." Without releasing him from her gaze, she added, "That is why we are here. The police in both jurisdictions and the United States government all have a serious interest in this case. Do you understand now?"

Geno seemed to pale slightly at the reminder of Amber's federal status.

"I didn't abduct anybody," he said, his eyes wide with innocence. "I don't know anything about any abduction. I swear." He put his palms up to plead his case.

Still patient, still holding that smile, Amber spoke in comforting tones. Her unmoving eyes, however, had a hardness that Geno didn't miss. "We don't think you abducted her, Geno. But we think you made it possible."

"No," Geno said, waving his hands spasmodically. "No. I didn't do anything like that. Who is this lady you're talking about? I don't even know her. Last night? I was playing my game all night. You can ask my friends."

Jefferson sat forward. "Let's not talk about last night. Let's instead talk about last week. You worked one day at Silver Hills Electric?"

"Two days," said Geno. "I quit cause the guy was a jerk."

"I wasn't done," said Jefferson. "And stop trying to pretend this was legit. We know you gave a fake name. Then you worked on exactly one job, fixing the broken outdoor lights for Mr. Devey, something you seem to have some skill in, as pointed out by Detective Hatch. Then you made the excuse of needing to use the bathroom to get inside the house. What did you really do when you went inside?"

Geno shrugged. "I went pee."

Hatch reached into an accordion-style folder and pulled out an evidence bag. "Do these look familiar?"

"Those are cameras," said Geno. He tried to say it casually, but his voice sounded thick, as if his mouth had gone dry. Grabbing the water bottle, he took a drink.

"They are yours, Geno. We already know that, so I will not beat around the bush," said Jefferson, his adrenaline pumping again. He resisted the urge to grab the idiot by his shirt collar. "Who paid you to plant them, and who received the stream?"

"I didn't—"

"Stop!" Jefferson slammed the table with both his fists. "Stop jerking us around. We know you put the cameras in the house. Who sent you! Who watched the stream?"

This time, Amber did not hold him back. Instead, she and Hatch watched Geno's reaction with interest.

"I-I don't know. I swear." He wrung his hands together.

Jefferson stood and leaned over the table, getting as close as possible to Geno's face. "I don't believe you. We," he said, looking back at the other two, "don't believe you. You set up the cameras so that the men who abducted M̲ would know her plans, where she would be. Tell us the truth!"

"No. I didn't know what the cameras were for," Geno whined. "You're right. I put them inside the house. But he didn't tell me why or who would be watching. I swear. I'm sorry about the lady, but I didn't know what he was going to do."

"Who. Is. *He*?" Jefferson spat out. "And don't even think about lying."

Geno shook his head, shrinking back as if he feared Jefferson's reaction to his answer. "We only talked on the computer. I never met him, I swear."

Hatch slapped his notebook on the table, ready to write whatever came next.

"Email? Social media? What?"

Geno was back to wringing his hands. "Oh man, look, this is like so bad. Me telling you, it means I'm dead. So dead."

"You're only chance is to help us right now," said Amber. "If we have to find the source without you, you have no promises of safety."

Flinging his head back, Geno groaned at the ceiling. When he next looked at them, the desperation in his eyes almost made Jefferson feel for the guy.

"What will you do? How will you protect me and my mom?" His voice cracked, and his eyes were filling with tears.

Amber folded her hands on the table. "We'll put you in a safe house until this investigation is complete. Then we can reassess whether continued protection is warranted. If it is, then witness protection. But know that the government will probably require your testimony if it will help with prosecution in this or related cases."

With a deep, ragged breath, Geno nodded. "Okay." He rubbed his palms down his thighs and shifted in his seat. Then, he took another drink of water.

With another deep breath, he started. "So, there's this site. It's on the dark web. People go there to get jobs. They're not really legal jobs, so you get paid a lot of money for them. I've seen some weird stuff on there." He let out a nervous breath. "People looking for hit men and stuff. I never answered none of those. That's crazy stuff."

"What's the website called?" asked Hatch.

"Hired.onion."

With his hand hovering over the notepad, Hatch raised his eyebrows. "That's it? Just hired?"

"Yeah. That's it," said Geno. "I've pulled other jobs from there, did my thing, got paid. No big deal. But this one," he shook his head. "This guy is a mean, scary dude . . . something different . . ." His words trailed off as he stared at the wall.

"Do you know his name?"

It took a second for Geno to return to the conversation. "Uh, just a screen name. But I've checked since then, and he's not there anymore. Even my chat with him is gone."

Hatch glanced at Amber. "Is this something your guy can find?"

"He'll certainly try," she said, glancing at her phone. What she saw there elicited a deep breath before she put it away. "Tell us as much as you can, Geno. Anything helps."

Jefferson hadn't missed her reaction, and he desperately wanted to know what news she'd received.

Feeling his intense focus on her, the agent glanced up. "Not now," she whispered.

He'd have to be happy with that. At least she hadn't dashed from the room, dragging him with her in a move that could only signal his worst fears realized. No, whatever she'd seen was important but not life-changing. His heart could beat a little longer.

Geno pulled at his ragged attempt at a chin beard. "He went by DirtySpines. I saw him on the board looking for electricians — I mean, not real ones. I don't have an actual certification cause I dropped out of the electrician's course after my kid brother died." Shifting in his seat, he tapped the table with his fingers before continuing. "My mind was all over the place."

"Sorry about your brother, man," said Hatch. "That stinks."

Geno nodded, his attention focused on the table in front of him.

"Anyway," he said, clearing his throat. "This job was different from the start. He wanted me to get hired at Silver Hills and even gave me fake credentials. Usually I just do sort of, not really legal stuff for people who don't want to involve city or county inspectors." With a side-eye at Detective Hatch, Geno shrugged one shoulder as if knowing he was outing himself but also sensing the people across from him had bigger fish to fry.

"I immediately wanted out of the job. It felt way too risky." His jaw tightened as he clenched a fist on the table. "That's when I got the note on my door." His head moved back and forth in slow motion as air hissed from his nose. "It said if I backed out, my mom was as good as dead."

"How did you know it wasn't a bluff? Mom is pretty generic. We all have them," said Jefferson.

Geno stared back at him, his eyes blazing. "Because at the bottom of the note," he said, stabbing the table with his pointer finger, "he'd printed a picture of my mom. A picture he'd taken from her front yard, into her living room window."

The three law enforcement figures said nothing, silenced by the level of organization and malevolence revealed by Geno, combined with what they already knew about the workings behind MJ's abduction.

"Shoot," Hatch finally said, breaking the silence. "How did he know so much about you, using the dark web and all?"

"That's what I mean," said Geno. "This guy is different. Dangerous. I wanted out, but now you see why I couldn't."

"Do you still have the note?" asked Amber.

The man responded with a slow nod. "Back at my apartment."

"We'll need that," she said. "Also, you said he gave you a fake certification. How did he get that to you? Did you have meetups, drops?"

"I never met him. When I came home from my buddy's place one night, I found an envelope on my counter. In. My. Kitchen. How did he get into my apartment?" Geno asked, his eyes wide with fear.

Hatch stopped writing. "Wouldn't be that hard, really. More importantly, he just wanted you to know he can get to you. Keeps you scared."

"Well, it worked," said Geno. "After I finished the job, I didn't even care if I got paid, man. I just wanted it over. And I swear, I did not know why they wanted the cameras in there. All I did was hide them and turn them on. Where the feed went, I couldn't say."

"Did you get paid?" asked Jefferson.

"Bitcoin," said Geno, "but I haven't touched it."

"What all was in the envelope, and do you still have it?" asked Hatch, his pen ready.

With his elbows on the table, Geno ran his hands over his ears and neck, shaking his head. "No. Sorry. His instructions said to burn it all, except the cameras, but I'm guessing you have those." Geno's eyes bounced up to Hatch.

"We sure do," said the detective.

"Yeah, so the envelope had an electrician's certificate, a resume, and a script for what I should say about myself."

"That's pretty thorough," said Jefferson.

"You're telling me," said Geno. "I'd never have gotten hired on my own. But Silver Hills just ate that crap up."

"We'll need access to your Bitcoin account, your hired.onion account, and maybe some others," said Hatch, ripping a blank page from his notebook and passing Geno his pen. "Start writing accounts and passwords."

***

After Geno finished writing details of his various accounts, an officer escorted him to a holding cell. There he would wait for his mom to arrive at the station. Mother and son would then have a brief meeting, after which Agent Dawn Clark would move Ms. Cook to an FBI safe house.

Jefferson followed Amber and the Las Vegas detective into Hatch's office, immediately closing the door behind them.

"What news did you get?" he asked Amber as he leaned against the door, his arms folded.

She pulled out her phone. "We should sit down. Ryan, can you connect this to your computer screen?" She held her device out to him.

"Sure can." He took it and rummaged on his desk for a chord snaking from the side of his computer monitor.

Jefferson hadn't moved from the door.

"Sit down, Jeff," she said, motioning to a chair next to her. "You're going to want to be close to the screen."

Unfolding his arms and pushing away from the door, the detective took the chair offered. "What is it?"

As her phone's home screen appeared on the computer, Amber took the device back from Hatch. "It's the interview," she said as she navigated her phone. "Nico and the marshals."

Hatch took a step back. "What?" His incredulous eyes flicked between the two of them. "How did you get that?"

With one more click on her screen, a bird's-eye view of a cramped interview room opened on the computer monitor.

"Don't worry about it."

"Holy crap, Amber. Am I going to need a lawyer after hanging out with you?"

"Oh dear," she said. "You have turned dramatic in your old age."

Leaning forward, Jefferson curled his hands into fists on the desktop. There was Nico, his wrists restrained and chained to the thick table. The image remained frozen, but the smirk on the man's lips was unmistakable. Without warning, Jefferson saw himself tackling Nico, his hands around his throat, squeezing until Nico's smirk turned into a scream.

"You ready?" Amber asked, studying his expression.

With his eyes pinned to the screen, he seethed, "Push play."

Instead, she let out a frustrated sigh and sat back in her chair. "I understand how much you hate this man, Jefferson. Nico needs to rot in prison for the rest of his miserable life. That's what I want too, but right now, I need you to be a detective. Not a boyfriend. Not a brother. You need to watch with an eye for detail. Otherwise, step outside because you are going to distract me."

Splaying his fingers on the table, Jefferson tore his eyes from the computer, the image of Nico's screaming face burned into his brain. He closed his eyes, willing himself to breathe normally.

"I understand," he said, fighting to keep the tremor from his voice.

"Good, because I don't know how long I'll have access," she said, picking up her phone. Then, without another word, Amber started the video.

For the first few seconds, Nico sat alone in the room, that self-satisfied smirk just waiting for someone to impress. When the two marshals entered the room, Nico sat back like a king accepting visitors at court.

The marshals, however, were not playing his game. The video did not provide a clear look at their faces, but both wore black T-shirts. One appeared younger with a close-cropped, military-style haircut, while the other had short silver hair.

"Good morning, little Nico, how's your stay been so far?" said the younger deputy as he took his seat across from the prisoner.

The smirk stayed, but it looked forced now. Nico's dark eyes followed the deputy's movements as if plotting the ways he might hurt him when he got out of prison. If any man said such a thing about the trafficker's size out in the real world, that man wouldn't live to see the next five minutes. This sensitivity about his size likely fueled Nico's early adoption of ruthlessness, needing to prove he could take on anyone. His appearance alone inspired little fear. Short and carrying a nice-sized paunch, the thirty-something Nico looked closer to fifty with his receding hairline and flabby body.

"That's okay," the deputy said. "You don't have to answer. We don't really care how you're doing."

The other deputy chuckled. "Now come on, Deputy Grimes. Be nice." He set a file on top of the table. "Nico, I'm Deputy Rex, and you've met Deputy Grimes. The deputy who escorted you read your rights?"

"Yes, he did, but I don't plan on talking, so it's all good, amigos."

Rex nodded. "Okay, well, today we need to do some extra background checks before the trial, make sure we can keep you and others in the courtroom safe from known associates who might want to, you know, take advantage of you being in court."

Nico raised a suspicious eyebrow. "This seems unusual. Background checks? Anything I would tell you, which isn't much, you already know. There is nothing else for me to say."

"I get that, but despite Deputy Grimes's rude greeting, it's our job to ensure the court proceedings are safe for everyone involved. Data show that transport to the courthouse poses the most significant threat to your safety. Some higher-ups in your organization might get nervous and try taking you out, you know? What better opportunity?"

With a snort, Nico rolled his eyes. "You and your data know nothing."

"Maybe. Maybe not," continued Deputy Rex. "But we want to go over some new information. Uh, rumors, you might call it, about some threats coming out of California."

Nico folded his chained hands together with a stoic look of patience, like a parent expecting a lie from a naughty child. "Like I said, you know nothing. But tell me this great rumor you've heard."

Deputy Grimes leaned over and whispered something to his partner.

"Ah," said Rex. "Sorry, Nico. I got that wrong. Not California. Police arrested someone in Las Vegas, and he had some strange connections to you."

At the mention of Las Vegas, Nico's expression shifted for a millisecond — a subtle change that most humans would recognize in others, but wouldn't be able to identify.

"Rewind it," said Jefferson.

"Already on it," said Amber.

As they watched Nico's response again, the signals became even clearer.

"Crinkling around the eyes, slight twitch of the lips," said Amber

"And look at his hands," said Jefferson. "He's released them and is drumming the fingers of one hand, showing the mention of Las Vegas disgustingly excited him."

"I don't get it. Didn't you already know it was him?" asked Hatch.

"Yes, but we could only claim that someone had abducted and threatened MJ on Nico's behalf," said Amber. "Now, I think we can safely say Nico knows all about it."

"Let's keep going," said Jefferson.

Nico looked down at his hands and sighed.

Another way of hiding his delight, thought Jefferson.

"I don't know anyone in Las Vegas," said Nico. "Oh no, wait, I once had a cousin there, but I think he died. Some cop shot him or something."

Ignoring Nico's comment, Deputy Rex continued. "The guy they arrested in Las Vegas," he said, referring to the open file in front of him, "he was supposed to do something with a girl, like kidnapping or something, but he messed it up, I guess. Anyway," he waved his hand to change the subject. "He told a wild story about how the job was for you, and it was your last chance. If it didn't work, you were toast, or something like that. Now, I just think that's weird. How would kidnapping a girl help you in prison?"

Jefferson had to admire what the deputies had done. They initially let Nico think his plan had succeeded by mentioning Las Vegas. Now, they suggested his plan had not only failed, but that failure meant Nico's own life was in danger, that another plot existed he knew nothing about.

They were obviously banking on Nico not having received word of the abduction's success through whatever prison network he'd concocted. Judging by Nico's body language, they'd guessed correctly.

Nico worked to keep his lips twisted into a carefree smirk, but his entire face had frozen, revealing the false bravado behind it. There was something else there now. Not fear. Jefferson knew better than to think that. Nico always believed himself to be untouchable. Even sitting in prison, the man whole-heartedly believed his incarceration was a temporary interruption to his life and business. He'd been right most of the time. No matter how often things went wrong for Nico, some powerful person up the chain rescued him, and the scumbag always came out stronger and meaner than before.

Nico wasn't afraid. He was angry. If someone screwed up his plan, they would pay a heavy price.

"Sounds like someone is spinning tales to twist up the cops," Nico said, his hard eyes dead set on the deputy, his smirk changed for a teeth-bearing grin.

"And he just happened to pull your filthy name out of a hat?" said Grimes. "Come on, Nico. You can lie better than that."

Nico shrugged, his eyes dropping momentarily to his hands as he turned his palms up. "What can I say? I know many people, amigo."

"Yeah, you keep some interesting company," said Grimes. "And now we know it's weirdos who like to swipe women from the street. Awesome friends you've got there."

Nico shook his head with a chuckle. "You try so hard to get me angry, but I'm telling you, I know nothing of this kidnapper." Then his face stilled, taking on a serious, almost reverential look. "How is the woman? Is she okay after such an ordeal?"

"Fine," said Rex. "She was a little shaken up at first, but she's fine now, happy that the cops caught the guy."

"That's good," said Nico, another fake smile spreading across his face. "It's such a dangerous city these days, Las Vegas. Not so good for her vacation, I guess. But it is good she is safe."

The two deputies looked at each other. When they did so, Nico, realizing his mistake, pressed his lips together at the same time his eyes closed in an extended blink. The movement only took a second before it was gone, but the deputies didn't miss it, and neither did the three watching the video.

"Did we say she was on vacation?" Deputy Rex asked.

Nico unconsciously clasped his hands together to keep them still. "Simple guess. Why else would anyone be in Las Vegas?"

"People live there, too," said Grimes. "Like your cousin."

This elicited an appreciative snort from Nico. "You listen well, Deputy."

Rex plowed on. "We know women get kidnapped for trafficking all the time. That's nothing new, but the weird thing about this case is the sheer amount of organization involved. Someone put a lot of planning into it. So, I'm thinking there may be something credible in the guy's claim. The plan didn't work. And that puts you at risk."

Nico erupted in a gut-busting laugh that went on for a full minute. When he finally stopped, the man wiped his eyes as if the humor of Rex's words had brought him to tears. "Oh. You are a funny man, Deputy. Please do not waste your time worrying about me. No one is coming for Nico." He shook his head. "I trust the system. The trial will prove I am an innocent man."

"Wow," said Grimes, glancing at Deputy Rex. "That is so refreshing, isn't it? Let the system work. I totally agree." He sat forward, moving further into Nico's space. "But I'm sitting here wondering why you're not more curious, Nico. How was a kidnapping supposed to help you?"

Furrowing his brow, Nico seemed to search for an answer. "I guess that man must not be playing with a full deck, you know what I mean?"

"That could be true," said Rex. "But humor me for a minute while I play out a scenario. See, I'm thinking that this guy planned to kidnap the woman because she has an important connection to your case. Get rid of her, and the case falls apart." He put his palms up. "Now, I'm not saying you had anything to do with it. Someone may be trying to help you, but I mean, it could end up making your situation worse."

Nico stared at the man. "Well, like you said, I had nothing to do with this kidnapping."

"That's not exactly what I said," smiled Rex. "It's very possible you had something to do with it."

Grimes turned to Rex. "Of course he had something to do with it. He's a liar. Aren't you Nico?"

"You should learn to be more professional, amigo," said Nico, his dark eyes shooting daggers at Grimes. "That mouth will get you into trouble."

"Such a big man in your little orange jumpsuit," Grimes chuckled. "I don't think I'm going to be the one in trouble. You should know that witness tampering, especially if anything happens to that witness, can add life in prison to what will already be a lengthy sentence for you."

Nico glowered. "I am done here. This talk of kidnapping and witnesses means nothing to me."

"What was the plan, Nico? Why not come clean? Who else is involved? You need to tell us before they come for you." Grimes pushed.

The forced smirk was back. "I am so happy to know how deeply you care, Deputy. But your worry is for nothing. All is well for Nico."

Grimes ignored him. "Where did you plan to take her?"

"I know no—"

Jumping to his feet, Grimes shouted. "Where, Nico! Why her?" He grabbed a photo from the file and slapped it on the table. "Why *that* woman!?"

The other man stared down at the picture of MJ as if studying for a test. When he looked up again, the broadest, sickest smile had slithered across his face.

"She is so pretty. I see why the crazy man wanted to take her. He must have planned to have some fun with her."

Jefferson's eyes burned, and in that moment, he wanted nothing more than to get his hands on Nico, punch his face until nothing remained of that disgusting smile. Instead, the detective sat miles away simmering with hatred, and the most intense helplessness.

Amber rested a hand on his clenched fist. When he met her eyes, there was no hiding the angry tears forming in his own.

She squeezed his hand before turning back to the video.

"You are a sick, dirty piece of garbage," seethed Grimes, still standing over Nico. "A woman like that wouldn't look twice at an overweight toad like you. She definitely wasn't your girlfriend. So why her?"

The deputies definitely knew everything having to do with MJ's abduction. They were expertly mixing truth and fiction.

Nico tried to laugh off the deputy's insults, but the sound was a hollow one. His flushed face said he was anything but amused.

"Ahhh, she is a sweet-looking maestra. She may be some man's fancy." He shrugged, rattling the chains that bound his wrists. "Not mine."

Grimes sat down, and turning to Rex he said, "You know Spanish better than I do. Remind me what that word means."

"What? Maestra?" replied Rex. He turned to face Nico. "It means teacher. Isn't that right, Nico?"

Grimes leaned forward and laughed. "I always knew you were a stupid screw-up."

For the first time, naked anger boiled on Nico's face. They had him, and he knew it.

The deputies let him simmer before Rex spoke with deadly calm. "Now tell us where."

Nico's eyes narrowed. "If the kidnapping failed, why do you care so much?"

"Let me remind you," said Rex, "witness tampering in its mildest form will get you thirty years on top of your other charges. If anything happens to a witness, especially if the witness dies, that becomes life in prison, my friend."

Nico bunched his lips as he nodded, his eyes still narrowed as he considered this.

"I know nothing about this kidnapping, but I think you are not telling the truth. This woman — she is missing?"

"Tell us the place, Nico," said Grimes. "You are already going down. Be smart for once in your miserable life."

Nico's face relaxed. Then, a grin, that could only be called evil, stretched across his face.

Chapter
Twenty-Three

L ander County Sheriff's Deputy Lance Michael glanced at the printed out BOLO on his passenger seat. He knew that car. Just a few weeks ago, he'd seen it in a driveway when looking for a missing kid.

After the entire sheriff's department spent days driving random streets in Austin and around the county, another deputy found the kid. The stupid twelve-year-old brat went camping by himself without asking or even saying where he was going. His teacher had read a book to the class about a kid who survives a plane crash in the wilderness. The story inspired the missing kid to try living off the land like a character in the book. He was lucky the temperatures were still relatively mild. If he did that now, the kid would freeze to death.

The problem was the deputy couldn't remember exactly where he'd seen that car. He didn't want to call it in to the Las Vegas Metro PD. They'd think he was an idiot if he turned out to be wrong.

He'd already checked three of the areas he remembered searching. Now he was miles from town in the fourth area. Everything looked different now. Snow covered the road and rooftops, blending everything together in one shade of white. This was the last area he would check. His shift ended in thirty minutes, and he was hungry for some of that beef stew his mom had brought over. The perfect meal for a chilly night.

His rig made the only tracks on the snow-covered gravel road. This area contained mostly manufactured homes, occupied by people who lived in this solitary place for reasons known only to themselves. But this road was more solitary than most. Only one house sat at the end, miles from the rest. Deputy Michael didn't get it at all. As soon as he had a few years under his belt with Lander County, he planned to transfer to some place closer to Vegas, maybe Henderson. He had a buddy who moved there, and he said it was pretty cool.

Reaching the end of the road, he pulled in front of an off-white or pale yellow manufactured home. Or maybe it used to be white. He couldn't tell. A memory flashed in his mind, and he remembered thinking that the car and house matched, both a bit beat up and dirty.

The only car in the driveway had a tan canvas over it, snow covering the flattest parts.

He should call for backup before getting out, except that backup would take at least thirty minutes to get here, and he didn't even know if he actually needed backup. Besides, he wanted to be eating stew in thirty minutes.

"Ah, screw it," he said to no one.

He'd get out, check under the cover, and if it looked like the right car, he'd leave and call it in when he had some distance between him and whoever lived here.

Leaving the car running, he quietly stepped out. He touched the flashlight on his belt. Though still daylight, the blanketing clouds made it feel like early evening. A little extra light might be needed to read the plate. And this place gave him the creeps.

The young deputy's boots crunched in the new snow as he stepped toward the car. Snowflakes littered his beanie, and a few fell into his eyes. He wiped them with the back of his leather glove.

Once at the back of the car, he crouched down, lifted the cover and pointed his flashlight underneath.

White. Battered bumper.

Deputy Michael pulled out his phone, trying to swipe with his gloved fingers to get his camera up. After a few seconds, he used his teeth to remove the glove. Finally getting the camera open, he held it up to the license plate.

Before he clicked the picture, he heard a faint crunch of snow behind him. As he turned, a metal pipe flashed in his peripheral vision. He raised his right arm to block the blow, but too late. His world went black.

***

MJ bolted upright.

Was that a car door?

Throwing back the sleeping bag, she rose to her knees and plastered her ear to the metal wall. The cold shocked her skin, and she pulled back, touching the now-frozen spot on her ear.

Hastily pulling her shirt up by the collar, she covered the ear and listened again.

She tried to control her breath, in and out, so that her heart might quit hammering, filling her head with its intense thump-thump-thump.

The cold seeped through her shirt until she pulled away.

Nothing. Not a sound.

But she'd heard it. Someone was out there.

Moving to her back, MJ pulled her knees to her chest before sending her feet slamming into the wall with as much force as she could muster. Then she pulled back and did it again. And again. And again.

She stopped. Someone was outside.

A sharp bark reached her ears. She lay back with a sigh. It was just Corky, and probably Robbie.

The adrenaline dropped away, leaving MJ shivering. She climbed back into the sleeping bag, zipped it up, and scooted to her taped-up portal.

When she looked into the yard, she found a confusing sight.

Robbie was outside, sitting cross-legged on the ground near the old pickup. He rocked back and forth, his hands covering his ears, muttering to himself. Corky sat in front of him, barking every few seconds, then whining as he skittishly approached the man, sniffing his hair and then jumping back and barking again.

MJ almost whispered Robbie's name, but before she could, a door slammed and another figure stormed into the yard.

"You need to shut that stupid dog up, or I will," the man said, stepping threateningly toward Corky.

The dog jumped back, but his barking continued, more defensive now than worried. The man took another step, and Corky bared his teeth, a low growl rumbling from deep in his throat.

That voice. MJ would know it anywhere. It carried the masked man's deep and deliberate way of speaking. No mask covered his head this time. At the moment, he had his back to her, revealing only his hair, sandy brown, turning gray, just like Robbie's.

"You'll growl at me, will ya?" the man sneered. Then he kicked out, the toe of his boot catching the dog on the right side.

"Stop!" cried Robbie. He'd stopped rocking, looking on in horror. "Don't hurt Corky!"

Corky yelped and ran, slithering under the truck for safety.

"Then keep him quiet," hissed the man. "And don't you say anything about what you saw. You got it?"

Robbie covered his ears again. "But I don't like it when you hurt that man. I don't like it." Within seconds, he began rocking again.

"Fine. Stay out here and freeze with your stupid mutt."

The man turned, and MJ quickly replaced the tape. She desperately wanted to see this man's face, but she couldn't risk her little secret viewing spot being discovered. It was her only contact with the outside world. With Robbie, who might be her only hope.

***

The door slammed again. The man was gone.

MJ opened the cooler. It contained the same lineup of food as before: peanut butter and jelly, sliced apples, chips, and water.

She broke a few pieces from the sandwich.

"Corky," she whispered through the open hole, adding a soft whistle.

Neither the dog nor Robbie seemed to hear her.

"Corky, boy," she whispered again, slightly louder this time. Then she stuck a sandwich piece through the hole.

A rustle of dirt and gravel. She had the dog's attention.

Pulling the food back, she made another appeal. "Come on, boy. It's okay. Come on, Corky."

After sticking the sandwich piece out again, she heard the slow and faint padding of paws on the snow.

She didn't dare pull the food back now. The dog had risked coming out of his hiding spot for her.

Then she heard the unmistakable sound of the dog's quick sniffing. A warm chomp of his lips; the food was gone.

"Good boy, Corky." She fed him a few more pieces, all the while trying to see past his head to Robbie.

One opportune glimpse showed her that Robbie had quit rocking. Instead, he watched Corky with an expression twisted with confusion and pain, his hands still covering his ears.

"Robbie," MJ whispered. "Are you okay?"

He probably couldn't hear her. The dog's superior hearing and smelling capabilities made him easy to lure. Robbie would be harder, especially given his dysregulated state.

"I'm sorry Corky got hurt, Robbie."

She was almost out of sandwich pieces. Corky was a hungry dog.

"Robbie," she called a little louder. "Can you hear me?"

Suddenly, quick steps were coming toward her. She pulled her hand back, afraid it was the other man returning. Had he heard her?

"Shhh! Please don't talk. He won't like it. He might hurt you."

MJ looked through the hole to see Robbie kneeling down, one hand grasping Corky's collar.

"Did he hurt someone else?" she asked in a quieter whisper.

"I can't say. He told me not to say."

Licking her chapped lips, MJ tried to calm her heart again.

Don't push him, she thought. *Take your time. He will tell you.*

"I don't want to get you into trouble, Robbie. But if you want to talk, I won't tell anyone that you told me."

Robbie's hands flew to his ears again, releasing Corky. Rather than running away, the dog stuck next to the man, sticking its nose into Robbie's face and licking his cheek.

"He hit him," said Robbie, his eyes squeezed tight. "He hurt the policeman."

MJ's heart lurched at the word policeman. He couldn't possibly mean Jefferson, could he? No, it had to be a uniformed officer, someone Robbie would recognize as a policeman. Did the local police know she was a prisoner in this place? She resisted the emotion welling up, not wanting to nurture the hope of rescue. Despite the effort, tears burned her eyes.

"Robbie," she said, her voice shaking slightly. "Is there a policeman here?"

The man's head moved violently back and forth. "In the trunk. In the trunk."

With a sharp intake of breath, MJ sat back from the wall.

Did he kill the policeman? Was there a patrol car? If a policeman came here, someone else had to know where he was — that she was here. Please God, let someone know the police officer was here, for his sake and hers.

MJ's mind whirred. What could she do? This might be her only chance of escape. She had to make a move, but she did not know what move to make. One thing she knew for sure, she could do nothing trapped inside this container. Step one: find a way out of this prison.

"Robbie," she said, shifting so she could look at him again. "I know how much you dislike when people—or dogs—get hurt. I want to help. Maybe I can check on the policeman and see if I can help him."

He didn't look at her, his hands still trying to shield his mind from the upsetting scene he'd witnessed.

MJ pushed on. "I'd really like to help, but I need to get out of this room first. Do you know how to open the door?"

No response. The head shaking had stopped, but Robbie now sat cross-legged on the ground, bent over at the waist, holding his head. Corky lay down next to him, nuzzling his neck every few seconds.

They heard it at the same time: the door slamming followed by angry, heavy footsteps.

Robbie's head shot up, and his eyes, wide with fear, met hers through the hole in the wall.

"What are you doing?!" bellowed the other man.

MJ quickly slapped the tape over the hole, but she didn't need to see it to know what happened next.

Robbie screamed out in pain as Corky barked furiously. Then the dog yelped, and MJ heard a thud against the wall.

"Corky!" Robbie's anguished cry broke MJ's heart. Her hands flew to her ears as tears coursed down her cheeks.

Desperate fear started an acidic ache churning deep inside of her, but it wasn't just fear. Anger added a flame that made her hands shake. And before she could stop herself, she'd ripped the duct tape away again.

"Stop it! Leave him alone!" she shouted.

Without warning, there was a deafening kick to the wall, making MJ jump. One massive, enraged dark eye looked through the hole.

"I will deal with you later," he hissed in his deep, unhurried way.

"I'm sorry. David, stop! David don't hurt me," Robbie pleaded, his voice moving farther away as the man dragged him from the yard.

Chapter Twenty-Four

B efore Franco even had the sense to ask for one, an attorney showed up at the station claiming to represent the drug dealer.

Low-level dealers like Franco usually tried to talk their way out of jail time, admitting to the least egregious illegal activities while claiming a variety of sob stories, all crafted to explain their dive into criminal life. Having an attorney from the get-go was highly unusual.

And having an attorney that wasn't a public defender — that was almost unheard of.

So, it appeared to the West Sound detectives that someone more important than Franco would pay the attorney's bill. Someone more important and with more to lose.

When the lawyer finally arrived, Rory and Larson gave him a few minutes with Franco before entering the room.

The attorney was not someone either detective had worked with before. He didn't look like any of the public defenders who usually sat across the table during an interview with someone like Franco. The attorney wore a navy blue suit with white plaid running through it; the clothes hugged his thin frame with the custom fit of an expensive brand. His tie, a silk paisley in sunset shades of pink and purple, disappeared into the snug-fitting vest beneath his suit coat.

Even Jefferson would think this guy had outdone himself, thought Rory.

Franco sat next to his attorney, regarding him like an injured bird might regard a wolf, as if the man were there to eat him instead of help him.

Larson set a file folder on the table, watching the lawyer as he and Rory sat down. "I'm Detective Larson, and this is Detective Jackson."

"Hello, gentlemen," said the thin-faced man with a slight bow of his head. His black, slicked-back hair caught the light as he moved. "My name is Caesar Milano. My client is happy to cooperate at this time; however, I expect the judge to release Franco on bail at his preliminary hearing, and I have advised him not to answer questions related to the murder charge until we have had more time for consultation."

"So much for cooperating," muttered Larson. "I'd say bail might be a long shot on this one."

The attorney folded his hands on the table with the unperturbed grin of a man confident in his position. Despite his immaculate physical presentation, the man's voice had a high, nasal quality that was instantly irritating.

"We understand your position," said Rory, "but we have questions about Franco's movements and his relationship to the victim, things we'd like to clear up that are not directly related to the murder."

With a dip of his chin, the lawyer signaled for the detective to continue.

Franco did not seem bolstered by this high-powered attorney's presence. He sat hunched over, his eyes pinned to the tabletop.

"Franco," started Rory. "How long have you known Brayden Shuster?"

The other man shrugged without looking up.

The attorney sighed. "My client does not know the victim personally."

"We'd like *him* to answer, if you don't mind," said Larson, his patience for stuffy attorneys on a shorter leash than Rory's.

With an impassive face, Caesar Milano showed a sliver of white teeth between his lips. "I'm sure you understand I cannot force the man to speak."

"True," said Larson. "But we have time to wait for his answer. No hurry."

Rory tried again. "Franco, we already know you've been selling marijuana on the street. So there's no point in arguing about that fact. Brayden Shuster, before he went into detention three years ago, bought his weed from Toby. Did you know Toby?"

The drug dealer finally lifted his head. "Yeah, I knew him." He sniffed and ran his hand across his nose.

"Are you aware that Toby died of a drug overdose?"

Caesar broke in. "How is this relevant?"

"If you let him continue," said Larson with a forced smile. "You'll figure it out."

A smirk worked up one corner of Caesar's mouth. "You may answer, Franco," he said, his eyes never leaving Larson's.

Franco cast a quick glance at the lawyer, then his eyes met Rory's. There seemed to be a pleading there that caught the detective off guard. If he was suspicious before, Franco's reaction convinced him that something was rotten in this attorney's sudden appearance.

"Uh, sure I know he OD'd," said Franco. "Everybody on the street does. Toby knew most everybody. He didn't get those drugs from me, though. I don't deal in—"

"That's enough, Franco." The attorney's sharp words silenced the dealer immediately.

Franco went back to studying the table.

Rory sat back, his right hand stroking his beard as his eyes moved between the attorney and the dealer. "Franco," he said, his eyes narrowing. "Did you hire Mr. Milano?"

The dealer's head shot up. "What?"

"Did you sign anything saying that you want this man to be your lawyer?"

Staring at Rory with goldfish eyes, Franco seemed stunned into silence.

"We have a verbal agreement," Caesar Milano said coolly. "Isn't that right, Franco?"

Franco's Adam's apple bobbed as he swallowed. "Um, yeah. That's right," he finally responded, his voice dry as a thirsty riverbed.

"Huh," said Rory with a thoughtful nod. "We'd really like to see a signed document."

"Of course," said Caesar. "We have had little time to attend to paperwork. When I have time, we will provide such documents if it would ease your mind."

The two detectives exchanged a glance. They clearly shared misgivings about this attorney. He seemed shadier than shade, and if this overdressed suit got Franco out on bail, they had to wonder if the dealer would be safe on the streets. The powerful someone paying the attorney's bill might also be very interested in keeping Franco quiet.

Unfortunately, unless Franco refused the attorney's services, there was little the police could do.

"We'd appreciate that," said Rory. "We like people to know they can engage an attorney of their choice, and if Franco would like a different one, he just has to say so."

This statement probably crossed a legal line, but Rory didn't care. He had a creeping feeling that this lawyer carried crime in his veins, that he worked for people who cared very little for the law.

"I think Franco is glad to accept my help. We are working pro bono." The man attempted a casual smile, as if humility had kept him from mentioning this earlier. "Isn't that right, Franco?"

The attorney did not look at his client, but his tone carried a warning. Franco didn't have a choice. Either way, he'd lose.

Two shades paler than when he entered the room, Franco swallowed. "Yeah," he whispered. "That's right."

Milano's grin broadened. "See. No issues," he said, spreading his hands out, palms up. "Please continue."

Pressing his lips together, Rory watched Franco, hoping he might look up and catch his eye again. He didn't, choosing instead to stare at the table.

Rory glanced at Larson, who shrugged. If the dealer wouldn't help himself in this situation, the two detectives couldn't interfere.

"Fine," said Rory. "Franco, after Toby died, you picked up most of his buyers."

The lawyer interrupted, but Rory put his palm up to stop him. "I m not asking you to confirm that," the detective said directly to Franco, ignoring the lawyer. "Your habitual drug dealing is not why we are here, though it's related. We are more interested in knowing whether you sold weed to Brayden Shuster and when."

"No, I never saw Brayden. Don't even know the dude," said Franco, risking a glance up.

Larson grunted. "So we won't find your DNA on the weed we found in his pocket?"

Caesar Milano maintained a relaxed, dismissive expression for most of the interview, but this question prompted the smallest twitch of his lips.

The dealer flicked a sideways glance at the attorney before shaking his head.

Larson sat forward, opening his file folder. "Is this your coat?" he asked, shoving a picture across the table. It was the jacket Franco had been wearing earlier.

Though he barely looked at the photo, Franco nodded. "Yeah. It looks like it."

Larson pointed to the picture. "How did you lose that button?"

Franco's features stilled as he studied the photo more closely this time. He swallowed again, this time avoiding the attorney altogether as he lost another shade of color. "I don't think I did. Maybe . . . Maybe that's not mine."

"Okay," shrugged Larson, sitting back again. "Like I said. DNA." He gave the dealer a wolfish grin.

Milano's eyes narrowed. "Gentlemen, I think we're done for today," he said. "My client and I need to prepare for his hearing tomorrow."

"Just one more question," said Rory. "Franco, where were you last night between the hours of 11 pm and 3 am?"

Without hesitating, Franco replied, "Sleeping."

"Where?"

"At my place down by the Shopsides."

"Can anyone vouch for you?"

"Don't answer that," warned Milano.

The attorney stood. "You have his answer. My client will not answer any further questions until we have had proper time for consultation."

Larson picked up his folder, standing to meet the attorney face-to-face. "You mean proper time to fake an alibi?"

Caesar Milano chuckled. "Detective, I am interested only in ensuring my client's rights do not get trampled. This is America, after all. Presumed innocent — that is the way, what we all believe, correct?"

"Well," said Larson, "there is that whole 'until proven guilty' part. I think we can prove enough to ensure your client stays in jail, no matter how eager you are for his release." He turned to knock on the door to get the attention of the officer outside. "How's Franco here going to pay a huge bail bond? Maybe the same person paying your fee is also interested in ponying up bail money?" Larson turned to Franco. "You got some rich relatives somewhere, kid?"

Before the dealer could respond, Caesar put his arm out to silence him. "It is a good thing that none of that is your worry, Detective. It is Franco's, and it is mine."

The officer entered, put Franco in handcuffs, and began leading him to the door. The entire way, Franco's eyes never left Rory's. They seemed to say. "I am a dead man."

Chapter Twenty-Five

R ory hung up the phone.

"So, what did they say?" asked Larson, drinking another cup of coffee.

Slouching down in his chair, Rory let his head fall against the back of it. "They said our evidence needs to be up to snuff if we want the judge to deny bail. We have to prove Franco is a continuing danger to the community. Otherwise, despite our concerns about Franco's safety, there's not much the prosecutor's office can do, especially if the stupid kid won't ask for help."

"I mean, I can't disagree. What are they supposed to do?" said Larson. "Play stupid games, win stupid prizes. Franco made his bed a long time ago. And don't go calling me cold and heartless. I think we should do what we can to help, but don't forget that this kid likely killed another kid in cold blood."

"I know," said Rory, looking at the ceiling as he turned in his chair. "It's not so much about Franco as it is about the big fish we never seem to get."

"Hey, we got Nico."

"But did we? How is he still plotting to abduct people from prison?" Rory shook his head. "When I think about these criminal gangs . . . It feels like they are more organized and better funded than we are. We're always just scratching the surface when we need to be digging out the heart."

"I hear you, man. No argument there."

Lost in their own thoughts, both detectives were quiet.

"On another note," said Larson, turning back to his laptop, "I had an interesting conversation with Daxton Dyer, the husband of the Shuster victim."

"Oh yeah?"

"Yeah. Dyer said that for the past few months he's found a random bag of cash on his front porch."

Rory pulled back with wide eyes. "What? Like how much cash we talking?"

Larson answered with his eyes on his computer. "Varying amounts. Sometimes as much as five thousand. Twenty-five thousand in all. He's talked to the police about it, but they seem to think it's some random member of the public who wants to help him and his other two kids."

"I mean," said Rory, "that's not a bad theory."

"No, it's not," said Larson. "And if it weren't for the Shuster's murder, I wouldn't think much of it. Some people want to help anonymously but don't trust those donation apps. I get it. But it's worth checking out, and Dyer just sent me the footage from his doorbell camera."

He turned his laptop so both he and Rory could see it. "You ready?"

"Let 'er rip," said Rory.

Over the years, home video cameras had improved to capture remarkably clear images. This one was no different as the detectives watched a thin, medium height man creep up three steps to the covered porch. Clutched in his gloved right hand, they saw a paper bag with the top rolled down. The man wore his hood pulled down over his head, making his face impossible to make out. All his clothes were black and nondescript. Once he reached the top of the porch, he lunged forward and dropped the bag on the welcome mat before dashing back down the stairs and disappearing around the front of the house.

"That is so much different than what we usually witness on people's porches," said Rory. "What do you make of it?"

Larson sighed. "I don't know, but I think we should add it to the case. I'm going to email the video to Meyers and have him print a still photo of the guy dropping the cash. Dyer says he still has all the money. He's been afraid to do anything with it. But this guy," he said pointing to the screen where the video had frozen, "seems careful, with the gloves and all. I doubt we'd get anything off the bills or bag, but it might be worth a shot."

"I agree," said Rory.

Suddenly, Ron jumped from his chair on the other side of the room, a paper held in his hand, and punched toward the ceiling in a victory stance.

"Ah-ha!" he shouted. "I got the little bugger."

"This sounds promising," said Larson.

The two detectives went to investigate.

"What you got, Ronnie?" said Julia as she rolled her chair to the big man's desk.

Ron returned to his seat, a massive grin splitting his face.

"Here," he said, pointing to the paper he'd slapped down on the desk. He turned it around so they could all read it right-side up. "This is our guy. I'm sure of it." His finger hovered next to the underlined name of Javier Garcia-Tenedor.

"This guy entered the United States on a flight from Mexico City to Phoenix two weeks ago. He stayed in Arizona until two-days before MJ's abduction. That's when he rented a car. He goes off the radar after that, probably using cash for everything, but this is the guy. I'd stake my life on it. Well . . . I'd stake Larson's life on it."

"Thanks," said Detective Larson.

"So what does this mean?" asked Rory. "How does this help find MJ?"

Julia ran a finger under the name. "Someone had to orchestrate this whole thing. I'd guess this guy is our conductor, making everything happen but keeping Nico out of it."

Rory sat up. "So if we find him, we find everyone else?"

"Precisely," said Ron. "But that part, my friend, will be up to the folks in Las Vegas." He pulled out his phone. "Amber needs this ASAP."

"Before you call her," said Julia, picking up the paper and reading the name again, "check for an upcoming or recent outbound flight. Let's hope we haven't missed him."

Ron rolled his eyes. "Don't be such a downer. Think positive thoughts, Agent Liufau."

With a mock huff of irritation, he pulled his computer to him and began typing. "That is a good idea, though."

"Thanks, Ronnie."

"Don't mention it, sister from a different mister."

Larson lifted his arms in a long stretch. "We should go update the chief on our lack of progress with Franco," he said, directing his words to Rory.

Rory knit his brows together. "I am going to agree with Ron. Think positive thoughts. Go have another fancy coffee if it helps."

"I am thinking sleepy thoughts," said Larson. "And they are about to become sleepy, grumpy thoughts."

"Fine, whatever you say. But let's ask for a short briefing. We need to comb through the forensics reports and have Meyers update the board. Any connection we make between Franco and Shuster will shore up our case for keeping Franco in jail. That missing button might not be enough."

Larson gave him a lazy salute. "Yes, boss."

The other detective's smile broke through his ginger beard. "I'm glad you finally understand the order of things."

"Whatever," said Larson as he walked toward the chief's office.

Before following Larson, Rory grabbed his notepad and wrote something down. Then he ripped it out and passed it across the desk to Ron.

"Can you check out this guy, too? I have a weird feeling about him."

Ron picked up the note. "Caesar Milano, attorney. Sure thing, boss." Then he cracked a face-engulfing smile.

"Hey," said Rory, dragging out the word. "I see what you did there. And I kind of like the sound of it," he said, eyes narrowing thoughtfully as he gave a couple of tugs at his beard. "But," he said, already walking away. "I'd better follow the guy who thinks he's real boss before he barks at me."

The FBI agents returned to working quietly. A few officers moved in and out of the hub, but no one batted an eye. Everyone had grown accustomed to seeing the agents hunkered down near the detectives' desks. For joint operations, it made more sense for the FBI to work out of the police station than the other way around, since the West Sound field office made the hub look spacious as a football field.

After a few minutes of light tapping, Jared sat back in his chair, staring at his screen.

"I have something," he said almost to himself.

"What was that, Jared?" asked Julia, rolling her chair to his desk.

The young man turned his laptop to face her. "The partial plate," he said, the words tumbling out as if he'd gone so long without speaking that he had forgotten how to pace himself. "I couldn't find anything in the current Nevada licensing records or police database. But then I ran it through the FBI database, because . . ." He stopped and swallowed, as if letting his words catch up with his brain. "It is unusual in a civillian abduction for the perpetrator to include an FBI agent in communications."

"That's true," said Julia, waiting patiently for the punchline. By this time, Ron had left his seat and joined them at Jared's desk.

"Because of that anomaly, I ran the partial plate through all of Amber's past FBI files. This is what I found."

He pointed to the screen.

Julia and Ron leaned forward to read the information on Jared's computer.

After a few seconds, Julia turned her dark eyes on Ron. "What the heck? Have we been barking up the wrong tree all along? Is this even about Jefferson?"

"That is too weird to be a coincidence," said Ron.

Julia blew out a breath. "Get all the names and contact information from that report. I don't care how old it is." She walked back to her desk. "It's time to call Amber."

Chapter Twenty-Six

Amber turned off the video.

Without a word, Jefferson stood and walked out of the room. He needed to move. He needed to see something besides the searing image of Nico's snake-like face grinning at him. With his hands clenched at his sides, Jefferson sped down the hallway, through doors and into new hallways, past confused officers, and down a stairway until he didn't have a clue where he was.

Golden sunlight streamed through the hallway window where he landed. He walked towards it, dismayed by how low the sun hung in the sky. The hours were fading. Nico was winning.

What if Alex didn't testify? Would it be so bad? Maybe the people who had MJ would let her go. He had to consider it. Saving MJ was worth any price.

And if Nico got out of prison . . . He'd deal with that, too. There were other ways to take care of men like Nico.

Jefferson watched the traffic passing on the street below. So many people went about their day oblivious to the treachery instigated by a little lowlife like Nico. Few understood what it took to protect the country, their communities, their families from that kind of evil. Perhaps Jefferson had not fully understood what he would have to do to get rid of Nico.

Now he understood. You had to be like Nico to beat Nico.

All his life, the detective had played by the rules, done the right thing even when it would have been easier or more fun to pretend the rules didn't exist. MJ was the one rule he'd broken. Letting her work with him to solve cases — he'd hated it at first, convinced she would get herself or someone else killed. A civilian helping to solve crimes seemed like the most ridiculous and risky idea in the world.

But he'd been wrong. MJ had a way of making connections that eluded him. And she never let an idea go. Once something got inside her head, she would follow it until she figured out what it meant.

A bitter laugh escaped as he remembered. MJ was always stubborn and always beautiful.

Maybe it was time for a different mindset. If he kept following the rules, he and those he loved would continue to be threatened.

What was it Nico had said? "Let the system work." Jefferson had to wonder which system Nico was talking about — the system of law and order, or the system of drug cartels, traffickers, and their associates subverting the law repeatedly.

Could he count on the doing the right thing to be the best course of action anymore?

He turned from the window and pulled up his sleeve. Ten hours left.

Something, or someone, had to give. Maybe that someone was him.

***

Jefferson, surprisingly, found his way back to Hatch's office with ease.

Amber was on the phone, pacing the office with a rare look of disbelief on her face.

"Yes, text me everything. Good work, Julia. Tell Jared and Ron the same."

When she ended the call, Amber's eyes fell on Ryan Hatch with a dazed look of shock and confusion.

"What's going on?" Hatch asked, walking to her in alarm.

She opened her phone and clicked to a different screen, holding it up to him. "Do you recognize this name?"

Hatch took only a second to read it. "You're kidding, right?"

"I wish I were." Her gaze flicked to Jefferson. "This is a strange update that I'm not sure I can explain. In fact, I'm not even going to try right now, because I think we know where MJ is."

"What! Where?"

"North." Amber turned to Ryan. "We are going to need a chopper."

"I will see what I can do," he said, heading to the door.

Just as he was about to walk out, Amber said, "And I want to pick up some friends along the way."

Hatch turned back briefly with a raised eyebrow. Then, he just shook his head. "I'm not even going to ask."

"Wait," said Jefferson. "How does he know where we need to go?" he asked, his head directed toward Hatch. Then he shifted back to Amber. "How do *you* know where we need to go?"

The agent and the Las Vegas detective shared a look.

"It's ancient history," said Hatch. "But I'll leave it to Amber whether to tell you anything more."

Then he left without answering Jefferson's question.

Amber took out her phone and started speed texting.

"We have a lot to consider before we get up north," she said. "I'll tell you more on the way."

***

Even if they flew by chopper, it would take almost three hours to reach their destination, which was somewhere around Austin, Nevada.

Time continued to tick, only now it seemed to race along with Jefferson's pulse, erratic and wild with both hope and desperation. This location had to be the major break they needed. They couldn't be wrong. Being wrong meant potentially being hundreds of miles from MJ's actual location.

Getting to the air services hangar took less than ten minutes in a patrol car, blue lights wailing across the desert. An aircrew of two met the detectives and Amber when they climbed into the helicopter.

"Thanks for the lift, guys," said Hatch as he took a seat.

"Don't thank us yet," said one pilot, sucking in a breath through his teeth. "It's going to be a long, loud ride. And we've got a storm up north blowing some snow around. I'm the command pilot, by the way. Steve Black," he said with a quick salute. "And this here is our tactical officer, Lucy Delgado."

"Hi, guys," said the woman.

The three passengers introduced themselves as they started clipping on their harnesses.

Steve Black worked the controls upfront, clicking and preparing whatever pilots needed to prepare. "I don't know what you've been told," he said, "but we'll need to stop for fuel if we want to make it all the way there and back."

"That fits right into our plans," said Amber. "We have agents who will join us at that stop. If I've been informed correctly, we'll touch down at Tonopah Airport to refuel?"

The pilot turned to cast a curious glance her way, clearly wondering how she knew that. "Your information is correct." He reached back with a bag of orange earplugs. "We've got headsets for you all, but it doesn't hurt to double up, unless you need to talk. Just remember that everyone hears everything in this bird's communication system, for safety's sake."

Jefferson studied Amber with curious eyes. He also wanted to know who was meeting them at the airport. Who could she have contacted that would already be in such a desolate place? The Las Vegas FBI field office served the entire state; there wasn't a random field office in the remote mountains of Nevada.

Before he could ask, the rotors started, drowning out any words in the intense noise of the whirring blades.

He'd get nothing out of her now.

Then his phone buzzed. He opened it to see Amber had sent him a text.

"K and team. Headed that way earlier today."

Now he was even more confused. He looked up to catch her eye, but the agent had turned to the window. Despite his questions, Jefferson did the same, watching Las Vegas disappear into the distance like a shimmering mirage of lights.

Being a chopper passenger didn't seem to agree with the Las Vegas detective. Hatch sat in the row behind them, eyes closed, head against the seat, with his hands clutching a winter police jacket. They each had one, compliments of the Las Vegas Metro PD supply room.

Jefferson could sort of relate. He'd only flown in a helicopter once before. Every year, Rainier County offered a fly-along to the police in the county. It sounded interesting to him as a young patrol officer, so he'd taken the opportunity.

The smoothness of the flight surprised him. He'd expected a lot of buffeting and movement. The experience taught him how a bird's-eye view helped officers on the ground. Flying also helped him realize that being stuck in a helicopter every day wasn't his cup of tea. But the guys who did it absolutely loved their jobs.

Today, he appreciated the noise. The constant droning made it nearly impossible to focus on anything for more than a few minutes. So, he followed Hatch's example by closing his eyes and letting the thwack, thwack, thwack take over as the chopper carried him closer to ending this nightmare.

Chapter Twenty-Seven

The shivers that wracked MJ's body were deep in her bones. Cold alone didn't cause the rattling of teeth, the nausea, the fog of confusion that swept over her as she waited.

He would come back. The rage she saw in that wicked eye assured her that when he returned, her life would be in danger.

She feared what he'd already done to Robbie.

Even the smallest sound outside, like the wind throwing snow or dead sticks at the metal walls, sent her mind into a spiral. It was him. He was coming.

Her state of mind continued to deteriorate as time passed. Had it been five minutes, an hour? Time seemed unreal and yet finite. Something she used to track and know down to the second. Now, it cycled in breaths, and MJ didn't know how many she had left.

A train of sobs broke from her as she remembered the pure terror on Robbie's face as he was being dragged away. Only the cruelest of hearts could treat such a gentle soul in that merciless way.

Right after the door slammed, she'd looked for Corky only to see the dog lying motionless against the wall of the shipping container. She'd detected a slight movement in his rib cage, as if he still breathed.

But it was also possible that her terrified mind played tricks on her, and the dog was already dead. She hoped he was alive, but it didn't look good.

When MJ first found the hole, first made friends with Corky, and then had her first stolen conversation with Robbie, she'd felt the hope burning inside that they would be her ticket to freedom. It kept her from sinking into helplessness and despair. Until now, she hadn't realized just how much of her survival she had pinned on those two, Robbie and Corky. And now, MJ felt all sense of hope slipping away, sliding through her fingers like the desert sand.

She would die in this disgusting place. He'd probably wrap her in that filthy blanket and bury her underneath the rusting truck. She'd never see her father again. She'd never know if her mother had survived. And she'd never know if her love for Jefferson had the staying power she hoped it did. Since realizing she loved him, MJ had let herself dream of their life together. But now, she couldn't see past this moment in time.

Is this what happens when people know they are going to die? Does the future disappear right before their eyes?

Pulling her knees to her chest, MJ rested her head there and cried. She wanted to rally herself, to think of some ingenious way to get free, but it was too late. Everything she'd hoped would work had failed. And no one was coming to save her. The only person coming for her was a man bent on causing her harm, pain, and death.

As her tears wet the fabric of the sleeping bag, MJ tried to push the terror from her mind by bringing up images of her family and friends. She wanted to send them something of her spirit, the things she would most want them to know if they never saw her again. Would it reach them? Would they feel her presence even if she ceased to exist in this world? She prayed they would.

Dad, she thought, *you have been my rock all of my life. I love you so much for being the kind of man who leads with love. I have always tried to be like you, failing a lot, but having such an example to reach for has been the best part of being your daughter. I love you and am so proud to be yours.*

As the tears poured out, MJ ignored them, letting them fall uninhibited. The pure love that produced them felt cleansing, calming her heart in a way she hadn't expected.

Mom, I am so sorry for what happened to you. Seeing you fall . . . I felt like a terrified little girl in that instant. I can't imagine my life without you. We haven't always seen eye-to-eye. It's a mother-daughter thing, I think. But through it all, I know that you only wanted to see me happy. And I was happy, because we finally built a relationship where we appreciated each other for who we are. I hope you are fine and that you get to spend many more years with Dad. You will need each other. I love you, Mom.

Shannon, my dearest beautiful friend. How would I have survived teaching eighth graders without your insight and compassion? No one cares about kids like you do, and you always kept me centered in that way. I'm sorry for pulling you into so many crazy situations, but I hope you had a little fun. My students will need you. They feel things so deeply and personally, like they did when Troy died. I know you will help them heal, just please take care of yourself, too. That's what you would say to me, right? I love you, Shannon. There's not a better friend in the world.

She took a deep breath, the reality of her last minutes weighing heavily on her mind. Oh, how she wished to say these things in person. To hug her mom and dad, to take Edgar on a walk, to hear Shannon's melodious laugh, to feel Jefferson's tender kiss again.

Jefferson. Where do I even start with you?

A clash of metal on metal. MJ's head shot up.

No! Not yet!

Her heart jumped to her throat. Suddenly her breath came hard and fast, making her head swim for a moment. Then she shot up, looking around for anything she could use to defend herself.

The cooler. MJ lunged to it, picking it up in her right hand. The water bottle still inside gave it only a little weight, but it would have to suffice.

With the cooler in hand, she moved to the wall beside the door. Surprising him would be her only hope. She'd have to swing the cooler at his head and run.

More rattling of the lock, and then the door swung open. MJ raised the cooler and was about to bring it down on the man's head, only it wasn't a man's head.

A woman screamed. "Don't! Please!"

MJ's arm fell to her side, but she didn't drop the cooler.

"Who are you?" she demanded, though her voice, trembling from the dread of this moment, sounded feeble even to her.

"Please, there's no time," the woman said, looking through the door behind her. "I don't know how long he'll be out. We have to go."

"Where is Robbie?"

"He's in the house. He's in a bad way. I-I couldn't move him." Her voice broke as her lips trembled. "We should just get help."

MJ shook her head. "We are not leaving without Robbie. Between the two of us, we can get him."

Doubt and fear clouded the woman's wrinkled eyes. MJ wondered if this woman with a long braid down her back and wearing a green apron had been the person cutting her sandwiches.

Despite her obvious terror at returning to the house, the woman nodded.

"Is there a police car outside?"

The woman's eyes narrowed in confusion. "A police car?"

"Robbie said David hurt a policeman. If that's true, the officer had to get here somehow."

"I-I don't know."

"There has to be," said MJ. "But let's get Robbie out first."

The woman's eyes watered. "I'm sorry I didn't help you."

MJ waved her off. "You're here now. So, show me the way. But at least tell me your name. I'm MJ."

The woman's eyes darted to the door as if she expected the man to appear any second. "It's Jeanie."

MJ squeezed the woman's hand. "All right Jeanie. Let's go."

Chapter Twenty-Eight

For the first time since being abducted, MJ saw the house — an unkempt manufactured home. Her limited vantage point from the shipping container had hidden how much junk littered the ground near the house. But she had no time to examine it now.

She and Jeanie crept through a side door; the same screen door that slammed each time David came out to harass Robbie and Corky. A dog flap at the bottom gave it an extra bit of weight.

The door led to a cramped utility room with a washing machine, dryer, and stacks of laundry in various phases of completion. Jeanie had been in front, but she stopped at the utility room door and shrank back.

"I can't go in there." Her haunted eyes were wide and hollow. MJ sensed the woman might go into shock. If they were going to make it out of there — with Robbie — she had to keep Jeanie focused.

MJ grabbed her by the shoulders. "Where is David?" she whispered.

The woman squeezed her eyes shut. "In the kitchen," she said, her eyes still clamped shut. "He went after Robbie. I couldn't take it, so . . . I-I hit him with the frying pan."

Glancing up at the door, MJ felt worry eating into her resolve. How hard could this tiny woman have hit him? Not hard enough to keep him unconscious for long, she feared. They had to move.

She put her face right in front of Jeanie's. "Do you know where David keeps his car keys?"

The woman's vacant eyes stared at the door, and MJ wondered if she had heard the question.

Before she could ask it again, the woman nodded. "In the pink dish . . . On the counter."

"Good," MJ said, encouraged by her response. "I'm going to get Robbie. You get the keys and go to the car. Make sure it starts. Can you do that?"

Terrified as she was, Jeanie blew out a deep breath. "Yes. I think so."

With a squeeze of the woman's shoulders, MJ said, "We are going to be okay, Jeanie. You understand?"

The woman nodded, but her skin had a dangerously gray tone. MJ prayed Jeanie would keep her wits if they separated.

"I will meet you outside. Now go." She leaned forward and opened the door, giving Jeanie a gentle push inside.

Jeanie gasped. That's when MJ saw him. David sprawled out, with a pool of blood extending from his head and seeping into the sun-flower-covered rug beneath the sink. On the counter sat a cast-iron skillet.

She glanced up at Jeanie's bird-like frame. The woman had picked the right weapon.

"Go," MJ whispered. Then they both skirted around the uncon-scious — or dead — man. They would not take the time to find out which.

Once around, Jeanie dashed to the counter with more energy than MJ expected. Then she turned back and held up the keys.

Their eyes met, and MJ felt a strange connection pass between them. Had Jeanie been a captive, too? Maybe not in the same way, but still a prisoner?

MJ nodded once, and then the other woman darted to the front door and disappeared outside, just as MJ turned away, on the hunt for Robbie.

***

Despite the junk outside, the inside of the house showed signs of care and cleaning. MJ chalked that up to Jeanie. She couldn't imagine David, or even sweet Robbie, pushing a vacuum cleaner, mopping, or bending over to scour the toilet bowl.

The place still smelled old and dusty, like a storage shed that no one had bothered to open for years.

MJ crept through the living room. The sun had fallen deeper into the sky, and no electric lights helped show the way. The dark wall paneling sucked up what little daylight still filtered through the sheer curtains. MJ could still see, but only barely.

Too slow, she thought. Time was not on her side, but she didn't want to risk waking David or scaring Robbie. Quickening her pace anyway, she focused on stepping softly as she turned into the hallway.

The door to the first room was closed. As she pushed it open, her heart pounded in her throat.

Why was she so scared? David was lying on the floor, possibly dead or dying. Robbie wouldn't hurt her.

The irrational fear clawed at her. The shadows spoke of the evil wrought by that man, an evil that seemed to permeate the walls the carpet, the air. MJ couldn't shake the very real dread of opening a door and finding a monster.

But she had to keep going. No better chance of escape would come her way. If David woke up and found her in the house, he would kill her, and probably Jeanie too. Maybe even Robbie.

Pushing the fear down, she peered around the door.

The bathroom. Empty.

She put a hand to her chest, willing her heart to cooperate. To be strong. To have the courage she needed.

Moving down the hall, she came to another door. This time, she heard something. Pressing her ear to the cheap, hollow door, she could easily hear the quiet rustle of movement, like a gentle but rapid rocking.

She'd found Robbie.

Reaching for the door handle, it struck MJ that Robbie had never seen her face. He might be terrified of her. If she rushed in, he could get completely stuck in his dysregulation, and then she'd never be able to move him.

However, he'd heard her voice plenty of times. She had to risk knocking.

Giving the door a series of gentle taps, MJ said, "Robbie, are you in there? It's me, MJ. From the shipping container outside."

She again pressed her ear to the door. The rocking continued, though MJ detected a slightly slower pace. Maybe. She couldn't be sure.

Taking a deep breath, she tapped on the door again, looking behind her for any sign that David had come to life.

What she heard shot a bolt of energy through her entire body. An engine revving. Jeanie. In the car.

The rest of the house remained quiet.

"Robbie," she called through the door, more urgently this time. "I'm going to come in. Remember, it's me, MJ, and we are friends, okay?"

When she pushed the door open and walked inside, the sight on the bed took her breath away.

Robbie sat with hands to his ears. When he raised his head to look at her, tear tracks streaked down bloodstained and bruised cheeks.

"Oh no, Robbie!"

MJ rushed to kneel in front of him. "Let me look at you."

The man had a nasty gash on his head, the source of most of the blood. One of his eyes had swelled almost completely shut.

"David got mad," he said through shuddering breaths. "He called me a stupid idiot. He'll be mad that you are here." His one good eye opened wide in terror. "Go back! Go back before he finds you!"

"No, Robbie. You don't have to worry about David right now. He's . . . He's asleep. So, we are going to go to the doctor and get you all fixed up, okay? Jeanie has the car ready outside."

"Jeanie?" Robbie's good eye narrowed. "How do you know Jeanie?"

MJ took one of his elbows. "I will explain later. Can you walk?"

"What about Corky? I have to go check on silly Corky. He'll be hungry." His eyes traveled to the door, and MJ could see that somewhere deep inside Robbie knew David had hurt his dog, even if he couldn't say it.

But they couldn't risk waiting. Going back for the dog would be an insane test of fate. They needed to take the window of opportunity offered and get out.

"I saw Corky before I came inside. He was hiding under the truck. You know how he does that," she smiled, hating the lie. "As soon as we get you all fixed up, we'll come back and make sure Corky has food and whatever else he needs."

That part might be true, but not if they didn't find some help fast.

"And Jeanie is waiting," she pushed. "So we really have to go right now."

Robbie didn't respond, but he allowed her to lead him.

MJ held tightly to his elbow as the two moved down the hall and into the living room. As they passed the kitchen, she turned her body to block Robbie's view of the kitchen as best she could, pointing to the door to guide his eyes in that direction. No matter how much David had hurt Robbie, seeing the man lying in a pool of blood would make him spiral.

"See," said MJ, "can you hear the car running outside? That's where she's waiting."

"I can hear the car," said a deep voice from behind her.

MJ froze.

Too late.

Chapter
Twenty-Nine

The chopper made better time than predicted, reaching the Toponah Airport in just seventy-five minutes. That was the good news. The plummeting temperatures? That was the bad news.

A tan, flat-roofed building next to the gas pumps offered the chance to take care of bathroom breaks and put on cold-weather gear as the chopper refueled.

Amber stepped inside first. Jefferson and Hatch followed. Waiting inside were four men, all in tactical gear and strapped with weapons. One extended a hand, which Amber took.

"Kota," she said, releasing his hand. "Thank you for making the trek."

Jefferson recognized one man with Kota as the door greeter from the Henderson motel. The other two were unknown to him.

"Of course," replied the DEA agent. "It's a good thing you sent us up this way. Puts us in an excellent position to help catch this piece of trash."

Amber pulled her jacket on. "I'm grateful you agreed to come. It's tough country out here, especially in the snow."

"Nah. We've definitely been in worse places." The surrounding guys chuckled, as if his words were a truth only they understood. "So, we've checked a bunch of video footage from businesses along this highway, as much as we could without attracting too much attention. The witness who heard the noise in the trunk . . . She was solid, but I don't think the sedan stopped more than that one time. And there is no guarantee they didn't change cars again. So until we heard from you, we were sort of out of ideas."

"Teamwork makes the dream work," said Amber, smiling at her own cheesiness.

"True," said Kota, glancing toward Jefferson. "Detective Hughes. Glad to see you're holding up."

Barely, Jefferson thought.

"Thanks," he said, finding it hard to meet the agent's eyes.

Unexpectedly, a wave of shame hit the detective. Seeing Kota and his team, battle ready and prepared to do whatever they had to do, reminded him that just a few hours ago, stopping his brother's testimony not only crossed his mind, he'd planned to make it happen.

He still didn't completely trust the system to deal with Nico, but so far, as Amber said, teamwork had done its job. They were close to MJ. He could feel it. If they found her safe and alive, he had this team to thank for it. He couldn't even consider the alternative.

"And this is Detective Ryan Hatch with Las Vegas Metro," Amber said.

As everyone greeted Hatch, Command Pilot Steve Black emerged from the men's restroom. His eyes popped when he saw the team standing with Amber.

"Oh boy," he said. "I'm not sure we can take on this much weight with the storm ahead," he said. "No offense, guys."

Kota grinned. "None taken. Two of these fellas will drive and be there to clean up if needed."

"Whew," said Black. "You had me worried for a minute there. It's going to be dicey with just the . . ." He did a quick count of the room. "With the seven of us. Winds are picking up, so we should get in the air while the getting is still good."

Dressed for the cold, the team boarded the chopper.

***

Just forty-five more minutes in the air would get them to Austin.

A bumpy sweep side-to-side had replaced the smooth ride from Vegas as the pilot worked to avoid the worst of the wind gusts. Steve Black said little during the flight, but when he did, his tight voice suggested he couldn't wait to land this bird.

Jefferson rubbed his eyes. What if they were wrong? His gut said they were close; everything pointed this way. But did he dare trust that feeling? He hadn't been himself since this whole thing began. In fact, his mind seemed to teeter on the edge of an abyss, and the wrong news would decide if he stepped back from it or fell inside.

He owed Amber big time. The lifeline she kept throwing out prevented him from going completely sideways. But even that lifeline felt tenuous the closer they came to the target.

What if they were wrong? What if they were right, but too late?

The light outside the chopper quickly faded as clouds and dusk banished the sun. He looked at his watch again. Less than seven hours until the deadline passed. If they were wrong, time would run through the hourglass before he found MJ.

Suddenly, her lifeless eyes flashed into his mind, her body stretched backwards over a log on a Pacific Northwest beach, a giant gash across her throat.

No!

He ground his palms into his eyes, his breath shallow and fast.

It isn't her. It isn't her.

"It isn't her. It isn't her."

Pushing harder with his hands, nothing worked to rid his mind of the hideous image.

He felt someone grasp his arm, pulling his hand away from his face.

"Jeff," said Amber, her voice coming over the headset.

Turning to see the concern in her eyes, the detective realized he had the attention of the entire cabin.

Had he said he words out loud?

The others quickly shifted their eyes elsewhere—out the window, behind their eyelids, or down to their hands or feet, anywhere but at the crazy detective who talked to himself.

Yes. He definitely said the words out loud. And everyone on the chopper had heard him.

Chapter Thirty

MJ could feel the menacing, hulking man behind her.

"Thought . . . you could . . . sneak out, did . . . you?" he rumbled, breathing heavily between words.

Slowly MJ turned around, pushing Robbie behind her and taking a step back into the living room.

David glared at them as he shuffled forward, a gun in his right hand.

MJ took another step back, moving Robbie with her. The man continued lumbering toward them. Then he paused as his eyes fluttered closed.

The frying pan to the head had taken something out of him. But the gun in his hand provided all the force he needed to keep them prisoner.

The bulky man lurched to the left, as if the room had jerked under his feet. Blood matted his hair above his left ear with a long red swoosh of it across his forehead. He'd always been a monster, but now he looked like one. A terrifyingly real monster who would never let them go alive.

David followed MJ's eyes to the weapon. "Nice of that cop to let me have this, don't you think? He won't be needing it," he said with a wicked grin.

Robbie whimpered behind MJ, and she could feel him beginning to sway.

"Just let Jeanie take Robbie to the hospital. He needs to see a doctor," MJ said, keeping her eyes on the gun.

A deep chuckle escaped the monster. "My brother will be just fine," he said, looking past her to Robbie's cowering frame. "But you and Jeanie. Now that's another story." He shrugged, swaying on his feet again. "I was going to kill you anyway," he said, "unless they told me not to."

He licked his lips in slow motion, as if he were about to fall asleep. Then he blew out a sigh, his hot breath hitting MJ's face. "But who are we kidding? They would never let you go. But I thought . . ." He said, turning the gun on its side and examining it. "I thought we had a little more time. I thought your FBI friend might show up, because I'd really like to see her again. We've got a little score to settle."

Despite her fear, MJ's eyes narrowed. Amber again. What in the world did this man have to do with Amber?

After another bout of dizziness, David leaned against the arm of the couch.

MJ took another step back, pushing Robbie gently. She could feel him rocking and hear him moaning. The poor man had locked himself inside his own head.

Perhaps that was best for now.

"Look, I don't know anything about you and Amber, but I know Robbie needs help. Please let him go," she said.

"Just . . . Just stop!" David shouted. Until this point, the man had maintained his usual flat way of speaking. Whether the situation or the head wound, the monster quickly became agitated.

"Robbie isn't going anywhere, so shut up about it!"

"Okay," she said, stepping back again. MJ sensed that David really wanted to talk about Amber. Maybe if she could keep him calm, they could find another chance to get out. Maybe he would pass out again. He clearly still suffered the effects of Jeanie's attack.

"I don't understand," she said. "Amber? Amber Wells?"

The gun rested on his hip, his finger wrapped around the trigger. He stared down at it as a grin twisted his lips.

"Imagine my surprise when her name popped up on all your . . . paperwork." He waved the gun in the air. "The name was different, but her smug face was the same." The man's expression hovered between amused and disgusted. He stared at the gun again. "But, she wasn't smart enough to find me out."

"What? Find out what?"

His eyes flicked up. "I'd say ask her, but that's not going to happen."

His unsteady gaze shifted to the door. MJ could still hear the car, but she wondered how long Jeanie would wait. If it were her, she'd have already gone for help.

"Jeanie," he said. "Actually, Jeannette, but I told her I liked Jeanie better. She was the first to stay in your room out there," he said with a slight movement of his head. "I was going to kill her. I was supposed to kill her, but then plans changed. So," he lifted one shoulder. "I just kept her."

MJ shivered at the cold description. He 'kept her,' as if she were a stray dog or an abandoned bike.

"Amber Wells," he hissed, carrying out the "s" with snake-like venom.

His head dropped suddenly to his chest, as if it had grown too heavy. MJ almost grabbed Robbie and ran, but David recovered quickly, his attention focused on her again.

"It was a long time ago," he said. "I guess you sort of reminded me of how Amber all but killed my cousin . . . made me lose my dirt business." He lifted a finger as he pointed lazily at her. "What else am I supposed to do for money out here? She just drove me to more crime. So, it's her fault you're here." He shrugged in a way that suggested he believed his own lie.

"But why are they paying you? What have I done?"

David's shook his head with a chuckle. "Just like a spoiled woman to think it's all about her." He looked her over as if seeing her for the first time. His lip curled in derision. "The people paying me to hold you here, they don't care about you, but they hate your boyfriend and that agent a lot. I just hoped to get Agent Wells as my bonus pay."

MJ stared at the man, shocked at the amount of information he had about Amber, Jefferson, and her.

"You probably think I'm crazy." He held the gun up to his head, lips twisting into an unhinged grin. "Maybe I am."

Those last words came out so slurred that MJ expected David to flop over any second. Instead, he lowered the gun and pinched his nose like someone trying to hold back a sneeze.

"You must be pretty disappointed," said MJ, a sudden wave of emotion stinging her eyes. She wouldn't cry. Tears would weaken her ability to escape. Curling her hands into fists, she fought the assailing crosswinds of fear and sadness. "I don't think Amber is coming. Nobody is coming."

David's face softened with mock empathy. "Yeah. I think you're right. After I take care of business, Robbie there will dig a grave in the backyard, big enough for both you and Jeanie. No one will be the wiser. Job finished. Then I get paid." He pinched the bridge of his nose again.

Suddenly, Robbie wailed behind MJ. "I won't. I won't do it. No, David. No hurting anyone anymore."

"Shut up, Robbie." David waved the gun in the air. "Your crying is just making me mad. You'll help unless you want to end up in the hole with them."

"It's okay, Robbie," MJ soothed. "It will be okay."

David shook his head with a dismissive chuckle. "No. No, it won't. Not for you." He pushed away from the couch and moved toward MJ. "But enough talk, I'm tired and my head hurts. Jeanie's going to pay for that."

He reached for MJ's arm just as the front door opened.

"No, Jeanie! Run!" MJ shouted as the woman's gray head peeked around the door.

David pointed the gun at the other woman. "Jeanie, step inside. We both know you don't want to leave."

"He's going to kill you! R—"

A blast of pain sent MJ's head jerking sideways. She stumbled and fell onto her hands and knees, blood dripping onto the carpet from her cheek.

David had swung with speed and force, the gun hitting her before she ever saw it coming.

"Stop!" Robbie screamed as he dropped to the floor next to MJ. Though he didn't check on her or try to comfort her, the man's wailing and rocking showed his distress on her behalf.

"Get in here," David sneered, aiming the gun at Jeanie, who whimpered in the doorway.

Putting her hands up, Jeanie walked into the room on trembling legs. "I-I'm sorry," she said. "Please don't hurt them. It's my fault. I got her out."

"I'm aware," he seethed. "That's why you'll go first. Get her up," he said, motioning with the gun toward MJ.

Jeanie bent down to take MJ's arm. "I'm sorry," she whispered.

As the woman helped her stand, MJ could feel blood trickling over her chin. Whatever he'd done to her, it was nothing compared to what was coming.

The man watched the two women with a dark expression, as if transforming into his most evil self. The version that could kill innocent people just because he wanted to.

Jeanie tried to pull Robbie to his feet, but the man wouldn't budge.

"Just leave him," ordered David. "I won't need him until the deed is done."

Far from passing out, the man seemed to regain his strength with each minute.

MJ's anger flared. With her eyes full of loathing, she wiped dripping blood from her chin. "You won't get away with this."

"Maybe not," he said. "But that hardly matters for you." He spread his lips in a teeth-baring mockery of her. "Now move. I'd just shoot you here, but without Jeanie to clean it up . . ." He shrugged, the sentence being too obvious to finish.

He can't get us outside. If he does, we won't have a chance. Fight where you are. That's what they say. Fight where you are.

In her mind, she saw the frying pan on the counter. There had to be knives. If she could hit him again, then maybe Jeanie would find a knife or grab the gun, and together, they could take him down. Better to die fighting than let him pick them off like animals.

He flicked the gun in the direction they were to walk.

Jeanie shook from head to toe, taking huge gulps of air. If she didn't calm her breathing, the woman would hyperventilate and be no help at all.

MJ grasped one of her hands. Their eyes met, and the teacher tried to pass some strength to the woman. *We're not done fighting!*

Either Jeanie didn't understand, or she wisely understood not to tip off David, because her erratic breathing continued. Whatever it was, they were out of time. David pushed them both in front of him, the gun pointing into their backs.

Robbie remained on the floor, curled almost completely into a ball, his face hidden in his knees while he repeatedly whimpered to himself, "No. No. No."

David gave both women a shove toward the kitchen.

Just knowing a bullet was inches from her back sent an electric pulse down MJ's spine as she walked. He could shoot them any minute. Did he really care if they got outside?

She closed her eyes for a second to control her breathing.

Control the fear. Fight. Fight for Jeanie, Robbie, and the people you love. Fight for your life.

They were already in the kitchen. In seconds, she'd have to make her move.

One. Two. Three.

With both hands, she grabbed the frying pan and turned to swing it at the man's head.

David's hand flew up, deflecting the iron skillet before it could find its mark.

"Do you really think I'm that stupid?" He pushed her against the wall. Then he raised the gun, pointing it at her head. "Bye, bye teacher."

In a flash, a body came flying at David, tackling him to the ground, snarling with fury, the furry body writhing and biting.

Corky! The dog attacked the man's legs as David tried to beat him off with the gun.

MJ knew they couldn't wait. She ran, grabbing Jeanie's arm.

They hit the living room just as Robbie uncurled himself. "Corky?"

"We have to go, Robbie. Grab his other arm," she told Jeanie.

Robbie resisted, but the two women had enough adrenaline between them to lift the man to his feet and drag him to the door.

As they opened it, a shot rang out. Corky yelped.

Robbie screamed the dog's name, but the two women didn't give him time to freeze, pulling him down the porch.

David would be right behind them. And he still had the gun.

Chapter Thirty-One

The flight turned into a white-knuckle ride through wind and snow, but to Steve Black's credit, the chopper landed safely in an Austin, Nevada, church parking lot.

The Lander County sheriff and two deputies waited with their vehicles, as well as a fire department paramedic rig.

As the team exited the helicopter, the slowing blades whipped up the already blowing snow so that it pelted their faces with extra force.

"Tucker?" asked Hatch as he reached out a hand to the sheriff.

"That's me," said a burly man in a beanie. "You must be Detective Hatch." He looked over the rest of the group, his eyes lingering on Kota and his fellow agent. "So what exactly is the operation here? Who has authority?"

Amber stepped forward, her credentials in hand. "I'm Special Agent Wells with the FBI. We are here to assist the Las Vegas Metro Police in finding the victim of last night's abduction." Her explanation went no further, and there was no introduction of the DEA agents.

The sheriff, looking only slightly mollified, still eyed them. "Well, let's get out of this weather and into the vehicles. I'll be leading, so whoever has the location should jump in my rig."

Kota stepped forward with his backpack in hand. "We've prepared maps for each of your vehicles. I've marked them with a suggested perimeter. We'll send in a small group, scope out the situation before moving in. If your guys stay outside the target and hold the perimeter, they'll catch any runners."

"And you are?" asked Sheriff Tucker.

Kota grinned but didn't respond.

"He's with me," said Amber. "Federal agent."

The sheriff just shook his head, training his eyes on Hatch. "I hope you know what you're doing, Metro."

"Ah, they're all good. No worries, friend."

With a huff of frozen air, the sheriff put out his hand. "Let me see the map."

Kota obliged. Tucker spent a few seconds studying it before looking up and calling his deputies over. After Kota passed the maps around, the sheriff gave brief instructions and barked assignments.

Then Jefferson, Hatch, and Amber followed Sheriff Tucker to his SUV. The rest of the crew loaded up, and they were off, driving into the blinding snow.

***

Jefferson's heart thrummed so hard against his ribs, he feared it might jump out of his chest and run to the location without him.

So much depended on their getting this right. The right location, the right approach, the right amount of force. Everything could go wrong, and yet everything could go right. His mind flip-flopped between hope and despair. They would save her . . . they would be too late.

Being too late would kill him. He wanted to be there for every second of this operation, but yet . . . He dreaded what might wait for him — a darkness so deep, it would drown him.

It didn't matter. He'd be there. He'd save her, and if the chance came, he'd make them pay.

Outside his window, the tiny town of Austin flew by in seconds, its western-style shops disappearing like a ghost town.

They followed a rough two-lane road, paved but potholed. Once out of town, the road seemed to go black as the sun and man-made light both abandoned them. The rig's headlights spotlighted short, scrubby brush on the side of the road, the snow making them look like cotton balls.

"We got about twenty minutes on this highway," the sheriff informed them. "So hold on. It's a bumpy ride."

Darkness continued to close in. The car's headlights cut through the black world, and flakes like dust scrambled in the air before them. They could see nothing in the distance, and it seemed to Jefferson as if they rode into a void.

Amber sat silently in the front seat. Though she appeared calm, Jefferson knew her well enough to recognize that she too felt the stress. Hers would be controlled . . . motivating. It would never show itself outwardly, but he knew the signs. More silent than usual, still hands, and an erect, stoic posture that signaled her mental preparation for whatever came next.

Since knowing the agent, Jefferson worked to emulate her composure. He had a lot of work to do in that regard, and it had pretty much gone completely out the window with MJ's abduction.

Hatch stared out the window with a detective's curiosity. Every so often they passed a house, and that's when he came to life. Looking back and staring after it, as if it had clues for them.

Only an occasional belching of sheriff's radio interrupted the silence.

"Unit 1, Lander County priority traffic."

The sheriff picked up his radio. "Go ahead, Dispatch."

"We have a possible officer needs assistance. Unit 252 Failure to 10-42. Last known location Shilo Road."

The sheriff turned to Amber. "That's where we are heading."

Jefferson and Hatch sat forward to hear the conversation. If their codes were anything like West Sound PD's, it sounded as if a deputy failed to clock out.

Amber pressed her lips together, glancing back at the two detectives and then back to the sheriff. "If your deputy is not responding . . ." She didn't finish the sentence.

Sheriff Tucker's expression turned grave. "Dispatch, Unit 1 is en route."

Chapter Thirty-Two

J eanie had left the car running. MJ almost cried with joy when she heard it still rumbling, saw its exhaust sending white puffs into the night. Another car sat next to it in the driveway, a canvas cover hiding it from view.

The police car.

If they had more time, the police radio offered their surest bet for getting help. But it was too late for that. Without keys, they had no way to help the deputy trapped in his trunk.

Survive first. Then get help.

Together, the women pushed Robbie into the back seat of the white car. There was no time to be gentle. He still wailed Corky's name, and the sound of it would have broken MJ's heart if not for the terror already claiming it.

The teacher jumped in the driver's seat, and just as she put the car in reverse, David stumbled from the front door, his hulking frame illuminated by the giant floodlight over the front porch.

Without a second thought, she slammed the gas pedal to the floor, pushing the car backward at an alarming speed. A shot rang out, hitting the front grille. Jeanie screamed. MJ hit the gas again, turning the car sharply around.

"Get down, Robbie!" she shouted, fearing a bullet through the back window.

David fired again. MJ felt the back left tire swerve as it took the bullet.

The gun sounded a second time, and then a third, the bullet hitting its mark as MJ felt the right back tire give.

"No!" she cried, still punishing the gas pedal.

The car jerked from side to side, sliding in the snow and slowing their speed as every ounce of air pressure died away.

She drove on anyway. Surely they had to hit a neighboring house soon. Somewhere they could get help, call the police, and finally be safe. Her cheek throbbed and blood stained the back of her hand from wiping at the blood that still trickled.

The headlights provided little aid in seeing the surrounding landscape as the car rumbled forward. MJ found the switch and flipped it to the high beams, casting a wider net of light over the desert.

If the car failed, they had to find somewhere to go. If not a neighbor, then somewhere to hide or a place where they would be better able to defend themselves.

"Jeanie," she said, her eyes scanning the empty land in front of her. "Are there any buildings or houses close by? I don't know how much longer this car will go."

A burning smell now emanated from the hood, and MJ feared David's first shot may have hit something inside.

"I think . . . I think there is an old abandoned barn somewhere on the left. I've seen it from the kitchen window." She sat forward and scanned the area.

"There!" Jeanie pointed out into the darkness.

At first, MJ saw nothing but scrub brush and snow. But then, in the furthest reaches of the high beams, she caught sight of a shadowy building.

Yanking the steering wheel to the left, she pushed the car onward, leaving the road and limping over the snow-covered desert.

Then they heard it. The unmistakable sound of another engine revving. MJ knew without looking it would be the police car, and David would be the one driving it.

She hit the lights, immediately sending the world into blinding darkness.

"What if he's already seen us?" Jeanie said, the terror clear in her voice. "Or sees the tracks in the snow?"

MJ plowed ahead. "Either way, we'll be better off in the barn than as sitting ducks in this car. Just think about finding weapons, just anything you can use to stop him. You already did it once, Jeanie. You can do it again. And this time, there are two of us. We are going to get out of this."

It didn't take long for MJ's eyes to adjust so that she could make out the barn in the darkness. They were close, and they needed to be, because the car had lurched under her foot, as if it were running out of gas.

Then, a flash of light caught her eye. Headlights from the road, from the direction they'd just traveled. And they were moving at full speed.

The white car lurched and jerked, bumping and sliding over the desert, but they made it to the barn. MJ willed the car to keep moving, to get them to the hidden side of barn.

Jeanie was right. He'd see their tracks, but they needed at least the little advantage of being out of sight.

The bigger problem was Robbie's continued wailing for Corky. She had to calm the man before David came hunting for them.

With gratitude for the last chugging breaths of the white car, MJ finally hit the brakes when they'd cleared the most visible parts of the building.

Once out of the car, she could hear the police cruiser flying down the road. With any luck, David hadn't seen them and would drive too fast to notice the tire tracks leading to the barn.

God, if you're up there, now would be a good time to send a little more help our way.

MJ jumped out of the car and rushed to pull Robbie out. Jeanie ran around to help.

The man lay on the back seat, his head in his hands, chanting Corky's name as if calling him from another world.

Despite their desperate circumstances, MJ knew that taking thirty seconds now could save five minutes in trying to coax or force him from the car.

"Robbie," she said. "Corky was very brave. He did a very brave thing to save you, and me, and Jeanie. He wants you to be safe, Robbie. That's why he did it."

The chanting continued, but quieter, and she hoped the man was listening.

"And if we get some help, we can go back for Corky and see if he's okay. You want to do that. Right, Robbie?"

He stopped moving but kept his hands over his ears. "Is Corky okay?"

She couldn't lie. The chances of Corky surviving that gunshot were next to none.

"I don't know," she said. "But if he is, we can't help him if David finds us. He is very mad and wants to hurt me and Jeanie, and maybe you, too. So it's very important that we hide and be as quiet as possible. Can you do that?"

Robbie sat up and nodded, wiping his tear-soaked face with his sleeve. "I can be quiet as a mouse."

Pain from David's earlier blow seared MJ's cheek as she smiled with gratitude, her lips trembling as she did so. If they made it out of this, it would be a miracle.

Chapter Thirty-Three

The three escapees hurried to the barn, the sound of the approaching police car haunting their every step.

The building's snow-capped roof seemed to float above the ground, but the rest of the barn blended into the darkness. They could barely distinguish the massive double doors from the walls.

As they approached, MJ's heart sank. A rusty padlock hung from the latch.

Jeanie let out a sob as she noticed the same thing. "It's locked. What are we going to do?"

MJ stepped forward, unwilling to accept this fate. They hadn't come this far to give up now. She grabbed the lock and pulled. To her surprise, it released. Either the old lock malfunctioned or non one cared to lock the place anymore. Or miracles still happen.

"Oh, thank God!" Jeanie breathed in relief.

MJ let out a slow breath of her own.

Thank God indeed.

She pulled the doors open to a rush of stale air. Jeanie held Robbie's arm, and the two of them stumbled inside. But MJ stayed behind, listening.

She could still hear the police car, but the sound seemed to grow more distant.

David had passed their tracks. He didn't know where they were.

His mistake had only bought them some time. She knew that. At his speed, it wouldn't take long for the man to realize they'd turned off. He'd be back.

Outside, the snow reflected the meager moonlight, but inside the barn, the darkness seemed to be a physical thing, a suffocating presence. As MJ stepped inside, she saw only blackness. Jeanie and Robbie were nowhere.

"Hey! Where are you guys?"

To her left, she heard Jeanie's voice. "Over here, behind the shelf."

What shelf? MJ couldn't see an inch in front of her. Just as she took a step toward Jeanie's voice, she had an idea. "Hold on," she said. "I'll be right back."

Running back to the car, MJ reached into the driver's seat and grabbed the keys still in the ignition.

If this was the same car, same trunk David used to bring her to this place, it had a lot of stuff in it. Perhaps even a flashlight. They needed some light if they were going to find anything to use as weapons.

Her hands were freezing by this time, causing her to fumble with the key before finally pushing it straight into the trunk lock. She had to rummage blindly, feeling for anything that might be useful.

Then her hand touched something long and metal. A crowbar or tire iron. She wasn't sure which, but it felt solid and deadly. It had to be the same solid bar that connected with her head when the man threw her in the trunk. Thinking of a little poetic justice, she stuck the freezing metal bar under her arm and continued searching, pushing aside random wrappers and empty paper cups. Finally, her hand landed on something square and plastic.

Just like the cooler, the feel of this thing brought back a memory. Camping in Bryce Canyon with her parents. Her mom carried the boxy flashlight. It had a handle on the side and a wide beam that lit their way to the bathroom in the middle of the night.

MJ stopped for a second, grabbing the edge of the trunk as a wave of emotion passed over her.

Not now! Don't think right now. Just do!

She shook the feeling away and grabbed the flashlight. Checking the batteries would have to wait until she was back in the barn. If the light worked and she turned it on in this black, empty desert, it would be like sending up a beacon to the man who wanted to kill them all.

Once she closed the barn doors behind her, MJ flicked the flashlight's power switch. A weak yellow light hit the floor.

They'd have to work fast. The flashlight obviously had little battery life left. The dying batteries could leave them in the dark again any minute. Not to mention the madman on their heels.

MJ turned to the left. There she saw a short workbench area with shelving. Jeanie poked her head up, and Robbie followed.

"Let's see if that is the best place to hide," MJ said, moving the light around, exploring the inside of the barn.

There was a loft overhead, but the barn was in such disrepair that MJ worried they could fall through the rotting wood. But still . . . Maybe it was their best option. David would have to climb the ladder to get to them, making him vulnerable in that moment.

"I'm going to try the loft. If it's strong enough to hold us, it could be the safest spot."

"I guess so," said Jeanie, who had come around to stand next to MJ, staring up the steep ladder. "Do you think we can get Robbie up there?"

MJ shone the light toward the shelving where Robbie still stood, looking transfixed by something on the worktop. Jeanie had a point. The man might not like heights, or he might struggle with climbing. They had to at least try.

"I'll check it out and see if it's even an option. Can you hold this?" She handed Jeanie the crowbar as she started up the ladder, holding the flashlight in her right hand.

"Be careful," Jeanie called up the ladder.

The rungs were stronger than MJ had expected. Solid underfoot, they held her with no problem. Her lungs were the problem. Just a few rungs in and she was already breathing heavily, her face throbbing and her head feeling woozy. The stress, the blood loss, the not eating, the intense terror — all were taking their toll.

With a deep breath, she finished the ascent, poking her head through the opening to the loft.

Besides a few random pieces of rope and rusty nails, there wasn't anything up there. MJ set the flashlight down and then pulled herself completely into the loft. A couple of tentative steps felt solid. The boards squeaked, but they held and, like the ladder, were stronger than they appeared.

She did a quick walk around, ensuring there were no surprise weak spots. Then MJ hustled back down the ladder.

"I think it's good," she told Jeanie. "Did you find anything we could use as weapons down here?"

"Not much," said the woman, wringing her hands. "Just some old rusty cans of food over there on the shelves."

"Better than nothing," said MJ. The two women joined Robbie at the workbench. That's when MJ shone the light and saw what had transfixed the man.

A tiny dead mouse lay on its side, slightly shrunken.

"Poor quiet mouse," said Robbie. "I sure hope Corky doesn't look dead like that guy. You said he might be okay." His sad eyes continued to stare at the dead creature.

"I hope he is Robbie, but I promise we will find out as soon as we are all safe."

As much as she might want to console the man further, they had to get moving.

"Jeanie, do you see a bag or anything you can use to carry some of those cans?"

"No, but . . ." She untied her apron from around her waist. "I can bag them up in here."

"Good id—"

An engine revving. He'd found them.

MJ's heart stopped, and she could feel fear wanting to take over, to freeze her on the spot.

"Oh no," whispered Jeanie as she dropped a can into her apron.

The terror in that whispered statement hit MJ's ears like a shout. Like a shock to her system, an overwhelming fury sent the fear scurrying away.

No one has the right to instill that kind of terror in another person. Not in Jeanie. Not in me. And not in Robbie.

"Over to the ladder. Quick!" MJ shouted, grabbing the crowbar and one of Robbie's arms. "Jeanie, you go first. Help Robbie pull up into the loft. I'll help from behind."

As they hustled to the ladder, pulling Robbie along, Jeanie started her ascent with the apron of cans in one hand. MJ shone the light up to guide her.

"Alright, Robbie," MJ said once Jeanie was a few rungs up. "Your turn. If we can hide up here, maybe we can get safe so we can go see Corky. Okay?"

"You promise?"

"I promise."

Then, with surprising speed, Robbie hit the rungs, almost running into Jeanie's feet. MJ started after him just as she heard a car door slam.

This was it.

Chapter Thirty-Four

I f he had a flashlight, he didn't use it.

MJ had turned hers off as soon as they were all hunkered down in the loft.

The barn doors slammed shut behind him. The man took no pains to be quiet.

"I know you're all in here," he said, his breathing labored despite walking just a few steps.

His feet scraped the floor as he lumbered through the barn searching for them.

MJ had to wonder if his head wound had come back to haunt him after all. She hoped it had.

She could feel Jeanie trembling next to her; however, the woman seemed as determined as MJ to fight despite her obvious fright. While she didn't know Jeanie's entire story, she knew the woman had suffered under David's brutality for a long time.

"I'm guessing you're in the loft," he said, his voice moving closer to the ladder. "Robbie? You up there? You should come down. It's just them two women I'm after."

"You hurt Corky!" shouted Robbie.

"No, Robbie," Jeanie whispered, trying to shush him.

"Ah. There you are," said David.

MJ could hear the satisfied, wicked smile in his words.

Then, a shot pierced the wood of the loft. Robbie cried out.

"No! No! Robbie," Jeanie sobbed.

"Dang it!" shouted David. "Did you make me shoot my brother?" Despite the evil nature of his deed, the man sounded casual, almost drunk. If he were crazy before, the head wound had him spinning out of control.

"Well, this is not good," he said lazily. "I want to make sure I shoot the right people and shoot them dead." The scraping of his feet across the floor moved closer. "You know, this might be better than shooting you in my backyard. No bloody mess for me to deal with."

He grunted with his first step on the ladder.

MJ let her breath out in a slow, steady stream. She looked over to see the shadowy shape of Robbie slumped over Jeanie's lap.

She wanted to cry. Her heart hammered in her chest, and her hands shook. She had to end this and end it soon if Robbie had any chance of surviving.

Just as David hit the halfway point of the ladder, the first can pelted his head, splitting the skin on his forehead. Then another hit him in the chest, and another on the wrist.

The man yelled out in pain, losing his grip and flying backwards until he hit the ground.

MJ was already halfway down the ladder, crowbar in hand. She did not know if he had the gun, but she didn't care anymore. He was still on his back, moaning, when she jumped down.

He hadn't seen her, and the first blow of the crowbar to his stomach caught him by surprise. Then another blow hit his legs.

Swinging in the dark, MJ let her blows fall wherever they would, screaming with guttural force each time she let the crowbar fly.

David threw a hand up, trying to grab the weapon, but he miscalculated, and the crowbar connected with his wrist. He howled in pain and then rolled onto his stomach to push himself to his feet.

That's when MJ hit the backs of his legs, then his back, and then the back of his head.

He must have lost the gun in his fall, because if he hadn't, MJ knew she'd already be dead.

David used his arms to drag himself forward, desperately trying to escape the barrage of blows MJ continued to deliver.

The back, the legs, the arms. The sounds coming from her own mouth were foreign to MJ. She'd never wanted to hurt someone or something the way she wanted to hurt this man.

He'd crawled a few feet forward, but Jeanie's first frying pan attack and now MJ's crowbar had taken their toll. David collapsed under his own weight, his wheezing breath coming quick and ragged.

MJ lifted the crowbar again. One more blow to the head, and he'd never recover. One more blow to the head, and he would never hurt another person. Ever.

Then the doors of the barn flew open, and a bright light shone in her face, illuminating her like a golden warrior about to strike the fatal blow.

"MJ?"

Could it be? She stared, the crowbar still above her head.

Then she dropped it and crumpled to the ground.

Chapter Thirty-Five

I n all the commotion, as the DEA agents ran in, rifles raised, the deputies behind them, all thoughts of revenge vanished from Jefferson's mind. The man half alive on the floor didn't exist as the detective tore off his coat, wrapped it around MJ and scooped her into his arms, holding back the emotion overwhelming him at the sight of her. The bruises and blood on her face told him too much.

"Robbie," she said, grabbing at his shirt frantically. "In the loft," she said between breaths. "David shot him. And Jeanie's there, too."

"Get the paramedics here now!" he shouted to the sheriff, who was still outside the barn.

"Already called them," he shouted back. "Found my guy in the trunk of his rig. He's in a bad way."

Amber, who had been watching as Hatch cuffed David, stepped closer to Jefferson and MJ. "Hi there, girl," she said with a smile. "We are so glad to see you."

MJ held on to Jefferson's neck, tears falling. She could only manage a trace of a smile for the FBI agent. He squeezed her tighter as her overwhelming emotion seemed to make words impossible.

The agent's eyes shifted behind them. Jefferson turned to see another woman descending the ladder.

"Jeanie," cried MJ, freeing herself from Jefferson's arms.

She ran to the woman and embraced her.

"I think he's alive," Jeanie said. "But I can't move him."

"We'll take care of him," Amber said, resting a hand on Jeanie's shoulder. Then she nodded to Kota.

"On it," said the agent, strapping a flashlight to his head. "Let's go," he said to the other agent.

They could hear the ambulance siren wailing outside the barn.

"I don't need to go," said MJ, turning back to Jefferson. "Just send Robbie. He's an emergency."

He felt a crooked smile inch its way up his face, his first genuine smile since MJ disappeared. She'd guessed what he was going to say.

Taking her in his arms again, he whispered in her ear. "Good, because I don't think I can let you out of my sight right now."

She stepped back, her eyes searching his. Her bottom lip trembled, and he could feel the weakness in her. He should make her go to the hospital, but what he'd said was true.

"I thought you weren't coming," she said, her beautiful blue eyes swimming.

He gently brushed her uninjured cheek before kissing her forehead. This time, Jefferson found himself unable to speak as a surge of love and gratitude for this woman choked off his words.

"Easy does it."

They both turned to see Kota and company slowly descending the ladder. Kota had Robbie slung over his shoulder like a sack of potatoes. A wide splotch of blood had spread across the injured man's backside.

MJ and Jeanie both rushed to see him.

"He's sort of conscious now," said Kota. "I think he just got hit in the backside and passed out from the pain. From the looks of it, he'll survive."

"Thank God," said Jeanie.

Hatch tried to drag David to his feet, but he only got as far as sitting him up. "I think this guy might need a little doctoring. You're quite a force with a crowbar, little lady."

Even sitting, the man swayed, his eyes groggy and his face marred with blood and swollen bruises. Despite that, his wayward eyes eventually focused on Amber.

"So she makes an appearance after all," he said in a lazy drawl.

Amber stood over him with a serene look of satisfaction on her face. "You should really stop picking on the ladies. I thought I taught you that lesson thirty years ago." She shook her head. "Looks like it took an actual teacher to get it through your thick head."

David scoffed. "You think you're so smart and clever. But I outsmarted you all."

The agent's eyes narrowed. Then she turned away, her eyes falling on Jeanie and studying the woman as if she were a ghost.

Walking away from David as if he no longer mattered, Amber approached the woman.

"Jeanie? Is Jeanie short for Jeanette?"

Jeanie nodded. "Yeah. He . . . He didn't like it, so he made me use Jeanie."

Amber's eyes grew wide. "Jeanette Resco?"

Covering her mouth to catch the escaping sob, Jeanie nodded.

***

MJ had two urgent things on her mind as she and Jefferson slid into the back of a police cruiser.

The first thing scared her. She had a question, and the answer could be devastating. She had yet to ask it.

Amber and the other guy, a detective she didn't know, rode in a different patrol car with Jeanie.

The ambulance had already sped off carrying the deputy found locked in his own trunk, and Robbie. The agent named Kota followed the ambulance in a different patrol car, keeping custody of David, who would also need the hospital. There was no room in the ambulance for him. The paramedics said taking him in the patrol car was better than not at all, which Kota had suggested.

The second thing MJ wanted was to keep her promise. That's why they were now on the road back to David's house—to find Corky.

As they bounced along the snowy, rutted road, MJ's hands twisted in her lap. No matter how many ways she thought of framing the words, they had refused to leave her mouth.

Jefferson's warm hand covered hers, quieting their constant motion.

"You haven't asked yet, so maybe you're not ready to talk about it. But if you are, I can update you on your mom."

She let out a breath that hitched with emotion, but still she couldn't ask.

"I will tell you this much, even without your permission," he said, squeezing her hands. "I think it will ease your mind." He gave her hands another squeeze, placing a gentle kiss on the top of her head. "She is alive."

At those words, the relief so overwhelmed MJ that sobs racked her tired body. Jefferson held her, stroking her hair as snow melted on the windows, a watery reminder of home.

***

They found Corky, not lying dead in the kitchen as MJ expected, but holed up under the rusty pickup truck.

When a deputy tried to coax him out, the injured dog snarled a warning.

It took MJ, kneeling before the truck with a piece of bread she'd found in the kitchen, to convince the dog to crawl out, one front leg bloody and useless.

More police cars arrived every minute, and soon crime scene tape encased the whole of David's house and surrounding property.

With Corky safe and Robbie on the way to the hospital, MJ's energy seemed to collapse. She sat in the patrol car, Corky on her lap, shivering.

Jefferson climbed in next to her. There was still so much to unpack, so much to know and do before they could consider the danger past, but right now, getting MJ safe and warm was all that mattered.

Chapter Thirty-Six

"Where is Meyers?" asked the chief, eyeing Evie Hanson as if she should know.

Which, as a matter of fact, she did. "He called and said his mom had fallen and needed his help. I'm going to take notes for him," she said.

"That is unfortunate. I hope his mom isn't injured."

"I'm not sure about that, sir," said Evie.

The chief sat back in his chair, his face crumpled in concentration as he mulled over the information Rory had just shared about Franco and his fancy attorney.

"I'm inclined to agree that this is an unexpected turn of events."

The boss's steely eyes turned to Fogarty and Hanson. "You two brought him in. Did he give you any sign he expected an attorney?"

"No, sir," said Evie Hanson. "In fact, he complained about not being able to pay rent if we kept him locked up. Not that he really pays rent," she said. "We're pretty sure he's living in that abandoned warehouse just north of Shopsides."

"But the other dealers were a little leery of talking about him, like he had some bad energy or something," added Fogarty.

"Bad energy?" scoffed Larson. "You been hanging out at the loopy-loo crystal shops?"

Hanson bailed out her partner. "I think what he means, sir," she said, addressing the chief, "is that the other dealers seemed afraid to talk about Franco, like he might be more dangerous or connected than the usual loose networks running drugs through the city."

"Well," said the chief with a sigh. "I can put in a call to the DA, but I doubt my call will get any further than yours, Detective Jackson. Do we have anything new on the forensics report?"

"Yeah," said Rory. "The button has DNA from both Franco and Brayden Shuster. That seems awesome for our case until you consider Jefferson found the button on the ground. Too easy for the defense to say it was there before the murder, and that's why Shuster's blood is all over it. The button connection is enough to hold him, unless that rat gets him out on bail. The lab has Franco's coat. If they find blood DNA on that, which I think they will, then we're in business."

"No weapon?" the chief asked.

Larson ran a hand over his bald head. "I think Evie is right about Franco shacking up with other bums at the warehouse. I'd like a warrant and a forensics team to search it."

With a long breath through his nose, the chief gave one solid nod of the head. "I'll sign off on that. You can arrange it." The older man drummed his fingers on the table. "Do you have any idea who would pay Franco's lawyer?"

"I'm not sure anybody is," said Larson. "The attorney says it's *pro bono*. Maybe he's doing someone a favor."

The chief continued drumming. "We have the button. We don't have a murder weapon. And we don't have a motive. I can't see why Franco would kill a customer, especially since he left the drugs behind."

"Maybe it's not about drugs," offered Fogarty. "Could be a girl or something."

Rory looked skeptical. "Nah. The Shuster kid had only been out for a week. I doubt he had girls hitting him up."

With his eyes on Larson, the chief said, "Doing someone a favor . . . You called all the family members?"

"Yeah," said Larson. "They all have alibis. But we got some interesting information." He explained the cash drops at Daxton Dyer's home. "I was counting on Meyers to print out a still photo of the delivery guy, so we don't have one for the board yet."

"If you send me the video, I can take care of that," said Evie, making a note.

"Thank you, Officer Hanson," said the chief. He turned inquisitive eyes on Larson.

"What are you thinking?"

"Dyer still has the money," said Larson. "I'll talk to the Everette detective about checking for prints. It's a long shot," he shrugged.

"Sounds like a solid plan," said the chief. "Also explore the idea of a hit for hire," said the chief. "I'm thinking bank accounts, legal connections between this attorney and other people in the family. With the warrant for Franco's place, get his phone and any other electronics examined. Let's see if he's had any contact with the family."

Rory nodded. "I see where you're going. And I like it." He looked down at his phone buzzing on the table. His eyes shot back up to the group.

"It's Jefferson."

"Well, answer it, you dweeb," said Larson.

Rory took the call. "Hey partner." Then his eyes closed as a gigantic, open-lipped, teeth-toting smile spread across his face. "They got her," he said to the group. "They got MJ."

Cheers went around the room just as Ron burst through the door, his face full of excitement.

"They—"

"Got her," everyone finished for him.

"Yeah, we know," said Rory, holding up his phone. "You hear that, Jeffey?" he said into the device. "We're ecstatic for you, man. Give that girl lots of love from West Sound PD . . . And our FBI partners."

"Darn," said the big man. "I really wanted to be the man of the hour."

Julia came up behind Ron, patting his shoulders. She had relief written all over her face. "You're always the man, Ronnie."

"I can't think of a more fitting end to this briefing," said the chief. "I say this calls for a celebration. Pizza on me. Larson, get it ordered."

"Sure thing."

"Hanson," said the chief, watching the young woman typing away on her laptop. "Get the most important Shuster case info on the board, but then it's okay to take a break and have some pizza."

"Yes, sir," she grinned. "I will do that."

"Good. We've all been on pins and needles since MJ's abduction. It's good practice to unwind a little when things go right. Understand?"

The young officer looked up and smiled. "Yes, sir. Thank you, sir."

Larson chuckled. "I can unwind like nobody's business."

"Just make sure you can wind yourself back up in time to get this Shuster case squared away," said the chief, his tone nowhere near as relaxed as when he spoke to Evie.

"Don't worry, Chief," said Rory. "I'm an expert Larson winder-upper."

The other detective walked to the door. "If only that weren't so true."

***

Four pieces of pizza later, Rory sat slumped down in his chair holding his stomach.

"I think I'm about to have a cheese baby."

Everyone else seemed to experience a similar state of fullness. Everyone except Ron, who had finished one supreme pizza by himself, plus a few pieces of the plain cheese variety. The food didn't faze him at all, and the agent continued pecking away at his keyboard.

Fogarty's pizza consumption was nowhere near Ron's, but he'd guzzled at least two-liters of root beer, and it showed. A huge belch rumbled out of him, which sent his cheeks into hyper-pink overdrive.

"Sorry," he said. "I guess I had too much soda."

"Ya think?" said Larson.

"It's a good thing our shift is over," said Evie. "You can go home and sleep that root beer off."

"Yeah. That sounds good," said Fogarty, fighting another belch eruption.

Officers for the next shift were wandering in, polishing off what remained of the celebratory pizza.

Jared barely nibbled one slice, preferring to live on energy drinks and his computer. Julia had eaten two slices, like a normal person, and then announced she was going home to spend some time with her little boy.

Larson stretched. "It has been a long day, and I am beat. I say we pack it in for the night. We can hit this Shuster case again early tomorrow."

"Yes, boss," breathed Rory, his lungs laboring under his overextended stomach. Grudgingly, he sat up. "I might take the file from Shuster's street-racing homicide home with me for a little nighttime reading."

"You do that," yawned Larson. "I wouldn't last five seconds." The older detective stood, putting his coat on and throwing away his empty paper plate.

Evie Hanson approached. "My shift is over and I'm about to head out, but if you send me the video, I'll do the photo first thing tomorrow."

"I didn't send it?" asked Larson.

"Nope," said Evie.

"Forgive him," said Rory. "It's the 'age' thing."

The officer smiled but didn't dare laugh.

"I will do that right now before I head out. Thank you for the reminder," said Larson, sitting back down.

"See you tomorrow," said Evie as she walked away.

Rory stuffed the Shuster file into his backpack before throwing his coat on.

"You two might want to slow your roll," said Ron, staring at his computer screen. "I got you a little Caesar salad."

"Salad?" said Rory, walking to the agent's desk. "Thanks, but I am really stuffed."

"No, you goofball. Not really a salad," said Ron. "It just sounded good. It has nothing to do with salad. But it definitely has something to do with Caesar. Caesar Milano. Or should I say Caesar Garcia-Tenedor?"

By now, both Rory and Larson were staring at Ron's computer. There they saw a Mexican passport for Caesar Garcia-Tenedor next to an American passport for Caesar Milano. The photos were unmistakably of the same person. And they were both pictures of Franco's fancy attorney.

"And if I need to remind you," said Ron, clicking his mouse until another passport appeared. The picture now on the screen belonged to Javier Garcia-Tenedor, the conductor, the man they believed had orchestrated MJ's abduction.

"What in the ever-loving . . ." said Larson.

"I'd say brothers," said Ron. "Maybe cousins. Partners in crime either way."

"This just went 'Twilight Zone,'" said Rory.

Instantly, they all heard the 'Twilight Zone' theme song in their heads.

"Is there a phone number or local address for Milano's law office?" asked Larson.

"He has a website," said Ron, typing away. "Says the office is on Oceanview Dr. I'll dial up the number."

Ron hit the speakerphone, making them all party to the shrill tone and robotic phrase, "We're sorry; you have reached a number that has been disconnected or is no longer in service."

The agent smirked and hung up the call. "Gents. I think we have ourselves an imposter."

"I knew that guy was shady," said Rory. "My shady-meter is never wrong."

Larson groaned. "I'll have a patrol car swing by that address tonight. I'm thinking it will be a dud just like the phone number."

"Most definitely," said Ron.

Rory rubbed his hands together. "I really hope he shows up tomorrow for Franco's bail hearing."

"You and me both," said Larson.

Chapter Thirty-Seven

The deputy found in his patrol car had a life-threatening head injury combined with hypothermia. Because of his dire condition, the paramedics called in a life-flight helicopter, which transported both the deputy and Robbie to a hospital in Battle Mountain, Nevada. The snowstorm had subsided, making the flight less risky and more advisable than a long ambulance ride.

The same paramedics insisted on cleaning and bandaging MJ's cheek before letting her go. David had given her a nasty gash. The paramedics applied butterfly bandages but suggested she see a doctor in Las Vegas as soon as possible.

Much to the sheriff's consternation, Kota insisted on taking custody of David after his visit to the hospital, claiming the man had aided an international drug trafficker, among the kidnapping, assaulting an officer, and other crimes still yet to be determined.

Despite their collective exhaustion, Amber, the two detectives, MJ, and Jeanie, all boarded the Metro Police chopper headed back to Las Vegas.

The noise, the intensity of the night, all of it made for a silent ride. MJ drifted off to sleep in Jefferson's arms. He held her tight, part of him afraid it was all a dream.

***

MJ desperately wanted to see her mom and dad. They still hadn't told MJ's father that they had found her, wanting to keep everything under wraps until the father and daughter saw each other in person. There would be a press frenzy once word got out, and Jefferson wanted MJ to have time with her parents before things became chaotic.

Amber dropped them at the hospital. She planned to get hotel rooms for herself and Jeanie. After a good night's rest, the agent needed Jeanie to tell her story. It could wait until tomorrow, but so many questions remained unanswered regarding Jeanie's disappearance all those years ago and David's part in it.

Jefferson wasn't sure of his plans. He'd play it by ear. For now, he would stay as long as MJ wanted him to. He knew this time with her parents would be intensely personal. If she asked him to go, it wouldn't bother him.

He loved her. He'd almost lost her, and it tore him to pieces. How did she feel about him? Could MJ even know that right now?

Experience told him that being abducted would play havoc with her mind. MJ's strength would help her fare better than most, but even MJ would struggle. Right now, she clung to him in a way that felt borne of desperation, of fear that her freedom would vanish.

He wanted it to be real, that she needed him because she loved him. Maybe part of it was love, or at least trust. He would not push her. They would have time to figure things out. That time was not now.

When they entered the hospital, it was well past visiting hours. The lobby was eerily quiet, in an apocalypse kind of way. Jefferson half expected to see zombies lurching down the hallway toward them.

Stepping from the elevator onto the intensive care unit amplified that feeling. The lobby lights were dim, as if reminding people it was bedtime . . . Or the end of the world. No one was at the desk, making it seem like everyone had completely abandoned the unit.

MJ pushed a button that signaled someone somewhere to come to the lobby.

After a few minutes, a hurried nurse appeared from the door directly behind the desk, her brows knit together in irritation.

Without waiting for them to speak, she said, "No visitors allowed at this time of night."

"I know it's late, and past visiting hours," said MJ.

Jefferson could hear the tremble already beginning in her voice. The sound triggered a spark of anger in him, and he stepped forward.

He pulled out his badge and slammed it onto the window. "Perhaps if you took a second to think, you might recognize Mrs. Devey's abducted daughter is standing in front of you. She would like to see her parents if it isn't too much trouble for you to make that happen."

It probably wasn't fair to the nurse, but then again, maybe it was. The trauma to MJ's face alone warranted a double take.

The woman's eyes flew open, and her hand went to her mouth.

"Oh! Oh, of course. Let me . . . Let me go get Mr. Devey." She turned toward the door and then stopped to look again. "He'll be so happy."

Then she ran through the door and was gone.

"Thank you," MJ said, her blue eyes wet with unshed tears as she looked up at him. The emotion in her gaze was so raw, so fragile. His heart ached that someone had taken the defiant flame from her eyes

. . that unrelenting side of her that had won his heart from their first meeting, even if he didn't know it.

He wanted to hold her and shelter her from all that would come next. Seeing her mom lying in a coma would tear her up. On the way here, Jefferson told her everything he knew about her mom's condition. But knowing and seeing are two different things. This would be rough.

The entrance door to the unit opened, and there stood Andy Devey.

MJ ran. Her father stepped forward, and they met in a sobbing embrace. The nurse had returned to the window, tears streaming down her cheeks. Soon another nurse was there, and then another, and more until no one else could fit behind the desk. All had wet faces and smiles.

"My baby. My baby," sobbed Andy as he squeezed MJ and stroked her hair. "I didn't think I'd ever see you again."

MJ cried, her face buried in her father's chest. Words were too much.

Andy looked over MJ's head and met Jefferson's eye. He mouthed the words, "Thank you."

Wiping his own eyes, Jefferson gave a nod, accepting the man's gratitude but knowing that this moment didn't happen because of him. This moment came because a team of dedicated people worked every hour to bring MJ home. And in no small measure because of MJ herself.

As father and daughter held each other, reunited at last, Jefferson backed away and slipped out of the lobby.

This was their time.

Chapter Thirty-Eight

Rory didn't sleep well. He tried, but he spent the night tossing and turning. Then the baby started to cry. He'd hurried to the crib and rocked her back to sleep as his mind whirred with what he'd learned from the Shuster speed-racing homicide.

The detective wasn't sure what it meant. Maybe nothing. If it were nothing, why wouldn't the officer have mentioned it?

When he finally rolled into the office, he opened his laptop and logged into the secure server.

He'd noticed the video footage from Rainier County Juvenile Detention yesterday, but hadn't taken the time to look at it. He and Larson both felt confident they had their man. But now Rory wasn't so sure.

It was still early, and his eyes burned from lack of sleep. He watched at triple speed as visitors entered and had their belongings scanned. If he saw that officer, they had a real problem on their hands.

After about thirty minutes, Rory stopped the video, his heart dropping to the floor.

There he was, chatting up the guard as she scanned people in. Before anyone had noticed, the officer worked his way inside without his person or anything he carried being subject to the scanner.

"Why so early?"

Rory jumped at Larson's intrusion into his deep thinking.

With a shake of his head, Rory let out a deep, regretful sigh. "We need to go see the chief. Is he here?"

"Yep, just saw him walk into his office."

"This will not be pretty."

***

They stood on the landing of Officer Meyers's apartment. Law enforcement in ballistic vests waited just below, ready to ram the door.

Once Rory read Jacob Meyers on the Shuster street-racing witness list, things started to fall into place. More pieces lined up after the detective watched video footage from the juvenile detention center. There he saw Meyers deftly chatting up a guard and then sliding through security without going through the scanner. Another camera caught him leaving a note in Schuster's mailbox.

The question of how the officer was involved with the murder remained to be answered. Finding the officer was the first order of business. He had answered no phone calls and had not come into work.

Larson banged on the door. "Meyers, open the door!"

Nothing.

Stepping away from the door, Larson motioned for the officer with the battering ram to move to the front.

"Wait," Rory whispered, holding a hand up. "Do you hear that?"

Larson put his ear to the door, catching the low moaning sound Rory must have heard.

He nodded to the officer with the ram. "We need to get in there."

The tactical officers lined up, ready to breach.

"Be ready for anything," Larson said to the group. "Meyers may be armed."

As the officer with the ram hit the door, a cacophony of shouted orders filled the tiny apartment.

Meyers stood holding a pistol but immediately dropped it, raising his hands in the air. In front of him, tied to a kitchen chair and gagged, sat Caesar Milano.

***

As he entered the station, Rory slumped under the weight of exhaustion. Emotional exhaustion. Nothing gutted a cop like discovering a dirty cop.

And it would be up to him and Larson to question Meyers.

It could wait a few minutes. Larson needed to get his coffee, and Rory needed to breathe.

Just as he plopped down at his desk, Evie Hanson approached.

"Detective Jackson?" she said, approaching cautiously. "I know things are busy right now, but I think you need to see something."

She set her laptop on his desk, not waiting for permission. On the screen, Rory recognized the Dyer porch video, frozen and zoomed in.

With an ink pen, Evie pointed at the screen. "See that watch? This is exactly the watch Meyers has been wearing lately. I wouldn't normally notice something like that, but he plays with it all the time."

"Play the video," Rory said.

She did as directed. Sure enough, the mannerisms, the build, it all fit.

"Thanks, Evie. This is excellent work."

"I wish it wasn't,' she said. "I hate this."

Rory nodded. "We all do."

Chapter Thirty-Nine

When the video finished, Rory reached over and hit stop on the laptop.

Meyers, sitting across the table, said nothing, just stared at the wall behind the detectives with defiant eyes.

"Explain this to me," said Rory. "Why give away so much money?"

The young man still said nothing, but his eyes shifted briefly to the laptop screen.

"I think he just felt bad for the family," said Larson. "What happened to the Dyers made all of us angry. Stupid kid, that Shuster," Larson said with unaffected venom. "Can you think of anything more selfish?"

Meyers bowed his head, staring at his hands. "Are you going to charge me for giving someone money?"

"Now that depends," said Larson. "Where'd you get the money?"

"I saved it," said Meyers, still not making eye contact.

"We've already pulled your bank statements," said Larson. "Care to try again?"

Apparently, he did not care to try again as he remained silent.

"What we *can* charge you with is false imprisonment, illegal use of your firearm," suggested Rory. "So forget the money for now. How do you know Caesar Milano?"

"I don't," said Meyers, with a shrug.

"You looked ready to kill him," said Larson.

Silence.

Rory sighed. "Look, Jacob, you're not helping yourself here. If you did not kill Brayden Shuster, then you need to tell us who did, because right now it is looking like we can get you on conspiracy to commit murder."

Meyers finally met Rory's eyes, but quickly looked away. "You know who killed him. Franco did it."

"Let's say that's true. Why did Franco do it?" asked Larson, sitting up and leaning across the table.

"Lots of people hated Brayden Shuster," Meyers said with cold calm.

Sitting back again, Larson said, "*You* hated Brayden Shuster."

"I did. I still do," said Meyers. His eyes grew distant as he stared at the table. "I was the first person at the Dyer's car after the crash. Not a cop. Just a normal person. A kid really." He closed his eyes. "You know the mom; she lived for about a minute. She asked me, 'Is my baby okay?' And I lied. I told her the baby was fine, and that she would be fine, too. But I already knew she was going to die and that the baby was already dead."

"I joined the police to stop people like Brayden Shuster. But then, he gets out in three years." He held up three fingers, his face incredulous. "Three years! As if three years in any way paid for the lives of two people brutally murdered."

Rory nodded, eyes narrowed. "I think I'm getting it. Brayden getting out so early didn't sit well with you, so you hired Franco to kill him."

Meyers rolled his eyes. "No. I did not hire Franco."

"So you just did nothing?" asked Rory. "You just let it eat you alive while he was out, roaming around free, smoking pot with his buddies. I mean, you threatened him with that note." His lips pursed in disbelief. "Come on, Meyers. You're not making sense."

"I wanted him dead. It's true. But I did not hire Franco." He folded his arms and looked at the wall.

"Then who did?" asked Larson. "Was it the father? Were you in some kind of collusion with him? You were giving him money."

"What?" said Meyers, his face screwed up in confusion. "No. No way. He's got nothing to do with this. I just wanted him and his kids to have some extra money after what happened. They don't have much."

"I don't believe you," said Larson. "I think you both wanted revenge. I'm not sure how the money fits into it, but I think you're in it together." He stood and turned to Rory. "I'm finished here. Let's go pick up the dad."

"No!" shouted Meyers. "Please! He doesn't . . ." With wild eyes, he said, "It was Milano. He gave me the money." His resolve seemed to collapse. "Please," he said, his energy gone. "Please don't bother the family."

They had him. Larson pushed. "Why did Caesar Milano give you money?"

Meyers covered his face with his hands and groaned.

"Tell us. Why?"

"I gave him information about the station, investigations, and about people that work here." He hung his head, and for the first time, he looked ashamed.

This was not what Rory had expected. He wanted to reach across the table and punch the guy in the face. "You told him about MJ and Jefferson."

"I swear I didn't know why he wanted it. He asked about everyone," Meyers whined. "He approached me, and I thought sharing a few things wouldn't really hurt. I could never get that kind of money on my own."

"And Shuster?"

He let his head hang back. "I must have said something about it, because he knew I hated him. But I swear, I never asked him to kill Brayden or hire someone to do it."

Neither detective responded nor gave any signal they believed him. In their silence, Meyers continued.

"I told him I couldn't give him any more information. He said okay, that was fine. Then, yesterday, I came home and found a bloody knife in my kitchen with a note."

The detectives didn't take their eyes off of Meyers, but they both knew it was the murder weapon.

"What did the note say?" Larson said, his eyes boring into the young man.

Meyers blanched. "It said, 'We took care of your problem as you requested. Silence buys silence.'"

"He didn't want you to tell anyone. So you think he was planning to frame you?"

Saying nothing, Meyers sat forward, his head in his hands.

"You idiot," said Rory, his voice full of suppressed fury. "Now, an innocent woman is lying in a hospital bed, fighting for her life. We're lucky MJ is even alive. You deserve whatever you get."

***

Rory sat at his desk twirling a pencil through his fingers, stewing in anger.

They'd all had cases where the punishment did not fit the crime, and almost always on the two-light side of the balance. But what Meyers did wasn't justice. It was selfish.

His actions put people at risk, traumatized those involved, and still could end up costing lives.

Dirty cops always think they have some kind of higher law than everyone else, that they have special foresight or hindsight or some darn thing. And Meyers had dirtied himself with the worst kind of dirt, even if he didn't know it. He'd been in the mud with Nico.

"Hey," said Larson, breaking into Rory's thoughts for the second time that day. "I know you are upset, and rightly so, but our next interview might brighten your day."

Rory dropped the pencil. "Milano?"

"Ready to eat some salad?" Larson raised an eyebrow at Rory.

"Let's go. I need a little fun."

Chapter Forty

C aesar Milano sported a crumpled, snazzy black suit with an embroidered flower pattern. It reminded Rory of his grandmother's sofa.

He looked worse for wear, his usually slick hair falling into his eyes.

With an air of mild curiosity, he watched the detectives on the other side of the table.

"Why am I here, gentlemen?" said Caesar, his dark eyes moving between them. "Clearly, I have been a victim of a wild and corrupt police officer."

Rory glanced at Larson, his eyes sad and downcast as if sharing this information caused him great pain. "Yeah, man. I don't know what to say. This whole thing with Shuster . . ." He shook his head. "It looks like an inside job."

Larson looked equally disturbed. "A cop," he whispered, shaking his head.

The man sat back, crossing his skinny legs. "So I ask again. Why am I here being held like a criminal?"

"So this cop," said Rory, "we think he hired Franco to kill Shuster."

Ceasar narrowed his eyes. "Oh, so you are still accusing my client of murder."

"Yeah, that hasn't changed," said Larson, leaning back in his chair and resting his foot on the opposite knee.

"Are you trying to keep me from my client?"

"No. Of course not," said Rory. "But we have to finish the story before you'll understand everything."

Ceasar folded his arms. "I'm listening." Even as he said it, his eyes traveled to the door. He wanted to get out of this room.

"The weird thing about this hire job is that no money exchanged hands," said Rory, his brow crinkled in insincere confusion. "All Franco wanted was information about West Sound detectives. And it seems he had a particular interest in Detective Jefferson Hughes."

"Do you know Detective Hughes?" asked Larson.

The lawyer's face had lost all movement. Only his lips moved in his response. "Why would I?"

"Right. Well, you're not missing much. A bit of a bore, honestly," said Larson.

"Hey!" said a disembodied voice. "A bore? Really?"

"Here he is now," laughed Rory, holding his phone up for the lawyer to see.

On the screen, Jefferson waved.

"Gentlemen," objected Caesar, standing. "I don't know what this is about, but I'm done with your silly games. I've had quite an ordeal, and I need to go home."

"Sit down, Mr. Milano," ordered Larson. "Or should I say Mr. Garcia-Tenedor?"

The man blanched before dropping unceremoniously back into his seat.

"You see," said Larson. "We really wanted to have you here when we had this little reunion video call. I think you will find the guest of honor even more interesting than our boring detective."

"Really? Boring again?" Jefferson chuckled. "You know you miss me, Larson."

"I miss you," said Rory, "and I am man enough to admit it."

Caesar's complexion had turned green.

"Anyway, is MJ Brooks there with you?" asked Rory.

"I'm here," said MJ as she appeared next to Jefferson.

The sound of MJ's voice and her face on the camera seemed to hit Caesar with a brutal one-two punch. His skin now matched his fancy white shirt, stark and deadly against the jet-black suit. It wasn't getting caught by the police that scared him. A man like Caesar didn't fear jail the way most criminals do. A man like Caesar, who works for men like Nico, feared failure. Failure gets you or your family killed.

"Wow, MJ, are you okay? What happened to your face?" asked Larson, feigning ignorance.

"Oh, it's nothing," said MJ. "You should see the other guy."

"So I heard," said Rory. "Well, you guys, it's been fun. Safe travels when you come back home."

The two on the screen waved goodbye, and Rory ended the call.

"Now do you remember Detective Hughes?" asked Larson. "Nico used you to target MJ. You and," Larson turned to Rory, "your brother?"

Rory shrugged. "Not sure. Maybe Caesar can tell us."

They both looked at him expectantly.

The man's eyes were solid black against his pale face, and he pressed his thin lips into an even thinner line. He pushed a shock of hair from his eyes. They were unlikely to get any more words out of Caesar Milano.

Rory was enjoying this far too much. "If you're not sure who we mean, then I think we have another video, don't we, Detective Larson?"

Larson set his phone on the table and swiped the screen. "We sure do." He set the phone up to give Caesar a clear view.

"For context," said Larson, "the uniformed police are Las Vegas Metro with a few TSA officers and FBI thrown in for good measure."

In the video, the man known as Javier Garcia-Tenedor was just about to board a flight bound for Mexico. When he saw the mass of law enforcement officers descending on the gate, he made a run for it, back into the terminal. This lasted for approximately five seconds before he was in handcuffs and being escorted away.

This video was the last straw. Rory barely made it to the man with a trashcan before Caesar Milano lost his lunch.

Chapter Forty-One

MJ was glad when Jefferson came back. She was also glad when he left last night.

That one act showed his ability to tune in to her.

She'd spent the night sleeping next to her mom's bed, her hand wrapped around her mother's. This morning, Toni's eyes rolled behind her lids when MJ spoke to her, as if she were trying desperately to wake up.

The decrease in intracranial pressure pleased the doctors. They didn't promise her mom would wake up, but their optimism was genuine.

As MJ and Jefferson sat together in the waiting room, she sensed he was holding back. Something colored his interactions with her, some other emotion that she couldn't place. He was gentle, everything she needed right now, but every once in a while, his sky-blue eyes would leave hers, as if he didn't deserve to look at her.

They'd just ended a video call with Rory and Larson. MJ didn't know all the details, but they had someone in custody who had helped orchestrate the whole abduction.

She still couldn't believe all the people involved in helping save her from that hellhole. All the while, she thought no one was coming, but in reality, so many people were coming and working on her behalf.

Now, she and Jefferson were waiting for Amber. The agent had called and asked to see both of them. MJ desperately wanted news about Robbie, and she hoped Amber knew something.

When Amber stepped from the elevator, Detective Ryan Hatch walked beside her.

"Whew," said Hatch. "I think every news crew in the country is downstairs."

"And there they will stay," said Amber. "Detective Hatch has a few officers helping the hospital security staff keep them wrangled."

Jefferson smiled. "Much appreciated."

"It's nothing," said Hatch. "They were happy to help. After everything this little lady and her mom have been through, they deserve some peace."

Amber embraced MJ. "How are you?"

"As good as I can be," she said. "I will be one hundred times better when my mom wakes up."

"She will," said Amber. "The woman that created a fighter like you has to have a deep well of strength."

MJ bit her bottom lip, fighting the sting in her eyes. "She is a tough lady."

They all sat. Amber and Hatch took chairs across from Jefferson and MJ.

"How is Robbie?" asked MJ, not waiting for Amber to start.

Amber grinned, tiny wrinkles making smiles in her hazel eyes. "Robbie is doing fabulously. He's been eating the hospital out of ice cream, and the sheriff is bringing Corky up to see him later today. The bullet went through the dog's leg hitting nothing vital, so he's going to recover as well."

MJ breathed a sigh of relief, her eyes shining once more. They'd been through so much together. One day soon, she'd see him again.

"Unfortunately," said Amber, her tone suddenly more somber. "The deputy didn't make it. The combination of the head wound and hypothermia caused too much damage to his heart."

This time, tears trickled down MJ's face. Jefferson wrapped an arm around her shoulders.

"That means David will face murder charges along with many others. If all goes as it should, he will be in prison for the rest of his life."

"Maybe it will go for him like it did for his cousin," piped up Hatch.

Amber scowled at him. "Ryan."

"What?"

She ignored him and continued. "MJ," she said gently. "This case is far more complicated than you know. Jefferson wanted to tell you everything, but I made him wait for me."

The teacher's eyes narrowed as she turned to Jefferson. "Okay . . . Why so secretive?"

Jefferson started to respond, but Amber put her palm up, stopping him.

"What I am about to share is extremely sensitive, but you deserve to know why this happened. Why it happened to you in particular."

"I already know it had something to do with Jefferson," MJ said, looking between the three of them. "So I think nothing you say will surprise me."

"Maybe not," agreed Amber. "Just remember, your silence on this topic could mean life or death for Jefferson's brother."

"Your brother?" She pulled back, searching Jefferson's eyes.

There it was again — that hesitation as his eyes darted away. "Yes. My brother."

Realizing that was all Jefferson would say, MJ turned back to Amber. "What does his brother have to do with my abduction and my mother being in a coma?" She didn't like the angry edge in her voice, but she couldn't take it back now.

Amber, patient as always, didn't let the emotion derail her. "You remember Nico, of course," she said.

"How could I forget?"

"Jefferson's brother, Alex, has turned witness on Nico and his entire operation. He's given names of people significantly higher in the chain than Nico. The DEA has been using that information to dismantle the network — one shipment, one storehouse, one speedboat at a time. And Alex's testimony against Nico will ensure that man never sees the outside of a prison."

MJ rested a finger on her lip, taking in the information as if a test would follow. "So, Nico wants to get to Alex."

"Yes," said Amber, the corner of her mouth lifting slightly at MJ's quick study of the situation. "But Alex is in protective custody. Even Jefferson has no contact with him. None of us knows where he is, which is exactly how it should be."

"So," said MJ, filling in the gaps, "Nico tried to get to Alex through Jefferson, and he did that by having someone abduct me?"

"Yes," the other three all said in unison.

She sat back in her chair, her narrowed eyes showing the workings of her mind. Then she glanced at Jefferson. He stared at the floor, not meeting her eye.

MJ sat up again. "What I don't get," she said, "is how Nico or any of his goon-faced people knew . . ." She cast another awkward glance at Jefferson before jabbing a thumb in his direction. "I mean, I love this guy, but nobody really knows that."

Jefferson's head shot up, and Amber laughed out loud.

"Woah," said Hatch, pulling his collar out. "It's getting hot in here."

Amber scowled at him again. "Why did I even let you come?"

"Purely for entertainment, I'm guessing."

Shaking her head, Amber tried but couldn't hold back the smile breaking through her normally composed expression.

"The other part you don't know," said Hatch, "is that you helped solve a decades-old missing persons case. That of Jeanette Resco, the case that introduced me to her ladyship, Agent Amber Holt, whom you all know as Agent Amber Wells."

"That was a lot of words, Ryan," said Amber. "Are you going to be okay?"

"You know, I talk just fine when you're not here," he said. "But go ahead. Tell the story."

MJ almost jumped out of her chair. "Wait! You mean Jeanie. He told me he kept her. That he was supposed to kill her."

Amber nodded. "I got the entire story from Jeanie early this morning. At first, he kept her locked away in that shipping container. She thinks it may have been two years she spent in there. Eventually, he brought her into the house, but he kept her chained to a bed when he wasn't there watching her. There had been a couple of sightings of her over the years, which is why I went to Austin all those years ago. He let her go into the store a few times. She thought about running, but David said he would kill her, and if he couldn't find her, he would kill Robbie."

MJ listened with rapt attention. As horrible as her captivity had been, it was nothing compared to what Jeanie had endured.

Amber continued. "She came to care a great deal about Robbie. Leaving him alone with that monster . . . She couldn't do it. So she waited for a day when they could both get away. That day never came, and she lost hope. She didn't think they would ever get out of that place." Amber reached across and took MJ's hand. "It wasn't until you came along that she found the courage again."

"I know it will take a long time for you to process all that's happened, all I've told you today," she said. "But I hope you know you saved and changed lives, MJ."

She dropped MJ's hand and sat back. "Jeanie is going back to her hometown. Her parents both passed, but according to her brother, they left her some property. They never believed she was gone. She wants Robbie to come live with her there."

Amber was right. MJ still felt slightly numb, like all that had happened was a nightmare. How it would rear its ugly head in the future, she couldn't say. But this news about Robbie and Jeanie, it sent a wave of joy through her heart.

***

With Amber and Hatch gone, MJ turned to study Jefferson.

"So that's it?" she asked.

He looked at her, confused. "What do you mean?"

"I mean the reason you can only look at me for a few seconds. You blame yourself for what happened."

He looked toward the waiting room window, seeking refuge in the blue sky.

"See, there you go again." She put a hand on his shoulder. "Jefferson, look at me."

Obediently, he let his eyes find hers. "Well, it is, isn't it? My fault? Look at you," he brushed her cheek. "And your mom . . . If not for me, none of this would have happened."

"That is absurd," she said, and for a second, he saw that blue flame of indignation flicker in her eyes. "Since when do you take credit for a scumbag like Nico's handiwork?"

"I'm not, but . . ."

"But you are," she said. "Look, Jefferson. I don't blame you. No one blames you. Stop blaming yourself. I mean, you came and saved me, which is very heroic."

She was grinning, but his face was deadly serious.

"But I didn't," he said. "Sure, I was there, but MJ, there were so many people that did more important things than me. If I'm honest, I was a head case when you went missing. I . . . I couldn't even think straight."

She touched a finger to her lips. "I don't think you understand. You saved me in the best way. I don't know what I would have done if you hadn't come when you did. You said my name, and it brought me back from the edge. Jefferson," she said, her eyes searching his. "I almost . . ." She dropped her eyes. "I don't know if I could live with myself if I'd done it. You saved me from myself."

He stroked her hair and pulled her close, grateful she never had to know whether she could live with it.

"But," she said, pushing back from him. "I want to hear more about this 'you couldn't think straight' business." She grinned at his expense. "Like you were going so crazy about me?"

He stopped, doing a double take. "Are you laughing at me?"

"No," she said, waving a hand in the air. "Of course I'm not laughing. Just tell me why you were so worried?"

His eyes widened, incredulous. "MJ, he was going to kill you."

"That's not what I mean. Why did it matter so much to you?"

She had moved closer without him noticing, but now, he could feel her breath on his cheek. Hatch was right; it was getting hot in there.

"Tell me, Jefferson."

He finally got it. He finally understood what she needed to hear.

With a softness he never showed another creature on earth, Jefferson placed a hand on each side of MJ's face, careful to avoid her injury.

"MJ Brooks," he said. "I almost went crazy at the thought of losing you, because I love you more than anything in this world."

"Bingo," she said.

When their lips met, the warmth of the other quenched their longing, the world melted away, and, at least for now, no more questions remained.

Chapter Forty-Two

Toni Devey saw her first ray of sunlight two days later.

MJ had been sitting next to her mom, reading jokes from an old Reader's Digest, when Toni's eyes fluttered open.

MJ's attention was on the magazine when she heard a hoarse whisper. "Can I get some water?"

The magazine flew as MJ jumped up. "Mom!"

Jefferson, who had been napping in a corner chair, immediately snapped to attention.

"MJ, keep your voice down," her mom croaked, her eyes darting from the ceiling to the bed and around the room in confusion.

MJ yelled, "Dad!"

"I'll get him," said Jefferson, running from the room.

Calming herself enough to grab the cup of water, MJ held the bendy straw to her mom's lips. "Here you go, Mom. You're in the hospital."

Toni sipped as best she could from her prone position. Then, she closed her eyes as she raised a shaking hand to touch the bandage on her head.

"That's going to bruise," she whispered, a weak smile trying to make an appearance. She stared up at her daughter. "Oh, sweetie. You're crying."

Wiping her eyes, MJ put the cup down and hugged her mom's shoulders. "Oh, Mom. I'm so glad you're back. We've been so worried."

Her mother's eyes crinkled with concern as MJ released her. With a shaking finger, she touched the bandage on her daughter's cheek. "What happened?" she whispered, the work of using her full voice too draining.

MJ just squeezed her hand, holding it to her heart. "It's a long story."

"Those men. They hurt you too?"

She nodded reluctantly, not wanting to explain anything right now. "But I'm fine, Mom. I had a lot of help."

Through the door came Andy Devey, tears already forming in his eyes.

"Toni?" he said, hurrying to the bedside.

"Were you expecting someone else?" It came out in a soft whisper, but the humor hit just the same.

Mr. Devey laughed through his tears as he bent down and kissed his wife. "I have never been so happy to hear your saucy self."

A nurse rushed in, with Jefferson close behind.

"Can I sit up?" asked Toni. "I don't like lying down."

"Of course," said the nurse. "You just let me know if you start to feel lightheaded."

She pushed the button to raise the head of Toni's bed. As she did so, the patient caught sight of Jefferson for the first time.

"Wait," said Toni.

The nurse stopped, a look of concern on her face. "Are you feeling okay, Mrs. Devey?"

"I'm seeing things," she said, staring. A quick cough stopped her, and MJ offered more water. Toni's eyes never left Jefferson.

"That detective is here?"

Jefferson felt the blood rush to his face. Maybe he should leave.

Without a word, MJ walked over and grasped his hand. "He's with me, Mom." Then she reached up and planted a kiss on his lips.

Jefferson offered a tentative smile. "I'm happy to see you again, Mrs. Devey."

"Thank you, Detective. I always knew . . . she'd pick you." She closed her eyes again before turning to the nurse. "I am a little light-headed. Maybe I should go back down."

As the bed descended, Toni whispered. "A mother always knows." She held a shaking finger to her temple.

MJ looked up at Jefferson, her blue eyes alive with happiness.

That was as close as he would get to her mother's blessing.

* * *

Epilogue

MJ held her mother's hand. Jefferson held MJ's other hand. Amber, on the other side of Jefferson, talked quietly with Kota Soucy.

Though the room felt somber with the heavy proceedings, there also existed an air of relief. The day had finally come, and no one could stop it.

MJ felt a light touch on her shoulder and looked to see her dad smiling at her. He had his arm stretched across the bench, behind both his girls. Toni still attended cognitive and physical therapy, but she'd progressed quickly. The doctors saw no signs there would be permanent damage.

The trial went well. They hadn't been able to attend all of it, but MJ insisted on being there when the verdict came down.

Today, Nico would be subject to justice, and she wanted him to know how badly he had failed.

She leaned her head on Jefferson's shoulder. Her own recovery would take some time. Sometimes she became impatient with herself, the harrowing dreams, the hesitation every time a car approached her. Everyone said it would take time. MJ Brooks hated waiting.

Everyone's attention turned to the front as the jury returned to the courtroom.

MJ tensed, and her eyes traveled unwillingly to the back of Nico's head. Smug to the last, he really thought himself invincible.

The court bailiff carried the verdict from the jury to the judge. He examined it for a minute before saying, "Thank you, Foreperson Anderson. Bailiff, you may present the verdict to the clerk."

The clerk declared the verdict to be in order.

"Thank you," said the judge. "The clerk will please read the verdict."

The court clerk cleared her throat. "The jury finds, in the case of Nico Lopez Guerrero versus Washington State, count one, manufacture of a controlled substance. Guilty. Count two, manufacture of a controlled substance with an intent to distribute. Guilty."

Guilty.

Guilty

Guilty.

Guilty.

Guilty.

Jefferson squeezed MJ's hand. All the way down the bench, none of them could hide the silent tears of joy.

Finally. Justice.